THE
BLACKSTONE
PROMISE

ROCHELLE ALERS

THE BLACKSTONE PROMISE

THE BLACKSTONE PROMISE

ISBN-13: 978-0-373-22999-4

Recycling programs for this product may not exist in your area.

Copyright © 2011 by Harlequin Books S.A.

The publisher acknowledges the copyright holder of the individual works as follows:

BEYOND BUSINESS
Copyright © 2005 by Rochelle Alers

A YOUNGER MAN
Copyright © 2002 by Rochelle Alers

www.kimanipress.com

Printed in U.S.A.

CONTENTS

Dear Reader,

You will enjoy another Blackstone story in
The Blackstone Promise. This time it is sexy widower
Sheldon Blackstone's turn to find that special love that
promises forever. Originally published under Desire,
Beyond Business isn't your traditional romance because
the older man–younger woman plot proves age is
nothing but a number.

The second novel in this 2-in-1 was also originally
published under Desire, and the title, *A Younger Man,*
says it all. What's good for the goose is equally good for
the gander when hunky ex-marine-turned-executive-
chef Kumi Walker turns up the heat while tutoring
widowed Veronica Hamlin in the kitchen *and* in the
bedroom.

For those who've written to say you want more
Blackstones—you will get your wish. Look for
Peyton Blackstone in the second book of the Hideaway
wedding trilogy, coming summer 2012. You can also look
forward to reuniting with Ana and Jason Cole when
they find love and their happily-ever-after when and
where they least expect it.

Sit back, put your feet up, grab your favorite beverage
and enjoy *The Blackstone Promise.*

Read, love and live romance.

Rochelle Alers

www.rochellealers.org

roclers@aol.com

BEYOND BUSINESS

Chapter One

"Please state your name," came the computer-generated voice through a speaker mounted on a post. A pair of electronic iron gates emblazoned with a bold letter *B* and closed-circuit cameras marked the entrance to the fabled Blackstone Farms.

Leaning out the driver's side window, Renee stared up at the camera. "Renee Wilson." Within seconds the gates opened and then closed behind her as she drove through.

New state, new job and a new beginning, she mused, driving past acres of white rail fences, stone walls and verdant landscaped grassland.

She smiled and returned the wave from a man sitting atop a tractor hauling bundled hay, sat up straighter and rolled her head from side to side. She was stiff—neck, shoulders and lower back. She'd made the trip from Louisville, Kentucky, to Staunton, Virginia, in a little more than eight hours, stopping only twice to refuel her car and eat.

"Yes," she whispered softly. She *had* made the right decision to accept the position as the administrative assistant for Blackstone Farms. Living and working on a horse farm would be a new experience for someone accustomed to the pulsating kinetic energy of Miami. And as much as she loved the south Florida city, with its personality and colorful residents, Renee knew she could not have remained there.

She had not wanted to risk running into her ex-lover who'd gotten her pregnant; a man who had conveniently neglected to tell her that he was married, she thought bitterly.

Slowing at a section where the road diverged into four directions, she followed the sign pointing the way to the main house. A towering flagpole with the American flag flying atop a black-and-red one lifted in the slight breeze.

It was late October, and trees were displaying their vibrant fall colors. The odor of wet earth lingered in the crisp autumn air from a week of thunderstorms that had left the Appalachian and Shenandoah Mountain regions saturated and lush.

Renee maneuvered her sedan behind a pickup truck in the driveway leading to Sheldon Blackstone's house. She had been interviewed and hired by his son Jeremy, who would eventually become her boss upon his father's retirement at the end of the year.

She turned off the engine, scooped her handbag off the passenger seat and pushed open the door. Her shoes had barely touched the ground when a tall figure loomed in front of her. Startled, she let out a soft gasp at the same time her head jerked up.

A pair of light gray eyes under curving black eyebrows in a deeply tanned olive-brown face pinned her to the spot. The afternoon sunlight glinted off streaks of red and flecks of gray in a full head of black wavy hair. Her breathing halted, her heart pounded erratically and a lack of oxygen made her feel light-headed. There was no doubt he was Sheldon. The resemblance between father and son was uncanny. But there was something in the elder Blackstone's gaze that unnerved her.

Recovering and letting out a soft exhalation of breath, she extended a hand. "Good afternoon. I'm Renee Wilson."

Sheldon Blackstone stared at the small hand before he shook it, her fingers disappearing in his larger grasp. He wondered how the woman with the delicate features in a nut-brown face and blunt-cut, chin-length hairdo would react once he informed her that she would have to live with him instead of in the bungalow she had been assigned.

Sheldon forced a smile he did not feel. "Sheldon Blackstone."

Renee eased her hand from his firm grip. "My pleasure, Mr. Blackstone."

Sheldon angled his head while raising an eyebrow. "Please call me Sheldon. Around here we're very informal."

The smile softening Renee's lush mouth deepened the dimples in her cheeks. "Then Sheldon it is, but only if you call me Renee."

His smile became a full grin. He found her dimpled smile enchanting. "Renee it is." Cupping her elbow, he led her toward the large two-story white house trimmed in black with an expansive wraparound porch. "I have something to tell you before you settle in."

Renee glanced at his distinctive profile. High slanting cheekbones, an aquiline nose, penetrating light gray eyes and a square-cut jaw made for an arresting visage. She stopped on the first step. "Jeremy told me everything about the position during the interview, including my duties and benefits."

Sheldon turned and stared down at her. "It's about your housing."

Renee closed her eyes for several seconds. She prayed the Blackstones would not renege on their promise to provide her with resident housing or on-site child care.

"What about it?"

Sheldon crossed his arms over his broad chest. "The bungalow assigned to you is uninhabitable. Unfortunately, lightning struck the roof, setting it afire. After we put the fire out, it rained. I had a contractor assess the damage yesterday, and he said he'll have to gut it before it can be renovated."

Renee's eyes widened with this disclosure as she curbed the urge to bite down on her lower lip as she usually did when upset or frustrated. "Are you saying I can't live *here*?"

Sheldon dropped his arms and reached for her elbow again. "Let's go inside and discuss your options."

She froze, her eyes widening again. She only had one option—if she couldn't live at Blackstone Farms she'd have to get into her car and drive back to Kentucky. And while Sheldon Blackstone wanted to discuss housing options she wanted to tell him that she was a thirty-five-year-old single woman, without a permanent residence *and* pregnant with the child of a lying man who had reconciled with his wife.

"Please, Renee, hear me out. Let's go into the house," Sheldon said in a deep, quiet voice.

She stared at him for several seconds before nodding. "Okay, Sheldon."

Renee would listen to what he had to say, but felt uneasy. Why, she asked herself, couldn't she find a man she could trust; they say one thing and do the complete opposite. It had begun with her father. Errol Wilson had been an alcoholic, liar, gambler and a philanderer.

She dated from time to time, and although she had offered a few men her passion, she refused to give any her love. But everything had changed when she met Donald Rush. She offered him everything she'd withheld from every other man, and in the end he, too, had deceived her. With the others she had been able to walk away unscathed with her pride and dignity intact, but her luck had run out. It wasn't until after she'd moved out of Donald's house and spent two months with her brother and his family that she discovered she was pregnant with a married man's child.

Renee followed Sheldon up the porch and into the house. An expansive entryway was crowded with a breakfront and beveled glass curio cabinets. Many of the shelves were filled with trophies, mementoes and faded photographs of black jockeys from the mid-nineteenth century to the present. She walked through a formal living room and into another large room with a leather seating arrangement. Streams of sunlight poured in through mullioned floor-to-ceiling windows.

Sheldon pointed to a club chair. "Please sit down." He waited for Renee to sit before taking a matching love seat several feet away. He crossed one denim-covered knee over the other. He didn't know what it was, but something told him that the woman Jeremy had interviewed and subsequently hired to computerize the farm's business records would not make it through her three-month probationary period. He'd read her résumé and although she'd been office manager for one of the most prestigious law firms in Miami, it did not compare to living and working on a horse farm. He wondered how long would it take for her to tire of smelling hay and horseflesh.

He doubted whether he would have hired Renee despite her experience and exemplary references, but that decision had been taken out of his hands. She would eventually become Jeremy's responsibility once he assumed complete control of running Blackstone Farms. The final transfer of thirty years of power would take effect January first.

His gaze moved slowly from her professionally coiffed hair to a yellow silk tunic, and down to a pair of black wool crepe slacks and leather slip-ons with a renowned designer's logo. Everything about Renee Wilson screamed big-city sophistication.

"As I said before you won't be able to live in your bungalow for a few months," Sheldon began in a quiet tone. "However, I'm prepared to open my home to you until the repairs are completed."

Renee sat forward on her chair. "I'll be living with you?" She'd vowed never to live with another man, even temporarily; but she also had to remind herself that Sheldon Blackstone would be her boss for the next two months, not her lover.

The beginnings of a smile crinkled Sheldon's eyes. There was no doubt his suggestion had shocked her. "This is a big house. We won't be bumping into each other. I have a housekeeper who comes in several times a week to clean and do laundry. You'll have your own bedroom with a private bath, and a makeshift office has been set up for you on the back porch. If you don't want to take your meals in the main dining hall, or have them delivered, you may use the kitchen. If you prefer cooking for yourself, just let me know what you'll need and I'll order it from the head chef."

Despite her consternation, Renee affected a smile.
"It seems as if you've thought of everything." Sheldon,
flashing a rare, open smile, nodded. "My living here
with you won't pose a problem for your..." Her words
trailed off.

Sheldon uncrossed his legs, clasped his hands together and planted his booted feet firmly on the parquet
floor. "Are you referring to another woman?" Renee's
averted gaze answered his question. "That will not be a
problem for either of us," he continued. "There are two
Mrs. Blackstones—my sons' wives, Kelly and Tricia."
Her head came up. "My wife died twenty years ago, and
I've never been involved with *any* woman who either
lived or worked on this farm."

Renee let out an inaudible sigh. "Well then, I'll
accept your offer."

Sheldon hadn't lied to Renee. There were no other
women in his life, hadn't been in months. He had married at seventeen, become a father at eighteen, was widowed at thirty-two and now at fifty-three he planned to
retire at the end of the year.

His retirement plans included fishing, traveling and
spoiling his grandchildren. He wasn't actively seeking
a woman to share his life, but if one did come along
who shared similar interests, then he would consider a
more permanent relationship—a relationship that was
certain not to include marriage. He'd failed once as a
husband and didn't want to repeat it.

He hadn't lived a monkish existence since burying
his wife, but at no time had he ever advertised his liai-

sons. All of his encounters were always conducted off the farm. No one, and that included his sons, knew any of the women who shared his bed after he'd become a widower.

"There is a slight problem," Renee said as Sheldon pushed to his feet."

"What's that?"

"I've ordered furniture and it's scheduled to be delivered here today."

"It arrived earlier this morning," he informed her, "and I took the responsibility of having everything stored at a warehouse in Richmond."

Renee sighed in relief and rose to her feet. "Thank you."

She'd sold the entire contents of her Miami condominium before moving into Donald's palatial Miami Beach oceanfront home, and the day she left him she'd walked away with only her clothes and personal items.

Sheldon smiled at the petite woman whose head came to his shoulder. "Let me show you to your room."

"I need to get my luggage from my car."

He extended his hand. "Give me your key and I'll get it."

Opening her handbag, Renee handed him the key. A slight shock rippled up her arm as her fingers made contact with Sheldon's. She stared up at him to see if he'd felt the same reaction, but his expression was reserved.

Slipping the key into the pocket of his jeans, Sheldon escorted Renee to a curving staircase leading to the second floor. Her fingertips trailed over the mahogany banister. Their footsteps were muffled in the carpeted hallway.

Sheldon walked past three bedrooms, stopping at the last one on the right. "This one is yours. It has its own sitting room and private bath."

Renee moved beyond Sheldon and into a large, sun-filled space, feeling as if she had stepped back in time. A massive mirrored pale green armoire, the only color in the near-white bedroom, was the room's focal point. An elegant antique, white, queen-size iron bed provided the perfect complement for the armoire.

She made her way to a door in a far corner. A bathroom with an old-fashioned claw-foot bathtub, yellow floral wallpaper dotted with sprigs of leaves and berries picked up the pale green hues of an upholstered chair in a corner. Antique wall sconces added the perfect finishing touch. She left the bathroom and reentered the bedroom, noting that the bathroom's wallpaper was repeated in the sitting room.

She smiled at Sheldon as he rested a shoulder against the open door, arms crossed over his chest. His pose reminded her of a large lounging cat. "It's perfect."

He flashed an open smile. He'd thought Renee would consider the bedroom too old-fashioned. After all, she had lived in one of the country's most cosmopolitan southern cities.

He straightened from his leaning position. "I'll bring up your luggage." He turned to leave, then stopped.

"Would you like something to eat or drink? Just for to-night, dinner will be served an hour later than usual."

Renee glanced at her watch. It was after four, and she was scheduled to eat again at six. Her obstetrician had recommended she eat five small meals instead of three big ones. She had just begun her second trimester, and she had gained an average of two pounds each month.

"What time is dinner?"

"Tonight it will begin at seven."

There was no way she would be able to wait three hours before eating again, not unless she wanted a pounding headache or a fainting spell.

"I'd like a fruit salad and a glass of milk."

Sheldon's expression stilled and grew serious. "Are you a health-food fanatic?"

Renee flashed a bright smile. "I decided a couple of months ago to eat healthy. No fast foods, gooey snacks or anything with additives or preservatives."

Light gray eyes studied her intently. "Perhaps you living with me will help me reconsider some of my dietary choices." His only weakness was ice cream—lots of ice cream.

"You look quite fit to me." The words were out of Renee's mouth before she could censor herself.

Sheldon gave her a direct stare. His last physical indicated he was in excellent health for a man his age. He stood six-one and weighed one-ninety, and with a break in the hot weather he'd begun the practice of leaving his truck in the driveway and walking more.

Sheldon and Renee regarded each other with a waiting that hadn't been there before. Again, Renee felt uneasy, as if she were a specimen under a powerful microscope. She did not know the owner of Blackstone Farms and she did not want to come to know him—at least not beyond an employer-employee relationship.

She would live in Sheldon's house until her bungalow was habitable, organize and computerize years of paperwork that had been done manually and come spring she hoped to deliver a healthy son or daughter. She refused to plan beyond the time her child would go from the farm's infant center to its preschool and subsequently to the day school.

Sheldon blinked as if coming out of a trance. "I'd better go and get your bags."

His deep, soothing voice shattered the silence between them, and Renee nodded in agreement. She stood in the same spot until pressure on her bladder forced her to retreat to the bathroom.

When she returned to the bedroom she spied her bags. Two sat on the floor next to a closet, while the largest rested on a whitewashed wooden bench at the foot of the bed. Sheldon had carried up all three bags in one trip where it would have taken her at least two, maybe three.

There was no doubt he was physically fit; he was tall, broad-shouldered with a trim waist and hips. It was the first time she'd encountered a man whose magnificent physique matched his face. Sheldon Blackstone was drop-dead gorgeous.

Slipping off her shoes, she decided to shower before eating. She would have to forgo what had become a regularly scheduled afternoon nap. There were times when she'd felt so exhausted that she could not keep her eyes open, but thank goodness up till now she hadn't experienced morning sickness.

The reality that she was to become a mother had changed her outlook on life. Everything she did and every decision she made was predicated on the tiny life growing inside her.

There had been a time when she was forced to give up her dream to graduate from law school. After her father drank himself into an early grave, she went to work to help supplement her mother's meager income. But her dream of graduating college was delayed for more than a decade. It had taken her six years as a part-time student, but she did it. She now held a degree in pre-law.

Renee closed her eyes and smiled. *Live for today, and let tomorrow take care of itself.* That had been her mother's mantra, and it was now hers.

Chapter Two

Sheldon drove past the area where a large white tent had been erected for the evening's pre-race festivities. Dozens of tables were covered in white linen; folding chairs, swathed white organza tied with either black or red satin ribbon, represented the farm's silks.

It had been several years since Blackstone Farms had hosted a pre-race gala. This year was different because Ryan and Jeremy had decided to enter Shah Jahan in the International Gold Cup race.

The Thoroughbred had become the farm's racing secret, along with its jockey. Seeing diminutive Cheryl Carney astride the magnificent black colt never failed to make Sheldon's heart stop whenever horse and rider crossed the finish line. Cheryl's uncle and head trainer, Kevin Manning, had clocked Jahan at one minute, fifty-nine and one-fifth seconds for a mile and a quarter—the distance run by three-year-olds in the Kentucky Derby. The record was one-fifth second faster than Secretariat's fastest winning time in Derby history.

Sheldon took a right turn and headed for the stables. He maneuvered into a space between his sons' SUVs. He left his truck and walked into the veterinarian's office.

"Isn't it a little early for celebrating?" he asked at the same time Ryan and Jeremy touched glasses filled with an amber liquid.

Dr. Ryan Blackstone smiled at his father. He lifted his glass. "Not early enough. Jeremy has good news for you."

Jeremy shifted on his chair and smiled at his father. "Tricia and I just got back from the doctor. She's pregnant."

Sheldon's smile matched his youngest son's. He pumped his fist in the air and howled, "Boo-yaw! Give me some of that sissy stuff you're about to drink. Once you come over to my place I'll give you a shot of my special blend."

"No, Pop!"

"Oh, hell no."

Jeremy and Ryan had protested in unison.

"I know someone at ATF whom I'm certain would like to test your so-called special blend," Jeremy teased with a wide grin.

Frowning, Sheldon shook his head. "I can't believe my boys have gone soft on me."

Ryan reached for the bottle of bourbon in a cabinet behind his desk and poured a small amount into a glass for Sheldon. His dark gray eyes crinkled in amusement. "You can keep that special blend. I'd rather drink something that doesn't double as paint thinner or drain cleaner."

Sheldon's expression softened. He was proud of Jeremy and Ryan. It hadn't been easy trying to raise his two adolescent boys after Julia died. That time had been a low point in his life because he'd worked around the clock to keep the horse farm solvent while attempting to provide emotional support for his grieving children.

Ryan had become a veterinarian. He'd returned to the farm to start his practice. It had taken Jeremy fourteen years, a four-year stint in the Marine Corps and a brief career as a special agent for the Drug Enforcement Administration before he'd settled down on the farm. After recuperating from an injury he'd sustained several months before during an undercover mission in South America, Jeremy had reconnected with his childhood sweetheart, Tricia Parker. Now he and Tricia would give Sheldon his third grandchild.

The three men touched glasses. Ryan and Jeremy took furtive sips while Sheldon tossed back his drink in one swallow. He set the glass down on the desk.

"Next time buy something that doesn't taste like Kool-Aid."

Ryan frowned from under lowered lids. "There's nothing wrong with this bourbon."

Sheldon rolled his eyes at Ryan and straddled a corner of the large desk. "Renee Wilson arrived about an hour ago," he said without preamble.

Jeremy sat up straighter. "How did she take the news that she would have to live with you until her place is renovated?"

Sheldon shrugged a shoulder, the gesture quite elegant for a man his size. "I suspect she wasn't too happy about it, but she didn't show it."

Leaning back in his chair, Ryan propped his booted feet on his desk and stared directly at his father. "Jeremy told me you cussed a blue streak when he suggested she live with you."

Sheldon glared at Jeremy. "You talk too much."

Jeremy returned the glare. "Well, you did, Pop. You said words I hadn't heard since Ryan and I were kids." There had been a time when he'd used foul language because he'd heard his father use it. He paid for the infractions whenever his mother washed his mouth with lye soap. But that ended once Julia Blackstone passed away. Jeremy stopped cursing and Sheldon stopped talking. Days would go by before he would utter a single word.

"Would you like to hear a few more?" Sheldon asked.

Jeremy held up a hand and shook his head. "No, thank you. What do you think of Renee?"

"If you're asking me whether she's qualified for the job, only time will tell."

A flash of humor glinted in Jeremy's smoky gray eyes. "Personally I think she's rather cute."

Sheldon gave his youngest son an incredulous stare. "Is that why you hired her? Because she's cute?"

Jeremy sobered quickly. "No. I hired her because she's qualified. In fact, her skills are exceptional. So much so that I wonder why she'd leave a position where she earned twice what we are going to pay her to live on a horse farm."

"Only time will tell," Sheldon responded. *Perhaps she's hiding from something or someone,* he added silently. "Is Jahan ready for tomorrow?" he asked, deftly changing the topic.

He did not want to think about Renee Wilson, because like Jeremy, he, too, found her cute—very cute and quite sexy. The last woman he'd found that cute and sexy he'd married....

"He's as ready as he will ever be," Ryan answered, bringing Sheldon's thoughts back to the present. "Cheryl had him on the track with three other horses a little while ago, and for the first time he didn't seem so skittish around them. In fact he was very calm once he was led into the gate."

Sheldon stood up. "Make certain Kevin knows he's not to race him without blinkers." Kevin Manning had been Blackstone Farms' head trainer for the past fifteen years.

"We have everything under control, Pop," Ryan said curtly.

Sheldon recognized the thread of irritation creeping into Ryan's voice. Ryan thought he was being controlling again. "I'm going back to the house to get ready.

I'll see you later." Leaning over, he patted Jeremy's shoulder. "Congratulations, son."

Jeremy raised his glass in a salute. "Thanks, Pop."

Sheldon glanced at his watch as he climbed the porch steps. He had an hour to ready himself before the residents from neighboring farms arrived for the social event that usually preceded a premier race.

He walked into the house, and felt her presence immediately. It had been a long time, since Jeremy and Ryan moved into their own homes less than a quarter of a mile away, since he'd shared his roof with another person.

He headed for the staircase, but then hesitated when he heard voices. Retracing his steps he walked towards the rear of the house. A slow smile softened his mouth. Renee lay sprawled on a chaise, asleep. A pair of blue sweatpants and an oversize T-shirt had replaced her tailored attire. The radio on a table blared a popular love song.

Soft lighting from a floor lamp flattered her delicate features. Sheldon moved closer until he stood directly over Renee. Her face, relaxed in sleep, appeared so peaceful, angelic.

Who are you? Why are you here? The two questions came to his mind unbidden.

He reached out and touched her shoulder. Her eyes opened and she came awake immediately. Her gaze widened until he could see the dark centers in a pair of heavily lashed eyes that were the color of rich golden sherry. Why hadn't he noticed their odd color before?

Smiling, Sheldon straightened. "I'm sorry to wake you, but you need to get ready for tonight's party."

Renee sat up and combed her fingers through her mussed hair. "What party?"

The lingering effects of sleep had lowered her voice until it was a velvety purr. Why, he asked himself again, hadn't he also noticed the sultriness of her voice? But he knew the answer even before his mind had formed the questions. It was because he did not want to be reminded that he missed female companionship. He had become so accustomed to living alone that he'd let loose with a string of virulent expletives he hadn't uttered in years the moment Jeremy suggested their new employee live with him until her bungalow was repaired.

"Blackstone Farms is hosting a pre-race party. One of our Thoroughbreds will be racing for the first time tomorrow afternoon."

Renee swung her sock-covered feet to the floor. "How often do you host these parties?"

"It's been two years since we hosted the last one. But if Jahan wins, then we'll hold a post-race celebration Sunday afternoon."

She stood up. "Do you expect him to win?"

"There is no doubt he'll win, although the odds are 12-to-1 against him."

"I know nothing about betting on horses."

"Don't worry, I'll show you."

She shook her head. "That's okay. I'd rather not."

"Are you opposed to gambling?"

Renee gave Sheldon a long, penetrating stare. A momentary look of discomfort crossed her face and filled her eyes. "Yes, because my father was an alcoholic and a gambler. A very lethal combination. He had a wife and children who needed his support."

The moment Renee had mentioned her father she was unable to conceal her vulnerability, and Sheldon's protective instincts surfaced without warning. He wanted to take her in his arms and hold her until her pain eased. However, he would not act on his impulse, because he doubted whether she would accept the gesture.

"There's nothing wrong with gambling or drinking, if done in moderation," he countered gently.

"Moderation wasn't in my father's vocabulary."

"You don't gamble or drink." His question was a statement.

"I drink occasionally."

Sheldon smiled. "If Shah Jahan wins tomorrow, will you share a glass of champagne with me?"

Renee shook her head. "I can't."

He sobered. "You can't or you won't?"

"I can't," she repeated.

"Does it have anything to do with you working for me?"

It should only be that easy, Renee thought. She hadn't disclosed her physical condition to Jeremy during her interview, yet knew it was only a matter of time before her pregnancy became evident.

"It has nothing to do with our employee-employer status." He raised a questioning eyebrow once she paused. "I am going to have a baby."

Her explanation hit Sheldon in the face with the force of a stone propelled from a slingshot. "You're pregnant?"

She nodded. "I've just begun my fourth month."

His gaze swept over her chest before dropping to her belly as if he could see under the cotton fabric to see her expanding waistline. "What about your husband?" The farm's employment application had been revised to exclude age and marital status.

Renee was hard-pressed not to laugh at Sheldon's shocked expression. "I'm not married. My baby's father was already married."

"You slept with a married man?" he asked, his tone coolly disapproving.

Pulling back her shoulders, Renee faced him down. "I didn't know he was married. Not until I came home early from a business trip and found a woman in my bed with the man whom I thought I would eventually marry."

A myriad of emotions crossed Sheldon's handsome face. "Does he know about the baby?"

"No." The single word was emphatic.

"Are you going to tell him?"

"No," she repeated.

"He has a right to know that you're carrying his child."

Renee took a step closer to Sheldon, close enough

to detect the lingering scent of his aftershave, close enough to see the stubble of an emerging beard on his angular jaw.

"That's where you're wrong. He forfeited that right when he conveniently neglected to tell me he'd married a Las Vegas showgirl when he'd attended a trade show convention there. I'd left Florida before I knew I was pregnant, and I have no intention of returning or contacting him. I don't need him for child support, so that lets him off the hook financially."

Sheldon saw a different woman than the one who had stepped out of her car only a few hours before. Under the delicate exterior was an inner strength that was not apparent at first glance.

She had come to Blackstone Farms to work and live, yet had not come alone. Now he understood why she sought out a position that offered on-site child care. A knowing smile touched his mobile mouth as he recalled the number of babies born to longtime employees who were now a part of the farm's extended family. His daughter-in-law Tricia had been a Blackstone Farms baby.

"I'll call the contractor Monday and have him add another bedroom to your bungalow."

Renee looked at Sheldon in astonishment, her jaw dropping. "Why?" The query came out in a breathless whisper.

Her reaction to his offer amused Sheldon. "Every child needs his or her own room, a place to call their own."

A dimpled smile curved her lush mouth. "You're right. Thank you, Sheldon."

He gave her a direct stare. "Your thanks may be a little premature, because I'm a hard taskmaster, Renee. You'll only have three months to bring Blackstone Farms into the twenty-first century. Everything, and that includes payroll and purchase orders, has been done manually for thirty years. And that translates into thousands of pieces of paper. Jeremy wants the farm's revenue and expenses computerized before he takes over in January.

"If you need someone to assist you on a temporary basis, just ask. More importantly, if you don't understand something, ask questions." His expression softened, his gaze as tender as a caress. "I may bark a lot, but I've never been known to bite."

Within minutes Renee recognized a maddening hint of arrogance in the owner of Blackstone Farms, but there was something in his manner that soothed rather than agitated her. There was no doubt they would be able to live and work together.

"I'll make certain to remember that."

He smiled again. "Good. Now, if you'll excuse me I have to get ready for a party."

She returned his smile. "I'll be ready by seven."

Renee still saw the broad shoulders under a pale blue denim shirt as she leaned over to turn off the radio. The enclosed back porch was the ideal workspace. Screened-in floor-to-ceiling windows faced the southeast. There would be an abundance of light during daylight hours. The area where she sat on the chaise had a wrought-iron table with seating for two, an entertainment center and an adjoining half bath. She could work, eat and relax without leaving the porch.

She would take the weekend to settle in, acquaint herself with the layout of the farm and its residents, before she began the task she'd been hired to do Monday morning.

Nightfall had descended on Blackstone Farms like a translucent navy-blue veil when Sheldon stepped out onto the porch to find Renee sitting on the rocker waiting for him.

His eyes widened in appreciation as she rose gracefully to her feet. She had pinned her hair atop her head, adding several inches, and a pair of three-inch black pumps added further to her diminutive height. A black dress and matching jacket pulled her winning look together. A pair of magnificent diamond earrings adorning her lobes supported Renee's claim that she could support her child on her own.

Sheldon forced himself to concentrate on her face and not her legs. A light breeze stirred the perfume on her body, and he froze. The fragrance had been Julia's favorite.

Renee saw his startled look. "Is something wrong?"

"No," he said a little too quickly. "You look very nice."

A wave of heat washed over her face, settling in her cheeks. "Thank you. So do you." Sheldon's dark suit looked as if it had been tailored expressly for his tall frame.

He moved closer, extending his arm, and he was not disappointed when Renee curved a hand over the sleeve of his suit jacket. "Thank you very much."

Renee was certain Sheldon could feel her trembling. There was something about the man that disturbed her—in every way, and she knew an attraction to him would be perilous to her emotional well-being. She hadn't missed the smoldering flame of awareness in the gray orbs when he'd stepped out onto the porch. The flame had flared to life before he'd successfully shuttered his gaze.

Sheldon looked good, smelled good and felt even better. Her hand rested lightly on his sleeve, yet she felt the power in his arm as hard muscle flexed under her light touch.

"Aren't you going to close the inner door?" she asked as he escorted her off the porch.

Sheldon covered her hand with his free one, squeezing her fingers gently. "My door always stays open until I retire for bed. The same goes for everyone who lives on the farm. That is one of the few mandates everyone is expected to follow."

She glanced up at him as he led her to a luxury sedan parked in the driveway behind his pickup truck. "What are the others?"

"One is that you leave the key to your vehicle in the ignition in case it has to be moved in an emergency, and the most important one is all residents must check in with one another during violent weather."

Sheldon opened the passenger side door and she slid onto the leather seat, mentally filing away the mandates. There was no doubt her life on the farm would be vastly different from the one in Miami.

Her mouth went suddenly dry as she watched Sheldon remove his jacket and hang it up on a hook behind his seat. Suddenly everything about him seemed so much larger, broader. He sat down and turned on the ignition and automatic seat restraints lowered over their chests and waists.

Turning his head, Sheldon stared at Renee. "Is the belt too tight for you?"

She met his gaze, the lights from the dashboard illuminating his eyes. "It's fine, thank you."

She was relieved that she had revealed her pregnancy; however, she did not want Sheldon to make allowances for her because of her condition.

Sheldon shifted the car into gear and backed out of the driveway. Within minutes they arrived at the area where tiny white bulbs, strung over fences, around branches of trees and the poles holding up a massive white tent, sparkled like flawless diamonds. He maneuvered into a parking space. Taped music flowed from large speakers set around the party perimeter in anticipation of an evening of dining and dancing under the autumn sky.

Sheldon slipped into his jacket, then came around the car to assist Renee, his right hand going to the small of her back. She stiffened slightly before relaxing her spine against his splayed fingers.

"I want to introduce you to my daughters-in-law before it gets too crowded," he said close to her ear. Lowering his arm, he reached for her hand, holding it gently and protectively in his warm, strong grasp.

Renee followed Sheldon as he led the way across the tent to a table where two women sat laughing hysterically. Sheldon cleared his throat and their heads came up at the same time.

Both were pretty, but the one with dark slanting eyes in an equally dark brown face was stunning. Her short curly hair was cut to complement her exquisite features.

Sheldon released Renee's hand, reached out and gently pulled Tricia Parker-Blackstone from her chair. Lowering his head, he kissed her cheek. "Congratulations. I'm so happy for you and Jeremy."

Smiling broadly, Tricia hugged Sheldon. "Thank you, Pop."

He held her at arm's length. "How are you feeling?"

"Not too bad. The nausea comes and goes."

He noticed the direction of Kelly's and Tricia's gazes. Shifting, he extended a hand to Renee. He wasn't disappointed when she placed her hand in his. "Kelly, Tricia, I'd like for you to meet Renee Wilson, our new administrative assistant. Renee, these are my daughters, Kelly and Tricia. Kelly is headmistress of Blackstone Farms Day School and Tricia is the school's nurse." The three women exchanged handshakes.

Kelly Blackstone had draped a red silk shawl over a

flowing black tank dress. She smiled at Renee. "It looks as if you came on board at the right time. Blackstone Farms is renowned for hosting the best pre-race party in Virginia's horse country."

The words were barely off Kelly's lips when a booming voice sliced the night. "Hey, Blackstone! I heard that you have a wonder horse better than the legendary Affirmed." A tall, florid-faced man with tousled silver-blond hair nodded to Tricia and Kelly. "Ladies."

Renee watched Sheldon's expression change, become somber. It was obvious he wasn't too fond of the middle-aged man.

"Someone has been lying to you, Taylor," Sheldon said quietly. "I'm certain you've seen the odds."

Kent Taylor, owner of Taylor Stables, stared boldly at Renee. "That's only because no one outside Blackstone Farms has seen him run."

"You'll see all you'll need to see tomorrow afternoon," Sheldon countered.

When it was obvious Sheldon wasn't going to introduce Renee, Kent Taylor's too-bright grin faded. "Are you saying I should put some money on Shah Jahan?"

"No, I am not." Sheldon's voice was a dangerously soft tone, his southern drawl even more pronounced. "I suggest you bet on something that is a sure thing."

Kent sobered. "Now that sounds like a challenge to me."

A mocking smile crinkled Sheldon's eyes. "That's why we have horse races, Taylor."

Kent nodded in agreement. "Tonight I'm going to

enjoy your food and liquor. Sunday afternoon I'll return the favor when I host the post-race victory celebration."

Sheldon's face was marked with loathing as his closest neighbor turned and walked away with an exaggerated swagger. He did not know why the man always attempted to turn the sport of horse-racing into a back-alley brawl.

Kelly grunted softly under her breath. "Now I see why he's been married so many times. No normal woman would be able to tolerate his overblown ego for more than a week."

Tricia waved a hand in front of her face. "He smells as if he's been sampling his own liquor cabinet before he got here."

Within minutes of Kent Taylor's departure Ryan and Jeremy arrived, carrying plates for their wives.

"Taylor just passed us, talking trash as usual," Ryan said, as he set a plate on the table in front of Kelly.

"He's a blowhard," Sheldon spat out.

Jeremy, leaning on a cane, extended his free hand to Renee. "Hello again, and welcome to Blackstone Farms."

She shook his hand before repeating the gesture with Ryan. Sheldon's sons had inherited his dramatic good looks and commanding manner.

Sheldon's arm moved up and around Renee's shoulders. He lowered his head and asked, "Hungry?"

Her head came up, her mouth within inches of his. "Starved."

Smiling, he winked at her. "Good. Come with me."

* * *

Renee lay on her side in the darkened bedroom, smiling. She was tired, but too wound up to sleep. Her first day at Blackstone Farms had become a memorable one. She'd attended her first pre-race party, met people whom she would get to know in the coming weeks and she'd found herself drawn to a man whose roof she would share until her own house was ready to move into.

She closed her eyes, a whisper of a sigh escaping her parted lips. Renee remembered, before sleep claimed her, the power in Sheldon Blackstone's arm whenever it circled her waist. There had been nothing sexual in the gesture, even though his touch communicated comfort and protection: two things she would need in the coming months.

Chapter Three

When Renee had gotten up earlier that morning she did not know she would become a participant in a spectacle resembling a fashion show rather than a horse race. She'd called her brother to let him know she had arrived safely, then waited another hour before calling her mother. Her mother had remarried two years before and had relocated to Seattle, Washington, with her new husband and stepchildren.

The weather was picture-perfect for a horse race. A bright blue sky with a few puffy white clouds, temperatures in the midseventies, moderate humidity, no wind and a slightly damp track from an early morning shower set the stage for Virginia's annual International Gold Cup.

She sat in a private box at the Great Meadow racetrack with Sheldon, Ryan, Kelly, Jeremy, Tricia and Kevin Manning, the trainer. Those in the grandstand representing Blackstone Farms had pinned red and black boutonnieres to their lapels.

Renee felt Sheldon's muscled shoulder as she leaned into him. "Why didn't you tell me I'd have to walk the red carpet to get to your box?" Many of the women occupying the private boxes were decked out in haute couture and expensive jewelry.

Sheldon gave Renee a sidelong glance. She had worn her hair down and the ends curved sensuously under her jaw, framing a rounded face that had enraptured him from first glance.

"There was no reason to say anything to you," he said close to her ear. "You have exquisite taste in clothing, and your natural beauty is a refreshing alternative to these plastic women with their designer labels, baubles and surgically altered features and bodies. Some of them have nearly bankrupted their husbands and boyfriends because they view aging as a terminal disease."

Renee did not have time to react to Sheldon's compliment as the voice blaring through the public address system garnered everyone's attention. The horses competing for the International Gold Cup were being led into position at the starting gate.

She peered through a pair of binoculars at the horses. A shiver of excitement coursed through her as she spied Cheryl Carney's petite figure in black-and-red silks atop the magnificent black stallion.

An eerie hush descended over the track as jockeys

settled their horses. After several anxiety-filled minutes the gates opened and the horses and riders shot forth.

Renee was on her feet like the others in the box, mouth gaping, heart pounding, legs trembling. Shah Jahan streaked around the track in a blur, his hoofs seemingly never touching the earth. Jeremy and Ryan were shouting at the top of their lungs while Sheldon pounded the railing of the box with both fists. Kevin stood paralyzed, eyes closed, hands fisted, praying silently.

Halfway around the track it was evident the other horses would never catch Shah Jahan. Recovering her voice, Renee screamed along with everyone else. Cheryl and Jahan raced across the finish line eight lengths ahead of the second-place winner, and Renee found herself lifted off her feet and her mouth covered with an explosive kiss that sucked oxygen from her laboring lungs.

Her arms came up of their own volition and curled around Sheldon's neck. She lost herself in the man *and* the moment. Without warning the kiss changed from shared jubilation to a soft, gentle caress and then to an urgent exploration that left her mouth burning with a fire where she literally swooned in Sheldon's arms. Somehow she found a remnant of strength to pull away. Her head dropped to his shoulder as she inhaled to clear her head and slow down her heartbeat.

"Sheldon." She'd whispered his name.

"Yes?" he gasped as he buried his face in her fragrant hair.

"Please, Sheldon," Renee pleaded, "let me go."

Slowly, deliberately he did let her go. Sheldon stared over Renee's head, his gaze meeting and fusing with Ryan's.

A smile inched up the corners of the veterinarian's mouth as he winked at his father. "We did it, Pop."

Sheldon set Renee on her feet and nodded. "Yes, *you* did."

Jeremy leaned over and pounded Sheldon's back. "We've just broken the track record!"

The words were barely out of his mouth when the employees of Blackstone Farms pumped their fists, shouting, "Boo-yaw!" The grandstand reverberated with their victory cry.

The chanting continued as Sheldon leaned over and handed Ryan two betting slips. "Take care of these after you and Jeremy stand in for me in the winner's circle." Kevin had left the box, heading for the winner's circle.

Ryan shook his head. "We can't, Pop. We're not the owners."

"Today you are," Sheldon countered. "You and Jeremy better go join Kevin and Cheryl."

Jeremy stared at his father. "You're kidding, aren't you?" He had expected Sheldon to leave the box and pose for photographers and talk to reporters from major cable sports channels, magazines and newspapers.

Sheldon shook his head. "No, I'm not."

"You can't, Pop!"

His eyes darkened like angry thunderclouds. "Please don't tell me what I can or cannot do." His expression changed like quicksilver, softening as he lowered his chin, smiled at Renee and reached for her hand. "Renee and I will meet you back at the farm."

Those in the Blackstone box stood numbly, watching as Sheldon led Renee away.

Jeremy stared at Ryan. "What's up with them?"

Ryan shook his head at the same time as he shrugged a broad shoulder under his suit jacket. "Beats the hell out of me, little brother."

Kelly looped her arm through Ryan's. "Stay out of it, darling."

He gave her a questioning stare. "Do you know something I don't?"

Kelly pressed a kiss to his smooth cheek. "I'm pleading the Fifth." She had noticed Sheldon staring at Renee, a look she was more than familiar with whenever Ryan looked at her.

Ryan opened his mouth again, but she placed her fingertips over his lips. "They are expecting the Blackstones to join their winning horse and jockey in the winner's circle."

Ryan grasped his wife's hand and followed Jeremy and Tricia out of the box. He shook his head, grinning broadly. "Pop and a woman," he whispered to Kelly. "I suppose there is hope for the old man after all."

Sheldon helped Renee into his car before rounding the sedan to sit behind the wheel. His decision not to talk to the media was based upon his initial opposition to enter Shah Jahan in the International Gold Cup race.

He'd felt the Thoroughbred wasn't ready to compete, but Ryan and Jeremy had overruled him and therefore the victory was theirs.

He started up the car and left the parking area, heading for the interstate. Once he set the cruise control button, he chanced a quick glance at Renee. She sat motionless, eyes closed and her chest rising and falling gently in an even rhythm. He returned his gaze to the road in front of him before risking another glance at her flawless face. Being pregnant agreed with her. She was exquisite, her skin glowing like brown satin.

He recalled the violent expletives he'd spewed after Jeremy suggested Renee live with him until her bungalow was ready. He guarded his privacy with the zealousness of a leopard secreting his kill from marauding scavengers. He did not want someone to monitor his comings and goings. Ryan had become accustomed to his declaration of "I'm going to be away for a few days." He had made it a practice of spending two or three days each week at his mountain retreat, but that would change because of the petite woman sitting beside him.

A smile stole its way across his face as he recalled the taste and softness of her mouth and soft fullness of her breasts when he kissed her. The action had begun impulsively before it changed into a deliberate, purposeful need to possess her mouth and more. The *more* wasn't sleeping with her—that he could do with other women, but an inclination to take care of her.

Why Renee, he did not know. But in the coming months he was certain he would find out.

A slight smile played at the corners of Renee's mouth as she turned her head slightly and stared from under lowered lids at the man sitting beside her. He had discarded his suit jacket and tie, and unbuttoned the collar to his crisp white shirt. He was so virile and masculine that she forced herself to glance away.

The memory of his kiss still lingered along the fringes of her mind. The initial joining of their mouths was shocking, unexpected. But everything had changed once she kissed him back with a hunger that had belied her outward calm. The caress of his lips and the solid crush of his body had sent spirals of desire through Renee that she hadn't wanted to acknowledge, because Sheldon was her boss—a man who wore his masculinity like a badge of honor.

"Where are we going?" she asked after seeing a road sign indicating the number of miles to Staunton. The farm was in the opposite direction.

"Somewhere to celebrate." Sheldon winked at Renee when she gave him a questioning look. "Do you like ice cream?"

"Does Don King need a hair transplant?"

There was a moment of silence before deep, rumbling laughter filled the sedan. Those who were familiar with Sheldon Blackstone would have been stunned by the sound, because it had been nearly twenty years since they'd heard his unrestrained laughter. He hadn't laughed out loud since he'd become a widower.

Renee found Sheldon's laughter infectious. She joined him, and within seconds they were laughing so hard he was forced to pull over onto the shoulder of the road.

Sheldon was still smiling as he rested an arm over the back of the passenger seat. Sobering, he gave Renee a long, penetrating look and marveled that she could laugh given her circumstances. She'd walked away from a position, one in which she'd been paid well, to work on a farm because a man she'd lived with had betrayed her.

Life had dealt her two losing hands when it came to men; first her father, then her lover. Had Renee been unlucky in love or had she unconsciously fallen in love with a lover with the same failings as her father?

In another five months she would deliver a baby and he wondered whether Renee would change her mind and contact her ex to inform him that he had become a father?

The questions bombarded Sheldon as his expression changed, growing tight with a realization he did not want to think about. There was something about Renee Wilson that reminded him of his late wife, something that evoked emotions he hadn't felt since he was seventeen.

An hour after he'd been introduced to Julia he'd known he wanted to marry her. But he didn't want to marry again. The truth was he wouldn't risk his heart again to the devastation he'd felt when Julia had died. He had failed Julia as a husband and he'd long ago vowed that he would never make that mistake again. He could not propose marriage to Renee as he had with Julia, but he intended to offer her and her child his protection as long as she was a resident of Blackstone Farms. He would do no less for any employee.

He removed his arm from her seat, put the car in gear and headed for downtown Staunton.

Sheldon escorted Renee into Shorty's Diner. The popular restaurant on Richmond Road had become a favorite with locals and tourists. All stainless steel with neon lights and colorful glass, it was an exact replica of a 1950s jukebox. They were seated at the last remaining table and given menus.

Sheldon watched Renee as she looked around. "It's not fancy, but the food is good."

"Fancy doesn't always mean good," she countered. "I once ate at a Miami Beach restaurant, which will remain nameless, whose construction costs exceeded three million dollars. The food was horrific."

"Are they still open?"

"Unfortunately, yes. People go there because the owner paid off the food critic, and right now it's the place to go to be seen. The paparazzi hang around every night, hoping to get a glimpse of the celebrities who congregate there."

Reaching across the table, Sheldon placed a hand

on Renee's, tightening his hold when she attempted to extract her fingers. "Do you miss Miami?"

She closed her eyes and shook her head. When she opened them she gave him a direct stare. "No, I don't. Once I decided to leave I knew I'd never go back."

He eased his grip, but did not release her hand. "What do you want?"

A slight frown furrowed her smooth forehead. "What do you mean?"

"What do you want for yourself? Your future?"

Renee could feel Sheldon's sharp eyes boring into her. His gaze was penetrating, but there was also something lazily seductive in the look. It had only taken twenty-four hours to feel the seductive pull of his spell. And if she hadn't needed a job or a place to live she would've driven away from Blackstone Farms and its owner minutes after coming face-to-face with him. Yet there was something in the light gray eyes that communicated that she could trust him to protect her and her child.

"I want to complete my probationary period without mishap, move into my own bungalow, go to law school and give birth to a healthy son or daughter. Not necessarily in that order," she added with an enchanting, dimpled smile.

A network of attractive lines fanned out around Sheldon's luminous eyes. "I certainly can help you with your probationary status. I'll tell Jeremy to waive your probationary clause."

"You can do that?"

Sheldon removed his hand. His strong jaw tensed. "I can. Besides, you don't need any added stress in your life at this time."

Renee was hard-pressed not to kiss him. A warm glow flowed through her as her features became more animated. "Thank you, Sheldon."

He angled his head and gave her a sensual smile. "You're welcome, Renee." There was a pulse beat of silence before he asked, "Are you hungry?"

She shook her head. "No. I can wait for dinner."

He closed the plastic-covered binder. "Then we'll have some ice cream."

Renee and Sheldon returned to Blackstone Farms to find Ryan sitting on the porch waiting for them. He'd changed out of his suit and into a pair of jeans, boots and a cotton V-neck sweater. He rose to his feet, his expression grim. He handed Sheldon a large manila envelope.

"I thought you should see this before it's aired later on tonight on ESPN. There's no doubt it will also appear in the *Virginian-Pilot*."

Renee turned to make her way into the house, but Ryan reached out and touched her arm. "You should also see this, Renee."

She hadn't realized her heart was pumping wildly until she saw the photograph of her and Sheldon locked in a passionate embrace in the box at Great Meadow. The picture was taken at the exact moment she'd put her arms around his neck. The kiss had only lasted seconds, but the image of her kissing the owner of Blackstone Farms would last forever.

"Who gave this to you?" Sheldon had spoken to his son, while his gaze was fixed on Renee's shocked expression.

"Eddie Ray."

Sheldon shifted his attention on Ryan. "Are you certain it's going to be televised?"

Ryan nodded. "Eddie freelances for several tabloids and he loves uncovering scandals."

"There is no scandal," Sheldon retorted. The scowl marring his handsome face vanished as he stared at Renee. "I'm sorry to have put you in a compromising position."

Renee's smile belied her uneasiness. "Don't beat up on yourself. Neither of us can undo what has already been done."

She peered closely at the photograph. Only her profile was discernible, but the diamond studs Donald had given her as a graduation gift glittered in her lobes. Biting down on her lower lip, she prayed no one would recognize her in the arms of the man who owned Virginia's most celebrated African-American horse farm—especially Donald Rush.

She had left Florida believing Donald would never follow her; but what if he linked her to Sheldon Blackstone of Blackstone Farms and uncovered that the child she carried was his? Despite his deception, would he be vindictive enough to wage a legal battle for custody? There was no way she could win against a man who had amassed millions of dollars as a toy manufacturer. Unshed tears glistened in her eyes.

"I have to go inside." She had to get away from Ryan and Sheldon before she embarrassed herself.

Sheldon watched the screen door open and close behind Renee's departing figure. He waited a full minute, then let loose with a diatribe that included what he wanted to do to Eddie Ray.

Ryan slipped his hands into the pockets of his jeans, rocking back on his heels. "Folks outside the farm are going to want to know who the mystery woman is."

"Who she is is none of their damn business!"

"There's already been talk, Pop."

"What about?" Sheldon snapped angrily.

"About you and Renee. You were all over her last night like white on rice, and today at the track the two of you looked like a..." His words trailed off.

"We looked like what?"

Ryan ignored his father's angry glare. "A couple."

"Is that how you see us, Ryan? As a couple?"

The veterinarian gave a sheepish grin. "From what I've seen of the two of you—yes."

Sheldon put the photograph into the envelope and thrust it at Ryan. "Go home to your wife and children," he drawled. Turning, he pushed open the screen door and walked into his house.

He had to talk to Renee and reassure her that he would do everything in his power to protect her from salacious gossip. Horse farms had all of the characteristics of a small town. Any rumor was a prerequisite for scandal. Climbing the staircase to the second floor, he made his way along the hallway. Her bedroom door stood open. He rapped lightly. There was no response; he knocked again, then walked in.

Renee sat on a chair in the sitting room, her bare feet resting on a matching footstool. Although her eyes were closed, he knew she was not asleep.

"Renee?"

Her eyes opened and she stared at him as if he were a stranger. Her lower lip trembled as she smiled through the moisture shimmering in her gold-brown eyes. "I'm okay," she lied smoothly.

The truth was she wasn't okay, because if Donald saw the photograph he would know the identity of the woman in Sheldon Blackstone's arms.

Sheldon did not believe Renee. She looked delicate, vulnerable. He moved closer, reached down and pulled her gently off the chair. He gathered her to his chest, resting his chin on the top of her head.

"What are you afraid of, Renee?"

She tried to slow down her runaway heartbeat. "What makes you think I'm afraid?"

"You're trembling."

The possibility that Donald would attempt to contact her at Blackstone Farms held her captive with fear. "I don't want him to find me," she sobbed against Sheldon's chest.

Cradling her face between his palms, he kissed her eyelids, his tongue capturing the moisture streaking her cheeks. "Don't cry, baby." She quieted as he comforted her, his hand moving over her spine. "Who is he, princess?"

She sighed softly. "His name is Donald Rush."

"What does he do?"

"He's a successful toy manufacturer."

Easing back, Sheldon anchored a hand under her chin and raised her tear-stained face. "You will be safe here. No one, and I mean no one, can come onto the property without being detected. And if he comes after you, then we'll have a surprise for him."

"What?"

"He'll be shot for trespassing."

Renee smiled despite her anxiety. "I hope it won't come to that."

"The decision will be his. Enough about Donald Rush." A frown settled into his features. "Now, we have to talk about you and me."

Her eyes widened. "What about us?"

"Ryan reports there's been gossip about us being a couple."

Her mouth dropped open. "But we're not," she said, recovering her voice.

"*We* know that. But, what's going to happen once your condition becomes evident?"

Pulling out of Sheldon's loose embrace, Renee walked over to a window and stared down at the leaves of a towering tree that had turned a brilliant red-orange. She turned and met his gaze.

"You think they'll believe I'm carrying your baby?"

Sheldon closed the distance between them. "I'm certain some people will believe that."

"What are we going to do, Sheldon?"

He crossed his arms over his chest. "Let them believe whatever they want."

She raised her eyebrows. "You don't care?"

"No. I stopped listening to gossip a long time ago."

"What do you propose?" Renee asked.

"Let me take care of you," Sheldon said without hesitating.

Renee's mind was spinning in bewilderment. Why was Sheldon giving her double messages? He'd said they weren't a couple—and they weren't. Then in the next breath he'd offered to take care of her.

"How?"

"Live here with me until the spring and become my hostess at all social events on and off the farm."

Her eyelids fluttered, her emotions spun out of control and she tried to digest his proposition. Not only would she work for Sheldon, but she would also live with him beyond the time he had projected her bungalow would be ready for occupancy. She would also become an actress whenever she stepped into a role as his date at social functions.

"Will this arrangement be on a strictly business level?"

Sheldon studied Renee thoughtfully for a moment. His eyes drank in her delicate face, unaware of the smoldering invitation in their silvery depths.

"It would be if I were your boss," he said in a deep, quiet voice.

She blinked once. "But you are my boss."

"Effective midnight, October thirty-first, I will officially retire as CEO of Blackstone Farms."

"But that's next week." There was no mistaking the shock in her voice.

Sheldon nodded. "I can't ask you to host a party for me if I'm your boss. That would be slimy *and* unethical."

Let me take care of you. His words came rushing back, and Renee stared at the man who within twenty-four hours had offered her what neither her father nor Donald had or could: his protection.

Tilting her chin in a defiant gesture, Renee gave him a challenging look. "You didn't answer my question, Mr. Sheldon Blackstone. Business or pleasure?"

He leaned in close, close enough for his breath to caress her cheek. "That decision will have to be yours, Miss Renee Wilson."

Renee felt in control for the first time since viewing the photograph. Sheldon was so compelling that her heart fluttered wildly in her breast. His nearness was overwhelming, presence potent.

Smiling, she said softly, "Strictly business."

Sheldon nodded, dipped his head and brushed his mouth over hers. He pulled back. "Business it is."

Renee stood, rooted to the spot as Sheldon turned and walked out of her bedroom. Once she realized what she'd agreed to, she floated down to the armchair and rested her bare feet on the tapestry footstool.

Living at Blackstone Farms would give her a chance to heal as she prepared for a new life for herself and her unborn child. However, she had to be very careful, because she had no intention of permitting herself to succumb to Sheldon Blackstone's intoxicatingly sensual spell.

Chapter Four

The televised footage of the International Gold Cup and the image of her kissing Sheldon were both aired on ESPN, compounding her anxiety that Donald might recognize her.

Renee existed in a state of fear, believing that Donald would show up at Blackstone Farms demanding to see her. One day became two and eventually a week before she was finally able to relax.

She found the cooler morning and evening temperatures a welcome respite from Miami's sultry heat and humidity, and the task of bringing Blackstone Farms into the electronic age challenging. It had taken a day to set up a system for an electronic payroll procedure and two more to program a database for purchase orders. Her respect for Sheldon increased appreciably once she realized the amount of money needed for a horse farm's viability. And despite the glitter and glamour of pre-and post-race parties the behind-the-scenes work was ongoing: feeding, grooming and exercising thirty-four Thoroughbreds, mucking out stalls, daily medical checkups for lameness and other equine maladies and the repair of paddocks and posts.

A knock on her office door garnered her attention. Swiveling on her chair, she saw Sheldon's broad shoulders filling out the doorway. Dressed in a pair of jeans, boots and pullover sweater, he presented a formidable figure in black.

She gave him a bright smile. "Good afternoon."

Sheldon winked at her. "Good afternoon. I came to tell you that Kelly has recruited us to help make jack-o'-lanterns."

It was Friday, Halloween and an official Blackstone Farms school holiday. The faculty and staff had organized a read-a-thon for students, in grades four to six, reading from the works of Mary Wollstonecraft Shelley, Bram Stoker, Edgar Allan Poe and J.K. Rowling.

Renee raised her eyebrows. "I've never made a jack-o'-lantern."

Sheldon studied Renee. He'd found her fresh-scrubbed face and her hair piled haphazardly atop her head innocently alluring. The image of her in his bed and her hair spread over his pillow popped into his head and popped out just as quickly. He did not want to lump her into the category of the other women who'd shared his bed, but would never share his life.

He had deliberately avoided her because he needed to know whether he was attracted to her because of her feminine sensuality or because he really liked Renee Wilson.

Even though he had kept his distance, he still could not stop thinking about her. It was October thirty-first, the day he intended to announce his retirement. After today, he intended to openly pursue her, hopefully satisfying his curiosity.

"It gets easier after you mutilate your first dozen or so."

The dimples in her cheeks deepened as her smile widened. "What happens to the ones that don't make it?"

"They become pies."

She wrinkled her nose. "How very convenient. Give me a minute to save these files."

Sheldon watched Renee shut down her computer and put her desk in order. If he had had any doubts as to her qualifications they were quickly dashed once she convinced Jeremy to set up the farm's payroll account with a local bank that offered service-free accounts to new depositors. Actual payroll checks would be replaced with electronic transfers, thereby eliminating the need for paper.

Renee turned off the desk lamp and stood up. "Where are we going to create these masterpieces?"

"The school's cafeteria." Sheldon glanced down at her feet. She had on a pair of sensible low-heeled boots.

"Do you feel up to walking?" The school was a quarter of a mile from his house.

"I don't mind walking, but I will need a jacket." The oversize cotton knit tunic was perfect for moderate afternoon temperatures, but Renee doubted whether it would be adequate after the sun set.

Extending his hand, Sheldon closed the distance between them. "If it gets too cool for you I'll get someone to drive you back."

"What about you?"

"The cool weather doesn't bother me."

Renee placed her hand in Sheldon's, smiling when he squeezed her fingers gently. There were calluses on his palms, indicating he was certainly no stranger to hard work.

Waiting until they had stepped out into the bright early afternoon sunlight, Renee asked, "How did you get into the horse-racing business?"

A faraway look filled his eyes as he pondered the question, contemplating how much he wanted to tell Renee about his past. He decided to be forthcoming.

"I hadn't planned on racing horses. My father was a tobacco farmer, as was his father before him. They grew and harvested some of the finest tobacco in the state, but that ended when my mother died from lung cancer. She had a two-pack-a-day cigarette habit that literally consumed her. As she lay dying she made Dad promise two things: marry her and stop growing tobacco."

"Did he marry her?"

Sheldon nodded. "Yes, but it was not what you would consider a legal union."

Renee glanced up at his distinctive profile. "Why not?"

A muscle in his jaw tensed. "My mother worked for him."

A tense silence enveloped them as they walked. "Your father was white and your mother black," Renee stated after a prolonged silence. Sheldon's eye color, hair texture and features were characteristic of someone of mixed blood.

The tense lines in his face relaxed, and Sheldon nodded again. "Virginia's miscegenation law would not permit them to marry."

"But you say they were married."

"There was no license nor any record of the marriage at the courthouse. A black minister who swore an oath of secrecy performed the ceremony. James Blackstone buried his wife, and three months later harvested his last tobacco crop.

"Dad took his life savings and bought twenty-two horses. It's ironic that he knew nothing about breeding horses, but told everyone he was a quick learner. And he was right. He made huge profits selling horses to farmers and for riding.

"He wanted me to go to college, then eventually take over from him. But I told him I didn't want to be a horse breeder. We argued constantly. After one particularly hostile exchange, I drove to Richmond and enlisted in the army."

"How old were you?"

"Seventeen. I know it broke Dad's heart because he knew I would be sent to Vietnam. I went to South Carolina for basic training, met a girl there, fell in love and married her before I was shipped out. I was assigned to Special Forces and trained as a sniper."

Renee remembered his comment about shooting trespassers. "Did you and your father ever reconcile?"

"Yes. After Julia wrote and told me she was pregnant, she went to live with Dad."

"Why didn't she stay with her folks?"

"They felt she had disgraced them by marrying out of her social circle."

Renee's delicate jaw dropped. "You're joking?"

"I wish," Sheldon drawled. "Julia's family, the Grants, believe they are the black elite, aristocrats of color."

Sheldon released Renee's hand, curved an arm around her waist, picked her up and moved quickly off the road. Within seconds a pickup truck sped past them.

She leaned into Sheldon; her heart pounded in her chest as he set her on her feet. She hadn't heard the truck. "You must have ears like a bat."

He smiled down at her. "If you live here long enough you'll be able to hear a frog croak a mile away."

Tilting her chin, Renee met his amused gaze. "I like living here. I thought it would be boring and much too quiet after living in Miami."

"I'm glad you like living here, because I like you, Renee."

"Thank you. It makes it easier to work together if we like each other."

His light gray eyes captured her warm gold-brown ones. "I don't think you understand my liking."

"What is there to understand, Sheldon?" she argued softly. "You *like* me."

Tightening his hold on her waist, he pulled her gently under a copse of trees. "I don't think you understand how much I like you, Renee. Maybe I should show you." Lowering his head slowly, deliberately, he brushed his lips against hers.

Renee clung to him like a drowning swimmer as his warm, moist, demanding mouth called, and she answered the call. This kiss was nothing like the one they'd shared in the box at Great Meadow. It was persuasive, coaxing. A fire she had not felt in a long time flared to life, and standing on tiptoe she opened her mouth to his probing tongue. Curving her arms under his shoulders, she communicated silently that she liked him, too—a lot.

She had spent a week telling herself that she had not been affected by Sheldon's kiss, that she did not find him attractive and that their agreement to pose as a couple was preposterous.

She had told herself that women gave birth to babies every day without a husband or a man in their lives, yet with each month bringing her closer to motherhood she knew that was not the kind of life she wanted for herself. She wanted someone with her whenever she went for her checkups; someone to massage her aching back and legs because she wasn't used to carrying the extra weight; someone with her in the delivery room to share her joy once she brought her son or daughter into the world.

She wanted that and so much more, but refused to think of the more.

Sheldon couldn't get enough of Renee. He kissed her mouth, the end of her nose, her eyes and then moved to the hollow of her fragrant throat. Nothing mattered except the woman in his arms.

He smiled when Renee giggled softly. "What are you laughing at?" he whispered in her ear.

"You," she whispered back. "I think you've made your point."

As he eased back, his gaze caught and held hers. "I don't think I have."

Her smile faded, and the pulse in her throat fluttered erratically, making swallowing difficult. "What are you talking about?"

Sheldon pressed a kiss to her ear. "I'm a little rusty when it comes to the dating game, so you're going to have to help me out before we make our debut as a couple."

Renee anchored her palms against his chest, pushing him back. "When?"

"Next month. I've committed to attend the wedding of a friend's daughter."

She rested her hands on her hips. "Next month," she repeated. "Tomorrow is next month."

"It's three weeks from now."

"Three weeks will give me enough time to shop for something to wear. My body is changing rapidly." He reached for her, but she moved out of arm's reach. "If you need me to act as your date or hostess you're going to have to let me know well in advance, because I'm extremely busy. After all, I do work nine-to-five, and I also have to have time to see my obstetrician."

The mention of an obstetrician sobered Sheldon as if he had been doused with cold water. Although Renee's body hadn't displayed the obvious signs of her pregnancy he was always cognizant that she was carrying another man's child—a man from whom she was hiding.

He nodded. "I'll give you the dates and events of my social commitments. I'll also take you to Staunton tomorrow so you can shop for whatever you need. Does this meet with your approval, princess?" he teased.

She affected an attractive moue, curtseying gracefully. "Yes, your highness."

Laughing, Sheldon reached for her hand and they returned to the road. "Look," he said, pointing upward.

Renee squinted up at a large bird flying in a circle. "Is that a hawk?"

"Yes. There was a time when we didn't see too many of them. But since it's illegal to kill them they've made a comeback."

Sheldon waved to two men in a truck going in the opposite direction, the cab of the pickup loaded with fencing to replace the worn posts along the undeveloped north section of the property, property he had deeded to his grandchildren.

He had purchased the two thousand additional acres because of rumors that a developer wanted to erect half a dozen subdivisions on the site. New homes meant an influx of people, cars and pollution that would impact on the natural beauty of the horse farms with stately manor homes, miles of forests divided by hedges, white rail fences and stone walls. He had joined the other farm owners whose mission was to halt the encroachment of development in the region.

Renee walked into Blackstone Day School's cafeteria to a flurry of activity as a group of women carved faces into pumpkins, while Kelly and Tricia Blackstone filled cartons with already carved specimens wearing funny and grotesque cutout expressions.

The school that had begun as an early childhood care center was expanded to include up to grade six. The children from Blackstone Farms and many others from neighboring farms had become recipients of a superior education taught by a staff of highly qualified teachers.

Kelly glanced up, flashing a smile when she spied her father-in-law and Renee. "Thank you guys for coming."

"How many do you have left?" Sheldon asked.

"About sixty."

Renee stared at the small round pumpkins lining the stainless steel countertop. Their stems, tops and seeds had been removed. "How many have you carved?"

Kelly wiped the back of her hand over her forehead. "I lost count after a hundred and thirty."

Sitting on a stool, Renee picked up a small knife with a wicked-looking curved blade. She stared at Ryan's wife. It was the first time she noticed the absence of a southern drawl in her beautifully modulated voice.

"Why do you carve so many?"

"You'll see why after they're lighted," Kelly said mysteriously.

Renee's curiosity was piqued. "Do you light them with candles?"

Kelly nodded. "Tea lights."

Sheldon sat down next to Renee and picked up a marker. "How artistic are you?"

She wrinkled her nose. "Not very," she admitted.

He handed her the marker. "Draw your face, then I'll show you how to use the knife."

Renee drew two hearts for the eyes, a circle for a nose and a crooked grin for the mouth. She gave Sheldon her pumpkin and within seconds he'd cut out a face sporting a silly-looking expression.

"Very, very nice, princess," he crooned.

"Thank you," she whispered back.

They spent the next two hours making jack-o'-lanterns. This year's jack-o'-lantern production differed from the prior ones. Only ten pumpkins would be turned into pies.

Renee sat at a table in the dining hall with Sheldon, Jeremy and Tricia, totally amused by the number of children outfitted as hunchbacks, werewolves, pirates, skeletons, vampires, princesses, clowns and a popular wrestler. It was the first time school-age children and their parents from the other horse farms had come for the Halloween holiday celebration.

The dining room staff had prepared a buffet feast reflecting the holiday: dem rattlin' bones spareribs; tombstone taters: baked potatoes with bacon, grated cheddar cheese and sour cream; creepy crawlers: shrimp served with a Cajun sauce in a spicy mayonnaise; deviled eggs; devil's food cake and peanut butter cupcakes. A large bowl was filled with warm nonalcoholic apple cider.

Sheldon stood up, waiting until the babble of voices became a hush, followed by complete silence. His silvery gaze swept over those whom he had come to regard as his extended family. They were hardworking, loyal people who were directly responsible for the farm's success.

A melancholy expression flitted across his features. "I'd like to welcome our neighbors to Blackstone Farms' annual Halloween celebration, hoping you'll enjoy yourself enough to come again next year. I say this because I will not stand here next year to meet and greet you because I'm retiring—tonight." His announcement was followed by gasps.

Ryan leaned back in his chair at a nearby table and stared at Jeremy; their expressions mirrored confusion. Sheldon nodded to Jeremy before repeating the gesture with Ryan.

Sheldon knew he'd shocked his sons with the announcement that he was stepping down two months early. He'd decided not to tell Ryan and Jeremy because he was certain there would be a confrontation. He'd spent the past year dropping hints that he wanted to retire because he'd tired of the day-to-day responsibility of running the farm, while they'd spent the past year denying the inevitable.

"I've waited thirty years for this day, and I'm blessed to have two sons who will accomplish feats I can only dream about. Jeremy, Ryan, I love and trust you to continue Blackstone Farms' quest for the Triple Crown."

Kevin pumped his fist, shouting, "Boo-yaw! Boo-yaw! *Boo-yaw!*"

The Blackstone victory cry reverberated throughout the dining hall as others joined in. Sheldon held up a hand until the room grew quiet again.

"Ryan and Jeremy will share equal control of the farm. Jeremy will be responsible for finance and personnel, and Ryan will provide day-to-day oversight." He had selected Jeremy as the chief fiscal officer because he'd earned a business degree from Stanford. Turning to Jeremy, he extended his hand. "Now, please get up and say something profound."

Renee watched Jeremy lean over and kiss his wife before coming to his feet. He'd brushed his rakishly long black hair off his face, revealing tiny diamond studs in his pierced lobes. There was no doubt the next generation of Blackstones would march to the beat of their own drum.

Jeremy flashed a crooked smile as everyone applauded. He gave Sheldon a quick glance. "My father asked that I say something profound. To tell you the truth I really can't come up with anything except to say that hopefully twenty years from now I can stand here and pass the torch to my nephew Sean."

Five-year-old Sean waved his fist the way he'd seen his father, grandfather and uncle do. "Boo-yaw, Uncle Jeremy." The room erupted in laughter.

Placing two fingers to his forehead, Jeremy saluted Sean. "Boo-yaw to you, too, champ. I know everyone wants to eat and celebrate the holiday, so I leave you with this. Shah Jahan and Cheryl will accomplish what no other horse has done in decades. They *will* win the Triple Crown." The Boo-yaws started up again as people came over to the table to wish Jeremy the best.

Looping her arm through Sheldon's, Renee asked, "Who or what is Boo-yaw?"

Sheldon covered the small hand on his arm. "He was our first champion." He had been their first Derby winner and the last race Julia attended. A week later she'd died in his arms.

He smiled down at her. "After we eat we'll take a hayride."

She glanced up at him from under a fringe of thick lashes. "I hope you don't think I'm going to roll around in the hay with you."

Throwing back his head, Sheldon let loose with a peal of laughter. The room went suddenly quiet as everyone turned and stared at him. He sobered quickly, returned their stares until their attention was refocused elsewhere. Renee tried to suppress a giggle, but she was unsuccessful. Burying her face against Sheldon's shoulder, she laughed until her sides hurt.

Curving a hand around her neck, Sheldon whispered, "I'm going to get you for that, Renee."

"I'm so-o-o-o scared, Sheldon," she said, still laughing.

"You should be," he countered. His hand trailed down her spine, coming to rest on a rounded hip. She went completely still as her gaze widened. "Now, say something else," he threatened softly.

The warmth of his hand penetrated the fabric of her slacks, and Renee was hard-pressed not to squirm in her chair. She met his gaze as he looked at her as if he were photographing her with his eyes. He had stoked a gently growing fire she was powerless to control.

She had left Florida because of one man, and had come to Virginia to start over. It had only taken a week and she found herself falling under the spell of another man who made her want him in spite of herself.

The very air around them seemed electrified with a waiting, a waiting for the next move. Sheldon's nearness made her senses spin as his potent energy wrapped around her in a sensual cocoon that made her want to take off her clothes and lie with him.

A hint of a smile softened her mouth as she fluttered her lashes. "Please get me something to eat before I faint on you."

Sheldon removed his hand, stood up and pushed

back his chair in one motion. She watched him as he cut the line. Three minutes later he returned to the table and set a plate on the table in front of her. "What do you want to drink, princess?"

"Milk. Please make certain it's fat-free and ice-cold."

Sheldon flashed a saccharine grin, then left to do her bidding. He didn't know whether he was good for Renee, but knew for certain she was good for him.

She made him laugh, something he hadn't done in years. And she made him look forward to his retirement with the expectation of a young child opening gifts on Christmas Day.

Yes, he thought, he was going to enjoy being a couple.

Chapter Five

Hundreds of lighted jack-o'-lanterns lined the roads of Blackstone Farms like an airport runway; a full moon, the second in the month, silvered the countryside in an eerie glow that added to the magic of the night.

The cool night air seeped through the fibers of Renee's bulky pullover sweater, and she snuggled closer to Sheldon, sharing his body's heat. She had taken her first hayride in a horse-drawn wagon. The driver stopped, dropping off and picking up passengers along a northbound route; children gathered on padded mats in the schoolyard, crowded around a large oil drum from which blazed a bonfire, listening to ghost stories while eating cotton candy, popcorn and candied apples.

She sat on the grass with Sheldon and stared up at

the star-littered sky. "The moon looks close enough to touch." Her soft voice whispered over Sheldon's throat.

Sheldon pressed his mouth to her hair. "The second full moon in any month is called a blue moon. However, Native Americans have named every full moon in the calendar."

"What are the names?"

"January is full wolf moon, February full snow moon and March full worm moon."

"What do they call October?"

"Full hunter's moon."

"How do you know so much about Native American folklore?"

"Growing up my best friend was a Delaware Nanticoke boy. His family moved to Virginia the year he turned four."

"Where is he now?"

There was a moment of silence before Sheldon said, "He died in Vietnam."

Shifting, Renee put an arm around his neck and rested her head on his shoulder. She was sorry she'd asked because each time she questioned Sheldon about someone the subject of death surfaced: his mother, his wife and now a childhood friend. His life was filled with the loss of loved ones while hers had been filled with disappointment.

"I'm sorry." The two words, though whispered, sounded unusually loud.

"I'm not sorry you're here," Sheldon mumbled in her hair.

A smile lifted her mouth. "Why?"

"Because you make me laugh, Renee."

"Are you saying I'm funny or silly?"

A chuckle rumbled in his chest. "No. It's just that you're good for me. You remind me that life shouldn't be so serious."

"I'm glad I can make you laugh."

Sheldon tightened his hold around her waist. "What do you want from me?"

Renee refused to acknowledge the significance of his query. Did he actually want her to tell him what she wanted from him as a man? That she wanted to trust a man enough to protect her and her child?

Could she tell Sheldon that the more time she spent with him the more confused she became? That her feelings for him intensified each time he touched or kissed her.

"I want a friend," she said instead. "Someone I can confide in, someone who will laugh and cry with me in the good and not so good…." Her words trailed off as she realized how vulnerable and needy she must sound to Sheldon.

His warm breath caressed her parted lips as he lowered his head and tasted her mouth.

"What do you want from me, Sheldon?" Her query was a shivery whisper.

Sheldon pulled her closer. "I want to be your best friend, I want to protect you *and* your child and I'd like you to live with me."

"But I am living with you," she countered.

"No, Renee, we are sharing a house."

Strange and disquieting thoughts swirled through Renee, his words not registering on her dizzied senses. "You want sex?"

A low, rumbling laugh bubbled from his throat. "Why do you make it sound so sordid?"

"Because I tell it like it is?"

Sheldon sobered. "You've misunderstood me, Renee. I've been widowed a long time, and until meeting you I had no idea how lonely I've been." His lips came coaxingly down on hers. "I want companionship, princess."

Parting her lips and swallowing his breath, Renee kissed Sheldon leisurely, lingering and savoring his scent, the feel of his firm mouth. There was no mistaking the hardness he pressed against her. She smothered a groan and bit down on her lower lip. The urge to roll her hips against him was so strong that it frightened her.

Her hands came up and cradled his face, thumbs sweeping over the elegant ridge of his cheekbones. He was offering her everything she wanted and needed, everything except marriage. But even without a promise of marriage she wondered whether she could trust him?

"I don't know, Sheldon." *I don't know if I can trust you,* she added silently.

He placed a forefinger over her lips. "You don't have to give me an answer. Come to me when you're ready."

"What if I'm never ready?"

"Then we'll remain best friends."

Renee lowered her hands, curving her arms under Sheldon's shoulders. They sat motionless, holding each other until the sound of the approaching wagon propelled them off the ground for the ride back to the main house.

The sound of tires crunching gravel drowned out the cacophony of nocturnal sounds serenading the countryside. A knowing smile curved Sheldon's mouth as he waited for his late-night visitors. Renee had retired to bed, but he hadn't been able to sleep. His mind was too active, too wound up after he'd bared his soul to Renee. He left bed, pulled on a sweatshirt over a pair of jeans, then came downstairs to sit on the porch.

Vulnerability, something he hadn't experienced in years, had slipped under the barrier he had erected to keep all women at a distance. The women who knew him were aware that he would offer them his passion, but never his heart. However, in the span of a single week a woman had unknowingly woven her way into his life and into his heart.

Sheldon sat forward on the rocker. The sound of doors closing was followed by booted footfalls on the porch steps. "What took you so long?"

Ryan climbed the stairs and sat on the glider, leaving his brother to take the chaise. "You were expecting us?"

Sheldon gave Ryan a long, penetrating stare. "But of course."

"Are you all right, Pop?"

Sheldon shifted his attention to Jeremy. "I'm fine," he countered sharply. "Why would you me ask that?"

Jeremy ignored his father's clipped tone. "You announced your retirement without giving us prior warning."

"I told you I was retiring at the end of the year. But with Jahan's win I decided to push it up."

Clasping his hands between his knees, Ryan leaned forward. "Are you sure that's the reason, Pop?"

Sheldon's jaw tightened as he glared at Ryan before pinning his angry gaze on Jeremy. "What's going on here?"

"Jeremy and I…we thought that something might be wrong and you were trying to conceal it from us."

Realization slowly dawned. Sheldon closed his eyes and shook his head. This scene was a repeat of one that had occurred twenty-one years before. He'd sat down with his sons and told them their mother was ill—terminally ill. Julia had discovered a lump in her breast, but refused to go to a doctor until it was too late. She'd waited until after Boo-yaw's Derby victory to tell her husband that she was dying. Her excuse was that she hadn't wanted to bother him.

It had been the first and only time he'd raised his voice to his wife. His tirade ended with him weeping in her arms because he hadn't been there for Julia when she needed him. That had been the first and last time he'd let anyone see him cry.

Sheldon opened his eyes. "There's nothing wrong with me."

Jeremy's dove-gray eyes narrowed. "Are you sure, Pop?"

"Do you want to see the results of my latest physical?"

"No, Pop." Jeremy reached over and patted Sheldon's shoulder. "I'm just glad you're okay."

"Me, too," said Ryan. "Sometimes it's hard to tell with you because your moods run hot and cold."

Jeremy winked at Sheldon. "I've noticed lately that you're running more hot than cold. Does a Miss Wilson have anything to do with that?"

There was a long pause before Sheldon said, "Yes."

Ryan moved off the glider and thumped his father's solid back. "Good for you."

"Boo-yaw!" Jeremy said in a loud whisper.

A flash of humor crossed Sheldon's face before his expression changed, becoming somber. "Thank you for worrying about your old man."

Jeremy swung denim-covered legs over the side of the chaise and stood up. "You're not old, Pop. We just don't want anything to happen to you. Tricia and I would like to give you at least three grandchildren before we turn forty."

Sheldon nodded his approval. "What about you, Ryan?"

"Kelly and I talked about having one more."

Sheldon nodded again. "Six grandchildren. I like the sound of that."

"Good night, Pop," Ryan and Jeremy said in unison as they prepared to take their leave.

"Good night," Sheldon said in a quiet voice. He felt as if a weight had been lifted from his chest. He'd even surprised himself after admitting to Jeremy and Ryan that he was attracted to Renee; he'd never disclosed his involvement with a woman to them before. He suspected his sons believed he had been celibate for the past two decades. That meant for twenty-one years he had successfully kept his private life private. All of that would change in a month once he attended the wedding with Renee, he thought with a wry smile.

Sheldon and Renee left the farm Saturday morning for Staunton. On the way they shared a gourmet brunch at the Frederick House, a small hotel with a tearoom in the European tradition.

Sheldon left her at a specialty boutique, promising to return in an hour. The one hour became two as she tried on undergarments, tunics, slacks and dresses that artfully camouflaged her fuller breasts and expanding waistline.

She finally emerged from the dressing room to find Sheldon sitting on a delicate chair reading a newspaper. His head came up slowly. Smiling, he stood up.

"Are you ready?"

Her gaze met his. "I have to pay for my purchases."

He took her arm. "I already paid for them. They'll be delivered to the farm Monday."

Renee tried escaping his firm grip, but his fingers tightened like manacles. "I don't need you to pay for my clothes."

"Let's not argue *here*," he warned in a dangerously soft tone.

"No. Let's not," she retorted between her teeth. Seething, she followed him through the rear of the boutique and into the adjacent parking lot. "I don't need or want you to pay for anything for me."

Sheldon opened the passenger side door to his pickup truck, caught her around the waist and swung her up to the seat. He glared at her, then closed the door with a solid slam.

Once it became apparent that he wasn't going to respond to her protests, Renee crossed her arms under her breasts and stared out the windshield. Sheldon took his seat beside her, turned on the engine and shifted into gear. The silence inside the vehicle swelled to a deafening pitch.

She did not want Sheldon to believe she was destitute. Although she'd lived with Donald she also had retained her independence. She paid her own bills, and when Donald offered to give her one of his many cars, she had refused it. In the end she was able to walk away with what had belonged to her and her dignity.

"I have to make a stop." Sheldon's voice broke the silence five minutes later. He pulled into a parking space at a supermarket.

"I'll wait here for you," Renee mumbled.

He shrugged a shoulder. "Suit yourself." He left the truck and made his way into the store. She was still pouting when he got into the truck and handed her a large paper sack.

"You can repay me for *that* if you want to."

Renee peered into the bag. It held two half-gallon bottles of fat-free milk. "Very funny, Sheldon," she said, biting back a smile.

"Think of it as a peace offering."

"How can it be a peace offering when we haven't had a fight?"

Suddenly his face went grim. "And we won't. We may not agree on everything, but one thing I will not do is fight with you." He had made it a practice never to argue with a woman. It was not his style.

"Why did you pay for my clothes?"

"Because I asked you to go out with me, not the other way around. Does that answer your question?"

There was a pulse beat of silence before Renee nodded. "Yes, it does."

His expression softened. "Good."

Resting his right arm over the back of her seat, he trailed his fingertips over the nape of her neck. "How would you like to hang out with me for the rest of the day?"

Renee shivered as much from the feathery stroking motions on the sensitive skin as from the gray orbs boring into her with a silent expectation. It was easy, too easy, to get lost in the way he was looking at her. She studied his face, feature by feature, committing them to memory while curbing the urge to trace the shape of his black curving eyebrows, the bridge of his aquiline nose and firm mouth with her fingers.

Desire, want and need swooped at her innards, and

she shuttered her gaze quickly before he read her licentious thoughts. Sheldon Blackstone was the first man she'd met who made her want him just by staring.

"Okay, Sheldon. I'll hang out with you." She heard his audible sigh. It was apparent he'd been holding his breath.

Leaning closer, he pressed a kiss to her forehead. "Thank you."

Sheldon took the sack with the milk off her lap and put it in a space behind the seats, then drove out of the supermarket's parking lot, heading in a westerly direction.

Renee woke up ninety minutes later surrounded by towering pine trees. The truck had stopped. Her lids fluttered as she peered through the windshield at the forested area.

"Where are we?"

Sheldon got out and came around to assist her. "Minnehaha Springs."

Dry leaves and pine cones crackled under their booted feet. "Are we still in Virginia?"

"Yes. But we're only fifteen miles from the West Virginia state line." Wrapping an arm around her waist over a lightweight jacket, Sheldon led Renee toward a house erected in the middle of a clearing. "Let's go inside the cabin, because once the sun sets the temperature drops quickly."

Renee glanced up at a structure that looked more like a chalet than a cabin. She waited as Sheldon unlocked the front door and touched a panel on the wall. Within seconds the entire first floor was flooded with golden light. She walked in, staring at a stone fireplace spanning an entire wall.

Sheldon reached for her hand. "This is where I hang out whenever I need to get away from the farm."

Her stunned gaze swept over a space that was comparable to the health spa she had frequented in South Beach. Ceiling fans, track lighting, skylights, gleaming wood floors, white-on-white furnishings, floor-to-ceiling windows and a wrought-iron staircase leading to a second-story loft provided the backdrop for a space that invited one to enter—and stay awhile.

"It's beautiful."

"It's peaceful," Sheldon countered. "Wait here while I get the milk from the truck, then I'll give you a tour."

The house contained three bedrooms. The master bedroom and bath took up the entire loft. There were two other bedrooms on the first floor. The larger had an adjoining bath with a massive sunken tub, freestanding shower and a steam room. A full, functional kitchen, living/dining area and a family room completed a space constructed for maximum living, dining and relaxing comfort.

Renee sat in the kitchen on a tall stool, munching on raw carrots, washing them down with milk and watching Sheldon as he rubbed ground spices onto the steaks he had taken from the freezer and quickly defrosted in the microwave.

Her gaze moved leisurely over his tall, slender body. He moved around the kitchen slicing and sautéing foods as if he'd performed the tasks on a daily basis. Then she remembered his mother had been a cook.

"Are you certain you don't want me to help you?"

He gave her a sidelong glance before he focused his attention to the temperature gauge on the stovetop grill. "Don't you know how to sit and relax?"

"I sit all day."

Drying his hands on a towel, Sheldon closed the distance between them and hugged her. "After you have your baby you'll look back on this moment and wish you'd taken advantage of it."

Renee went completely still. It was the first time Sheldon had made reference to her having a baby since the day of the race. She found it odd that he was willing to be seen with her in public when there was certain to be gossip once her condition became evident.

Tilting her chin, she stared up at him staring down at her. "You're probably right."

"I know I'm right. It's not easy for a woman to balance work and motherhood. That's the reason I set up the farm's child-care center. Some of the mothers wanted to go back to school to either begin or resume careers, but couldn't find anyone to watch their children. With Tricia as the school's pediatric nurse most of them don't have to miss days if their children aren't feeling well. It will be even easier for you because you work on the farm."

"Having on-site child care was the reason I accepted the position."

Sheldon wanted to tell Renee that he was glad she had been hired. Once he'd acknowledged his growing attraction for her he thought about her unborn child, asking himself whether he wanted to become involved with a woman with a baby when his youngest son, at thirty-two, was going to make him a grandfather for the third time. He had taken early retirement at fifty-three to kick back and relax, not play surrogate father.

The questions had bombarded him when he least expected them, and the answer was always the same: yes. Yes, because Renee made him laugh—something he hadn't done in a long time. And yes, because she unknowingly had elicited from him a profound longing for a woman he hadn't felt in years. What amazed him was that she hadn't flirted with him as some women did. She had just been herself. He had found her strong, independent, but whenever the topic of her ex came up she exhibited a vulnerability that made him want to do everything in his power to protect her.

Sheldon reached up and wiped a residue of milk from her top lip with his thumb. "Did you drink a lot of milk before you got pregnant?"

Dimples winked in her flawless cheeks as she gave him a warm smile. "No. Instead of craving potato chips and pickles like other women, I have an insatiable thirst for milk."

"Milk is a lot healthier than chips and pickles." He

kissed the end of her nose. "When are you scheduled to go to the doctor?"

A slight frown appeared between Renee's eyes. "Next Friday. Why?"

"I'll go with you."

She stared, complete surprise on her face, as an unexpected warmth eddied through her. She wanted to ask Sheldon why, but the word was lodged in her constricted throat.

Renee nodded her consent, not trusting herself to speak. He was offering her what she wanted, someone to accompany her when she went for her checkups. Her sister-in-law had gone with her the first three times, and she hadn't been able to ignore the rush of envy when she saw women in various stages of confinement with the fathers of their unborn children holding their hands or rubbing their backs. Afterward, she chided herself for being weak and needy.

Wrapping her arms around Sheldon's waist, she rested her cheek over his heart and counted the strong, steady beats. Unbidden tears filled her eyes and overflowed as she cried without making a sound.

Sheldon felt moisture soaking his shirt. He moved his hand over Renee's back in a comforting motion. "Shush, princess. Everything is going to be all right."

His attempt to console made her cry harder and Renee clung to him like a swimmer floundering in a dangerous undertow. She had tried telling herself she could go through nine months of pregnancy and deliver a baby alone, but when she least expected it her armor cracked, revealing her vulnerability and leaving her with a feeling of helplessness.

She pressed a kiss to his strong neck. *Live for today, and let tomorrow take care of itself.* Her mother's mantra echoed in her head. Right now Sheldon had offered her everything she needed for emotional stability. She needed to focus on the present instead of agonizing over whether their relationship would work out in the future.

"I'm ready, Sheldon," she whispered in his ear.

Sheldon froze, his breath stopping in his chest. When it resumed he was certain Renee could feel his heart beating. "Are you certain?"

"Very certain."

Pulling back and staring at her tear-stained face, Sheldon's heart turned over when he saw pleading in her eyes. "I don't want you to come to me because you're feeling vulnerable." His gaze softened. "I can't and won't take advantage of you."

"I am ready," Renee repeated. She pulled her lower lip between her teeth to stop its trembling.

Leaning forward, Renee pressed her mouth to his, kissing, lingering and savoring the taste and touch of his firm mouth. He kissed her back in a series of slow, feathery kisses that set her nerves on edge.

Mouths joined, Sheldon tightened his hold on her body. What had begun as a tender joining segued into a hungry, burning desire, the sparks igniting like brilliant showers of embers flung heavenward. Her sensitive nipples tightened, ached; her breasts grew heavy, swelling against the fabric of her bra.

"Please," she moaned as if in pain.

Sheldon tore his mouth from hers, laser-gray eyes glittering like quicksilver. He knew if he did not stop now he wouldn't be able to. He wanted Renee just that much. His chest rose and fell heavily as if he had run a grueling race.

"Okay, baby. I'll stop." He did not recognize his own voice.

She grabbed the front of his shirt in a punishing grip. Her eyes had darkened with her rising desire. "Don't you dare stop!"

He cradled her head between his large hands. "You know what this means, don't you?" She inclined her head. "If we make love, then there will be no turning back." She nodded again. "Tell me *now* what you want from me."

Renee closed her eyes, shutting out his intense stare. "I want you, Sheldon."

"For what?" he whispered against her lips.

"To protect me and my baby."

He nodded. "I can do that. What else, darling?"

"Become my best friend."

Lowering his head, he nuzzled her neck, inhaling the sensual, haunting scent of Shalimar. "I can do that, too. What else, princess?" Renee opened her eyes and something in her gaze gave Sheldon his answer.

"I want you to be the last man I sleep with."

He swept her off the stool, reached over, turned off

the grill and walked out of the kitchen. His long, determined strides took him across the living room, up the staircase and into the bedroom he had never shared with a woman. Whenever he brought a woman to the cabin in the woods they always slept together in one of the first-floor bedrooms. The loft had become his monastery—a private sanctuary—until now.

Shifting Renee's slight weight, he walked to the bed, lowering her to the mattress. The light from the emerging near-full moon cast a silver glow on every light-colored surface. He made his way to the adjoining bath before returning to lie next to her; holding her hand, he stared up at the shadows on the ceiling.

There was only the sound of measured breathing as seconds ticked to minutes. Sheldon pulled her over his chest with a minimum of effort. He met her gaze in the diffused moonlight. "I can make love to you without being inside you."

She willed the tears pricking the back of her eyelids not to fall. Why, she asked herself, did tears come so easily now when in the past she hardly ever cried? Sheldon had scaled the wall she had erected to keep all men out of her life and her heart with a quiet gentleness she hadn't encountered in any man she knew—in or out of bed. He had asked how to proceed because of the child in her womb.

She exhaled audibly. "What I had with Donald is over. Any love I had for him died the moment I walked out of his life. There will never be three people in our

bed, and this will be the last time I mention his name
to you."

Combing his fingers through her hair, Sheldon cradled her head and kissed her with a passion that threatened to incinerate her. Reversing their positions, he
supported his weight on his arms while at the same
time he pressed his middle to Renee's, communicating
his desire for her.

Slowly, methodically he undressed her, his mouth
mapping each inch of flesh he bared. Trailing his
tongue over her warm, scented flesh, he committed
her smell to memory. The throbbing between his legs
increased, yet Sheldon forced himself to go slow, slow
enough to give Renee the pleasure he was certain she
would wring from him.

The buttons on her blouse gave way and he stared
mutely at the swell of flesh spilling over her bra's delicate fabric. Reaching around her back, he released the
clasp and slipped off the bra. His breathing quickening, he swallowed a groan. Her breasts were as full and
firm as ripe fruit.

Renee felt the heat from Sheldon's gaze as he eased
her slacks down her hips and legs. Her panties followed,
leaving her naked to his hungry gaze. The pads of his
thumbs swept over her swollen nipples, sending pinpoints of exquisite pleasure to the pulsing between her
thighs.

Eyes wide, breathing heavily, Sheldon sat back on
his heels. "Sweet heaven, princess. You are beautiful,"
he whispered reverently.

His mouth replaced his hand, suckling her, and she rose off the mattress, her breasts heaving. She wanted to touch Sheldon, taste him the way he was touching and tasting her. Tears filled her eyes again as he lowered his head and trailed soft kisses over her slightly rounded belly. She crooned his name again and again while mouth and tongue worshipped her.

Renee sat up, her hands going to the buttons on his shirt. She managed to undo two, but was thwarted when he brushed her hand aside and accomplished the task in one sweeping motion; buttons were ripped from their fastenings.

Sheldon went to his knees, unsnapped the waistband on his jeans and pulled down the zipper in a motion too quick for the eye to follow. His jeans, briefs and socks lay in a pile with hers on the floor beside the bed.

He slipped the latex sheath over his aroused flesh and extended his arms. He wasn't disappointed when Renee moved into his embrace. Holding her, breathing in her scent, filled him with a sense of completeness. It was as if he had waited twenty years for a little slip of a woman to come into his life, a woman who would change him forever.

Why Renee and not some of the other women he had slept with?

What was so different about her that he had willingly pledged his future to her?

He prayed silently he would discover what it was before he got in too deep.

Supporting his back against the headboard, he

cupped Renee's hips, lifting her high enough to straddle his thighs. "Put your legs around my waist." She complied, lowered her forehead to his shoulder, her breath coming in short, quick pants. "Are you comfortable?"

"Yes," she gasped.

All of Renee's tactile senses were on high alert: the mat of chest hair grazing her sensitive breasts, heavy breathing against her ear and the hardness between her thighs. She moaned, then bit down on her lower lip to stifle another one as her flesh stretched to accommodate Sheldon's sex.

She rocked her hips against his, setting the pace. Each push, stroke, moan, groan and gasp of air became part of a dance of desire that sucked them into a vortex of sensual delight that had no beginning, no end.

Renee was drawn to heights of passion she had never known; her body vibrated with the liquid fire scorching her brain and nerve endings. Her lips quivered in the intoxicating desire she had not felt in months.

Sheldon could not stop the groans escaping his parted lips as flames of desire swept over him with the ferocity of a tornado touching down and sweeping up everything in its violent wake. He tried thinking of anything but the woman in his embrace, and failed— miserably.

Cradling her hips, he increased their cadence, their bodies moving faster and faster until the swirling ecstasy escalated and erupted in a tidal wave that swept them away to a private world of erotic enchantment.

Renee collapsed against Sheldon's moist chest, her

breath coming in deep surrendering moans. Filled with an amazing sense of completeness, she closed her eyes.

Sheldon loathed having to withdraw from Renee. Their lovemaking had become a raw act of possession. He belonged to her and she belonged to him.

Easing her arms from under his shoulders, he laid her gently on her side before he covered her moist body with a sheet and lightweight blanket. He sat motionless and stared at her, then moved off the bed and made his way to the bathroom.

He stood under the warm spray of the shower recalling what Renee wanted from him. He had been forthcoming when he told her he would protect her and her child. That he'd done with his sons.

However, he knew he could never promise Renee marriage, because despite his success as a father and businessman, he had failed as a husband. That was a failure he would not chance repeating.

Chapter Six

Renee lay in the drowsy warmth of the large bed reliving the pleasure and satisfaction she'd shared with Sheldon. His lovemaking—the warmth of his body against hers, his protective embrace and the touch of his lips on hers had left her aching and burning for more.

Even with spiraling ecstasy that had nowhere to go, she'd prayed for it to continue until she was sucked into a vortex that held her prisoner for an eternity.

Reaching over, she turned on a lamp, looking for her clothes. They weren't on the bed or floor. She left the bed and went into the bathroom. The bathroom was more than twice the size of her first apartment. A free-flowing master bath opened into a dressing area with built-in drawers and closets tucked into an alcove. She opened a drawer and took out a T-shirt with the logo of Tuskegee University. Sheldon revealed he had not attended college, and she wondered which of his sons had attended the historically black college.

Opening the cabinets below the vanity, she discovered a plethora of grooming supplies. Twenty minutes later she'd brushed her teeth, showered and moisturized her body. She pulled on the T-shirt, walked out of the bedroom and descended the curving staircase.

Renee hadn't stepped off the last stair when she saw Sheldon, his back to her, setting the table in the dining area. Light from an overhead chandelier created a halo around the damp black hair clinging to his head. He'd changed into a pair of jeans and a black cotton sweater. She smiled. Like her, he had elected to go barefoot.

"Are you certain you don't want my help?"

Turning slowly, Sheldon stared at Renee. She wore the T-shirt Ryan had given him after he'd returned from his alma mater as a visiting professor. The sleeves reached below her elbows and the hem below her knees. His gaze lingered on her shapely legs and bare feet.

A slow smile crinkled his eyes and deepened the slashes in his lean jaw. He moved toward her. Cradling her face, he dipped his head and brushed a light kiss over her parted lips.

"I'm certain. I wanted to set the table before coming up to get you. Are you hungry?"

She wrinkled her nose and nodded. "Starved. I'm sorry I'm not dressed for dinner, but I couldn't find my clothes."

"I put them in the wash." He kissed her again.

"They're now in the dryer." With an arm around her waist, he led Renee to the table. He waited until she'd pulled the hem of the shirt under her hips, then pushed the chair under her.

Sharing dinner with Sheldon was a surreal experience for Renee. He started a fire in the fireplace, dimmed all the lights except in the dining area and tuned on the stereo to a station that featured love songs.

He had prepared a four-course meal beginning with lobster bisque and a salad of tomato and mozzarella topped with freshly grated Parmesan cheese. A grilled steak complemented baked potatoes and blanched snow peas. She'd refused dessert because she had eaten too much at one sitting.

Smiling across the table, she closed her eyes and sighed audibly. "You can cook for me any time."

"Is that what you want me to do? Cook for you?"

Her eyes opened and she sat up straighter. "No, Sheldon. That's not what I want you to do. I wouldn't mind if you cook for me on occasion and I'll do the same for you."

"You cook?"

She affected a frown. "Of course." Her mother had taught her to cook, and by the age of fifteen she could prepare an entire meal by herself.

"No, princess." His voice was low, soothing. "I look forward to cooking for you."

The distinctive voices of Kenny Rogers and Sheena

Easton singing "We've Got Tonight" came through speakers hidden throughout the first floor.

Sheldon pushed back his chair, rounded the table and extended his hand to Renee. "Come dance with me. This is one of my favorite songs."

She hesitated. "I can't."

"Why?"

Renee stared over his head rather than meet his questioning gaze. "I don't have on any underwear."

A hint of a smile played around his mobile mouth. "By the time I go and get your underwear the song will be over. But, if you feel uncomfortable, then I'll take off my underwear."

She shot up from the chair and grabbed his hand. "No. Don't. Please."

Sheldon led her out to the middle of the living room, chuckling softly. "I just want you to feel comfortable."

Renee moved into his embrace. "I'm comfortable," she said a little too quickly.

He pulled her close to his body, spinning her around as he sang, "We've got tonight. Who needs tomorrow? Let's make it last."

She closed her eyes, listening to Sheldon sing. Was he saying that he only wanted right now—tonight and not tomorrow?

She wanted to tell Sheldon that tonight was all they had, because tomorrow was not promised. Sinking into his comforting embrace, she rested her head over his heart. The strong, steady beats kept time with hers. The song ended, but they did not pull apart. There was no need for words. Their bodies had communicated without words and what their bodies shared had nothing to do with business.

The clock on the fireplace mantel chimed the half hour as Sheldon and Renee climbed the staircase in the house at Blackstone Farms. It was one-thirty. He'd wanted to stay over until Sunday night, but she complained about having a sore throat.

"I think I'd like to sleep in my own bed."

Sheldon's stoic expression concealed his disappointment. They'd made love but would not sleep together. He nodded. "I'll see you in the morning."

Renee forced a smile. Every time she swallowed she felt as if her throat was on fire. "Good night." Rising on tiptoe, she kissed his cheek. She walked the length of the hallway and into her bedroom. She undressed quickly and slipped into bed.

Renee woke Sunday morning chilled to the bone. She could not stop her teeth from chattering. It was obvious she had come down with something.

It was ironic that *something* was the reason she'd gotten pregnant. A paralegal at the law firm had died from bacterial meningitis and everyone who had come in contact with her was prescribed a powerful antibiotic. Unknown to Renee, the antibiotic interacted with her low-dose contraceptive, decreasing its potency.

There were times after she'd relocated to Kentucky when she wondered what if Donald hadn't been married. Would he have offered marriage once she told him he was to become a father? The what-ifs had haunted her until she went for a drive, parked along the bank of a small river and screamed at the top of her lungs. The action was enough to purge her what-ifs and lingering angst.

Renee forced herself to leave the bed long enough to brush her teeth and take a hot shower. She made it back to bed on wobbly knees and went back to sleep.

Sheldon walked into the dining hall and saw Jeremy and Tricia sitting at a table with her grandfather, Gus Parker. Tricia motioned for him to join them.

Leaning over, he kissed her cheek. "Good morning."

"Good morning, Pop." Her dark eyes sparkled. "Grandpa has some wonderful news."

Sheldon sat next to his longtime friend. Augustus Parker had come to the farm as a groom two weeks after Sheldon purchased his first Thoroughbred, and retired as assistant trainer some thirty years later.

"What's the good news, Gus?"

Tall, thin and nearing eighty, Gus affected a mysterious smile. "I'm getting married." He and his first wife Olga were married for forty-seven years before she died twelve years ago.

Sheldon's shocked expression gave way to a wide grin as he pumped Gus's hand. "Congratulations. Who is the lucky woman?"

"Beatrice Miller."

"Your nurse?" Sheldon asked.

"My ex-nurse and soon-to-be wife."

Tricia rested a hand on her grandfather's shoulder. Gus had suffered a heart attack and been hospitalized in late summer, but had recovered enough to give her away in marriage to Jeremy Blackstone. It was apparent the middle-aged visiting nurse not only helped heal the older man's heart; she'd softened it as well.

"When is the big day, Grandpa?"

"I'm leaving that up to Beatrice."

"Do you plan to move off the farm?" Sheldon asked.

Gus shook his head. "No. I wouldn't even consider leaving now that I'm going to become a great-grandfather." He winked at his granddaughter. "Beatrice told me she would love to fill in for Tricia as school nurse once she goes out on maternity leave."

Tricia stared at Gus. "I'm not going out on maternity leave, Grandpa. The baby is due the first week in July. School is over by that time. I'll have two months to bond with the baby, then I'll see it every day at the school's infant center."

Sheldon thought about Renee and her baby. She'd told him she was in her fourth month, which meant she would probably deliver sometime in March. Although she would not have worked for Blackstone Farms long enough to make her eligible for maternity leave, he would ask Jeremy to allow her some time off.

He glanced down at his watch. It was nearly noon and Renee had not put in an appearance. If she did not come to the dining hall before he'd left it, he would bring her breakfast favorites to the house.

* * *

Sheldon rapped on Renee's bedroom door, listening for movement on the other side. He tried the knob, turning it slowly. The door opened silently and he walked over to the bed. She lay on her side, eyes closed. He touched a bare shoulder, then jerked his hand away. She was burning up!

Guilt attacked him. He thought she'd refused to share his bed because she hadn't felt comfortable sleeping with him at the farm. Reaching for the cell phone on his waistband, he dialed Jeremy's number. The call was answered after the second ring.

"Tell Tricia I need her to come and check on Renee. She's burning up with fever." Ending the call, Sheldon walked into the bathroom, wet a towel with cold water, then retraced his steps.

Jeremy and Tricia found Sheldon sitting on the side of Renee's bed, dabbing her face and neck with a cloth.

Tricia met her father-in-law's worried gaze. "Let me take her temperature."

Sheldon rose from the bed. He stood with his back to the window, watching intently as Tricia took Renee's temperature and blood pressure.

"Last night she complained of a sore throat," he said in a quiet voice.

Tricia glanced at Sheldon over her shoulder. "At least half a dozen kids have also come down with sore throats. The doctor tested them for streptococcus."

A frown appeared between Sheldon's eyes. "Did any of them have it?"

"No. All of the cultures came back negative."

"I can't take antibiotics," Renee said in a croaking voice.

Tricia met her gaze. "Why not?"

Renee closed her eyes. It hurt her to talk or swallow. "I'm pregnant."

Jeremy and Tricia turned and stared at Sheldon, whose impassive expression did not change with Renee's admission. They exchanged a knowing look. It was apparent the elder Blackstone knew about Renee's condition.

"I want her tested for strep throat," Sheldon ordered softly.

After tucking her stethoscope and blood pressure equipment into a small black leather case Tricia stood up. "You want the doctor to come out here today?"

"Call him, Tricia. *Now.*" Sheldon could barely control his annoyance. The farm's on-call physician was paid a generous retainer to come at a moment's notice.

Jeremy was more than familiar with his father's explosive temper. He had challenged him countless times as an adolescent, and had always come up the loser.

"I'll call the doctor, Pop." Turning on his heel, Jeremy walked out of Renee's bedroom.

Tricia, more than anxious to follow her husband, said, "Make certain she drinks lots of water to avoid dehydration. I'll wait downstairs for Dr. Gibson."

* * *

Renee lost track of time, but she remembered hearing the doctor tell Sheldon she had contracted a virus, and with bed rest, a light diet and plenty of fluids she should feel better in three to five days.

She slept for hours, waking to find Sheldon hovering over her while urging her to drink from the glass he held to her lips. Milk and blended fruity concoctions were added; these she sipped through a straw. What she did not remember was Sheldon washing her body as if she were a small, helpless child. Early one morning she woke up to find him asleep on the chair in the sitting room.

Renee sat up in bed Tuesday afternoon alert and ravenous. The first thing she noticed was that she wasn't wearing a nightgown, but a man's T-shirt; the second was the woman coming out of the bathroom with a pail filled with cleaning supplies. Even though she'd met Claire Garrett at the pre-race party, she'd only seen the housekeeper once before. She heard the hum of her vacuum cleaner, but failed to catch a glimpse of the tall elusive woman.

The third thing she noticed was the most shocking: her stomach. She'd lost her waistline the month before, leaving her belly slightly rounded; however, now it protruded above her pelvis.

Claire smiled, her bright green eyes sparkling like emeralds. "I'll let Sheldon know you're up."

"Thank you." The two words came out in a low

husky tone. Her throat no longer hurt, but whatever she'd picked up had affected her vocal cords.

Renee returned Claire's smile as she swung her legs over the side of the bed. Her feet touched the cool bare floor and she shivered. It wasn't even winter and she felt cold. It probably would take her some time to get used to the change of seasons.

Walking into the bathroom, she filled the tub with water, added a capful of bath salts, the scent of vanilla wafting in the air. She brushed her teeth, rinsed her mouth with a mint-flavored mouthwash and washed her face, then stepped into the tub. Sighing, she rested her head on a bath pillow and closed her eyes.

"Do you need me to wash your back?"

Sitting up and splashing water over the sides of tub, Renee spied Sheldon lounging in the doorway, smiling broadly. A swath of heat cut a path from her face to her toes.

"No...no thank you."

Sheldon could not move, not even to breathe. The sight of her full breasts and the timbre of her husky voice rendered him temporarily paralyzed. The increasing heaviness between his thighs was akin to pain, a pain he did not want to go away.

"Does your throat still hurt?"

Sinking lower in the water, she shook her head. "No. But I sound like a foghorn."

He fixed his stare on her dewy face, smiling. "All foghorns should sound so sexy."

Sheldon knew he had to leave the bathroom *now,*

or he would strip off his clothes and join Renee in the bathtub. "I'll see you downstairs."

He knew his feelings for the woman living under his roof were intensifying with every minute he remained in her presence. Sitting and watching Renee sleep while he waited for her body to heal had taken him back twenty years. Then he'd sat by another woman's bedside, waiting and watching her die. While the events in his life had changed in two decades, he hadn't—not until now.

In the past, he'd slept with other women because of sexual frustration. However, it was different with Renee because he did not need her as much as he wanted her. A wry smile tilted the corners of his mouth. It was time he opened himself to accept whatever life offered.

Chapter Seven

"Is this your first one?"

Sheldon pulled his gaze away from *The Washington Post* and looked at the red-haired man sitting on his right. A slight frown furrowed his smooth forehead. "First what?"

"Baby?"

His frown vanished. "No."

"Which one is it?"

As promised, Sheldon had accompanied Renee to her obstetrician the following week.

"This one will be the tenth," Sheldon replied, deadpan.

The man's face paled, leaving a sprinkling of freckles over his nose and cheeks before a bright pink flush eased its way up from his neck to forehead. "You're kiddin', dude?"

Nodding and hoping not to burst into laughter, Sheldon continued the charade. "Nope. I have nine sons. We keep trying because we're hoping for a girl."

"Holy…" The redhead's words trailed off.

Sheldon went back to reading his newspaper.

Renee walked into the waiting room at the same time he finished reading the business section. He placed the newspaper on a coffee table and rose to his feet. Her dimpled smile was as bright as a spotlight.

When she had come to Blackstone Farms he never would have suspected she was carrying a baby. Now three weeks later, a hint of a belly was apparent under her khaki-colored tunic.

He closed the distance between them, putting an arm around her waist. "How are you?"

She snuggled closer to his side, her arms circling his waist. "Wonderful. It's a girl!"

Lowering his head, Sheldon pressed a kiss to her forehead. "Congratulations."

The moment she had informed him she was pregnant and intended to raise her child alone he'd hoped for a girl. He'd been a single father, and there were times when his teenage sons tested the limits of his patience *and* sanity.

He'd found girls quieter, less aggressive than boys. The difference between his three-month-old granddaughter Vivienne and Sean at the same age was like night and day. Vivienne was content to coo and play with her fingers and toes, while Sean had demanded to be picked up whenever he wasn't sleeping.

"When's your next appointment?"

"A month from now."

"Is everything okay?"

"I'm fine, Sheldon. Let's get out of here," Renee said quietly. Seeing some of the women in their last days of confinement was a blatant indicator of what awaited her.

Sheldon escorted Renee through the waiting area, stopping only to tap the inquisitive man on his shoulder. "We can stop now. It's a girl."

He glared up at Sheldon. "What if it was going to be another boy?"

Leaning closer, his gray eyes giving off sparks like streaks of lightning, Sheldon bared his straight white teeth. "Then I'd keep trying, *dude.*"

Waiting until they were out in the parking lot, Renee placed a hand on Sheldon's arm. "Did I miss something back in the doctor's office?"

Sheldon opened the pickup's passenger-side door. "He asked me how many children I had and I told him nine." He bit back a smile when Renee's delicate jaw dropped. "I said we were going to keep trying until we got a girl."

Resting her hands on his chest, Renee shook her head. "You're bad, Sheldon Blackstone."

He moved closer, trapping her between his body and the truck's door. "How bad, princess?"

Tilting her chin, she stared up at him through her lashes. "Very, very bad, your highness."

Sheldon dipped his head. "Is that a good bad or a bad bad?"

Closing her eyes against his intense stare, she shook her head. "I don't know." The sultry hoarseness in her voice floated around them like a low, lingering fog.

"What would I have to do to help you make up your mind?"

Renee opened her eyes. "I'll leave that to your imagination."

Without warning, she found herself swept up in a strong embrace and seated in the truck. She did not have time to catch her breath when Sheldon got in beside her, put the vehicle in gear and drove out of the parking lot.

"Where are you going?" Renee asked as Sheldon parked the truck behind a gourmet shop.

Leaning over, he kissed her cheek. "How would you like to share a late afternoon picnic dinner with me?"

She ran the tip of her tongue over her lower lip, drawing his gaze to linger there. "Where?"

He raised an eyebrow. "Front porch, back porch, your bedroom or mine. It's your call."

Renee thought of his choices, then said, "How about outdoors?" The early frost had come and gone, and the Indian summer temperatures topped out in the low seventies during the daytime hours.

Sheldon regarded Renee for a minute. She was totally unpredictable, a trait he liked because he knew she would never bore him. "Outdoors it is."

Renee lay on a blanket in the same spot where she'd lain with Sheldon on Halloween. They sampled the most delectable foods, emptied a bottle of sparkling water, then fell asleep in each other's arms.

The sun had begun its descent and the air had cooled considerably when she stirred, her face pressed to Sheldon's solid chest, one leg sandwiched between his.

"Sheldon?"

He opened his eyes at her sultry query. "Yes, baby?"

"I want you to be bad."

There was a pulse beat of silence. "How bad?"

There came another pause. "Naughty."

Cradling her body with one arm, Sheldon rolled Renee over on her back. "Here?"

She nodded. "Yes."

"I can't protect you, because I didn't bring any condoms with me."

Renee giggled like a little girl. "It's too late for that, Sheldon. Remember, I'm already pregnant."

She was pregnant and he was disease-free. He had used a condom with her the first time because he didn't want Renee to think he was cavalier when it came to sleeping with women.

Sitting back on his heels, he reached down and pulled off his waffle-knit pullover. His gaze fused and locked with Renee's as he removed boots, jeans and boxers. He followed her gaze as it moved downward.

The first time they'd made love it had been in the silvered glow of a full moon, and now it was in the fading shadows of the setting sun. He had tasted and touched her like a sightless man, but this time everything she claimed would be presented for his viewing.

A cool breeze rustled the leaves on an overhead tree, leaves falling and littering the blanket like colorful confetti. Shifting, Sheldon removed Renee's shoes and striped trouser socks. He unbuttoned her tunic, his breath catching in his chest. Leaning over, he pressed a kiss to her distended belly.

"You're beautiful, princess."

Renee closed her eyes. "I'm fat, Sheldon."

Reaching for her hand, he placed it over her stomach. "You're filled with life, darling. Don't you realize how special that is?"

She opened her eyes, seeing unspoken pain glowing in his eyes and recalling the loved ones he'd buried. "Yes." Her voice was barely a whisper. "This baby is special."

He removed her tunic, bra and panties with a skill and familiarity indicating he had performed the action innumerable times.

Renee did not have time to ponder his statement when she found herself naked to his penetrating gaze. Extending her arms, she welcomed Sheldon into her embrace. She did not feel the full effect of his comforting weight because he'd supported it on his arms.

Under a darkening autumn sky with all of nature as their audience, they began a dance of desire that needed no dress rehearsal.

His eyes smoldering with liquid fire, Sheldon feasted on the woman who made him look forward to the next day, the woman who made him laugh without trying to be funny and the woman who made him want to be inside her every day, hour, minute, second.

He brushed featherlike kisses around her mouth. Her lips parted of their own volition, and his tongue entwined with hers like pieces of molten steel. He did not kiss her mouth, but devoured it before moving down to the scented column of her neck, lingering at the base of her throat.

Traveling southward, he tasted one breast, then the other. She gasped as if in pain and rose off the blanket when his teeth closed on a nipple, worrying it gently before giving the other equal attention.

Renee was mindless with the divine ecstasy wrung from her. The pulsing between her legs thrummed faster, harder, and she was afraid it would be over before he claimed her body. She reached for his hair, fingers tightening in the heavy strands.

"Please do it, Sheldon," she begged hoarsely. "Take me, *now!*"

He complied, easing his sex into her warm, pulsing flesh. The turbulence of her passion swept Sheldon up in a flood tide of the hottest fire, clouding his brain. He was lost in the flames threatening to devour not just a part of him, but all that he was and he had hoped to become.

Then it came upon him like the whispered feet of a cat out of the darkness of the night. Feelings, emotions, sensations he had locked away when he'd buried Julia surfaced. The love he'd had for one woman, the love he was unable to offer another, trickled through the chasm in his heart, bursting forth, rushing and sweeping him up in its turbulent wake of realization as he surrendered all to the woman in his arms.

Renee welcomed the powerful thrusts, meeting each one with her own. Her hands were everywhere: in his hair, trembling over his broad shoulders, tunneling through the thick mat of hair on his chest. She wanted to yield to the burning sweetness that held her prisoner, but knew it was only a matter of seconds before she was forced to surrender to the raging passion lifting her higher and higher until she floated beyond herself. Her breath came in long, surrendering moans, and she gave in to the ecstasy.

The sounds escaping Renee's parted lips became Sheldon's undoing. Lowering his head, he growled in her ear as the explosions erupted in his lower body. The aftermath left him gasping and fighting for his next breath. It was a full two minutes before he was able to move, collapsing heavily to the blanket.

Renee rolled over on her side and rested her head on his shoulder. He pulled her close, offering his body's heat. "Don't go to sleep on me, darling," he whispered in her hair.

"I can't move."

"You don't have to."

Renee lay motionless while Sheldon pulled on his clothes, then dressed her. During the short ride to the house, she managed to doze off. It wasn't until hours later that she remembered sharing a shower with Sheldon and his request to share her bed.

Around three o'clock she woke up and made her way downstairs for a glass of milk. She returned to the bedroom, finding Sheldon sitting up and waiting for her. There was no mistaking the concern in his gaze.

"Are you all right?"

Renee got into bed, straddled his lap, wiggling until she found a comfortable position. "I just went down to get a glass of milk."

"You shouldn't do that," he crooned in her ear.

"Do what?"

"Sit on me."

A sensual smile touched her mouth. "And why not?"

"Because you'll find yourself on your back and me inside you…"

Her explosive kiss cut off his words. It was her turn to gasp as Sheldon gathered the hem of her nightgown, pushing it above her waist. He lifted her with one arm and joined their bodies, making them one.

Instinctively, her body arched toward him. The crisp chest hair teased and tantalized her sensitive nipples and she welcomed the erotic sensation. Writhing, she moved closer, rocking up and down, back and forth over his hardness. Why, she asked herself as she came down to meet Sheldon in a moment of uncontrolled passion, couldn't she get enough of him? What spell had he cast over her that made her temporarily forget everything—even her name?

Sated, she collapsed against Sheldon, her lower lip trembling from the ebbing raw sensuality coursing through her. She did not know if the increase in her libido was from her being pregnant or from the realization that she was falling in love with Sheldon Blackstone.

In the six weeks Renee lived at Blackstone Farms, she had changed. The most apparent change was her body. Anyone who saw her knew she was carrying a child, and despite Sheldon's reassurance that he found her more beautiful than when she'd first come to the farm, there were times when she felt clumsy and misshapen.

Since they'd begun sleeping together it was always in her bed, because despite their intimacy she felt something was missing in their relationship. Each time she opened her arms to Sheldon the love she felt for him deepened. Each time he brought her to the pinnacle of desire she feared blurting out how much she had come to love him.

She had asked Sheldon for friendship, a confidant; his proposition included companionship and a promise to protect her and her child. Falling in love was not a part of their agreement—that went beyond business.

Late the next afternoon Renee mounted the porch, opened the door and walked into the main house. Heat greeted her as she went through the entryway and up the staircase.

The door to Sheldon's bedroom was slightly ajar and she heard him singing loudly. A knowing smile softened Renee's vermilion-colored lips as she walked to her bedroom. At first she'd found it odd that although she and Sheldon lived together, they rarely encountered each other during the day. It was only at night whenever Sean did not come for a sleepover with his grandfather that they slept together.

A strapless periwinkle-blue silk gown with an empire waist and slip lay across the bed; the matching quilted jacket hung from a padded hanger in the armoire.

Twenty minutes later Renee slipped her feet into a pair of sapphire-blue silk heels and walked over to the full-length mirror on the door of armoire. She did not recognize the woman staring back at her. Her hair had been pulled off her face and pinned into a chignon at the back of her head. The style was sophisticated without being too severe.

A slight gasp escaped her as another image joined hers in the mirror. Sheldon stood behind her, resplendent in formal dress. He wore a tailored tuxedo, white spread collar dress shirt and dark blue silk tie with an aplomb she hadn't seen on many men. Close-cropped raven hair brushed off his forehead and fell in layered precision against his scalp. The heat from his body and the tantalizing smell of his aftershave made her heart beat a little too quickly.

Sheldon placed one hand over the silk fabric artfully concealing her belly; the other circled her neck. His thumb caressed the skin over the nape of her neck as Renee's gaze met his.

His impassive expression did not reveal what he was feeling at that moment, what lay in his heart. He had deliberately avoided Renee because he'd found himself caught in a web of desire that held him captive. Each time he encountered her he was sucked into a force field, making him helpless and vulnerable. These were familiar emotions he had not wanted to experience again.

Renee shivered as Sheldon's forefinger toyed with the diamond stud in her right ear. Closing her eyes, she rested her head against his shoulder. The shiver became a noticeable shudder as he trailed kisses along the column of her neck.

"You look incredibly beautiful, smell delicious and taste scrumptious," he murmured against her velvety flesh.

Renee drank in his strength. "If we don't leave now, we're going to be late," she said not too convincingly.

"We won't be late, princess," he whispered, nuzzling her ear. "Thank you, darling."

She melted against his stronger body, her breath coming quickly. "For what, honey?" The endearment slipped out of its own accord.

"For being you, Renee." Sheldon's hands went to her upper arms and he turned her in his embrace. His hands came up and he cradled her face. His gaze widened, the gray orbs missing nothing. "I never thought you'd be able to improve on perfection, but you have. I'm going to be the envy of every man tonight." Her professionally coiffed hair and makeup highlighted her best features.

Renee reached for his hands, pulling them down. "Is that why you asked me to go with you and paid for this dress? To show me off like one of your prize Thoroughbreds?"

A warning cloud settled into Sheldon's features, his expression a mask of stone. "Is that what you think, Renee?"

"Yes."

He shook his head slowly. "You don't know, do you?"

Her waxed eyebrows lifted. "Know what?"

Without warning his expression changed, his eyes brimming with tenderness and passion. "I adore you."

Renee's body stiffened in shock, complete surprise on her face. Sheldon had given her everything she wanted, but she never suspected deeper feelings would become a part of their plan. She wanted to tell Sheldon she adored and loved him, too, but his confession caused the words to wedge in her throat.

"Thank you," she whispered, recovering her voice.

Inclining his head, Sheldon forced a smile, successfully concealing his disappointment. It was apparent she did not share his sentiment.

Threads of doubt nagged at him. Was she still in love with her ex?

"Are you ready?"

She nodded. "Yes."

Chapter Eight

Renee walked out of the chapel, her hand resting on Sheldon's sleeve. She had given him several sidelong glances as the bride and groom exchanged vows, wondering whether he had relived the moment when he'd married his young bride; however, his solemn expression had not changed.

Sheldon covered the small hand on his arm. Renee's fingers were ice-cold. "Are you all right?"

"Yes. Why?"

"Your hand feels cold."

"This is one time when I'm not cold." The temperature inside the mansion was comfortably set for the expanse of bared skin in low-cut and backless gowns.

The number of carats glittering from throats, wrists and ears of the other women present in the grand ballroom stunned Renee. The guests were Virginia's aristocracy, with a few Washington senators and other politicians in attendance. The wedding was touted as the wedding of the year, linking heirs to two of the largest and the most profitable horse farms in the state.

Sheldon found their table and seated her. Leaning down, he pressed his mouth to her ear. "What can I get you to drink?" Guests were quickly lining up at several bars set up around the ballroom.

Renee opened her mouth to say milk, but changed her mind. "Sparkling water with a wedge of lime."

Sheldon chuckled softly, his gaze straying from her mouth to the swell of breasts rising and falling above her revealing décolletage. "Does this mean that I'm going to have to be the designated driver tonight?"

"Hello again, Renee." A familiar voice interrupted their interchange.

Renee glanced over her shoulder. Kent Taylor leered at her chest, a lopsided grin on his face. His attention was temporarily averted when Sheldon grabbed his hand and shook it, while pounding his back.

"When are you racing Kiss Me Kate again?"

The high color in Kent's face deepened. He still had not recovered from his horse coming in second at the International Gold Cup. "I don't know." He eased his fingers from Sheldon's firm grip. "I hope you don't mind if I ask your lady for a dance later on tonight."

Sheldon's cold smile would've chilled most men, but Kent was too inebriated to notice. "I do mind."

Nonplussed, Kent blinked a few times, hoping he

hadn't heard what he thought he heard. Shrugging a shoulder, he turned and walked away.

"He's worse than a swarm of mosquitoes," Sheldon mumbled under his breath.

Renee's eyes narrowed. "I hope you're not going to growl at every man who asks to dance with me. I came here tonight to have a good time."

Sheldon hunkered down beside her chair, cradled the back of her head and pressed his mouth to hers. "And you will have a good time."

Her dimples winked at him. "You promise."

His smile matched hers. "I promise."

She did have a good time as she danced with Sheldon. A band whose repertoire included more than four decades of familiar tunes replaced a string quartet that played during the meal and many toasts.

Excusing herself, Renee whispered to Sheldon that she was going to the ladies' lounge. Making her way across the marble floor of the ballroom, she felt as if every eye was directed at her. Whenever Sheldon introduced her, he only offered her first name. Of course that made her more mysterious and others more curious.

Fortunately, she did not have to wait on line in the opulent bath and powder room. In the stall, as she adjusted her dress, she heard someone mention her name.

"Who is she?" came a soft drawling female voice.

"I don't know." This feminine voice was lower, more dulcet than the other woman's. "I thought you knew who she was. After all, you went to Sheldon's pre-race party."

"I don't remember her," the first woman admitted in a hushed tone.

"Where on earth do you think Sheldon picked her up?"

"I don't know. Maybe he joined some dating service, or he could've picked her up in one of those so-called gentlemen's clubs. You can find anything there."

"What do you mean anything?"

"Women who dance topless and swing around poles."

"Are you saying she's a whore?"

"She doesn't really look like a whore. But, one can never tell nowadays."

"The cut of her dress is a little deceiving, but I think she's in the family way."

"Bite your tongue, Valerie Marie Winston. I can't imagine Sheldon waiting until he's a grandfather to start making babies again."

"Bite your own tongue, Susanna Caroline Sullivan. You see what she looks like. The good Lord was certainly smiling on her when He handed out bosoms."

Renee could not move. If she left the stall, then the women would know she was eavesdropping on their conversation. But she also did not intend to hide behind the door indefinitely.

"No one has seen Sheldon with a woman since Julia died. Maybe he was having a problem with you-know-what," Valerie continued.

"Where have you been?" Susanna chided. "There are drugs for men with that kind of *problem*."

Renee had heard enough. Sliding back the lock, she left the stall. The shocked expression on the women's faces was priceless. It was impossible to tell their ages. They were the surgically altered women Sheldon had mentioned: perfect noses, collagen-enhanced lips, face-lifts and expertly dyed ash-blond hair.

Smiling, she washed her hands and accepted a towel from the bathroom attendant. It was apparent Valerie and Susanna thought the woman so insignificant they could gossip in her presence. Opening her evening purse, she left a bill in the plate on the countertop before she faced the elegantly dressed women who had taken a sudden interest in powdering their noses.

Renee cradled her breasts, her gaze meeting and fusing with wide-eyed stares in the mirror. "Yes, these are mine. And to set the record straight, Sheldon Blackstone doesn't have that particular *problem*."

Head held high, back ramrod-straight, Renee strutted out of the rest room, staring down anyone whose gaze lingered longer than was sociably polite.

She found Sheldon sitting with several men as she neared their table. Vertical lines appeared between his eyes when he saw her tight-lipped expression. He stood up, the other men following suit.

Rounding the table, Sheldon cupped Renee's elbow. "What's wrong?"

"I want to leave," she whispered.

"Now?"

Renee had clenched her teeth so tightly that her jaw ached. "Yes, Sheldon. Now."

Sheldon saw something in Renee's eyes that had never been there before, and he wondered what had set her off. He nodded to the other men. "Gentlemen. We'll continue our conversation another time."

"Give me a call next week, Blackstone, so we can get together."

"Will do," Sheldon said to a tall, lanky man who bore an uncanny resemblance to Abraham Lincoln.

He led Renee out of the ballroom and retrieved her jacket from the cloakroom. They waited, staring at each other in silence while a valet brought his car around.

Five minutes into the return drive to the farm, Sheldon broke the swollen silence. "What's the matter, Renee?" She told him everything, including the full names of the two women who had indirectly called her a whore.

"If this is a taste of what I'm going to have to confront every time we go out together, then I want out of our agreement. They know nothing about me, yet they have the audacity to call me a whore."

Signaling, Sheldon maneuvered the car to the shoulder of the road and stopped. He shifted into park. His eyes glittered like particles of diamond dust in the diffused light of the dashboard. "You know who you are, and I know who—"

"You know nothing about me," Renee countered, cutting him off. "You've slept with me, Sheldon, yet you know nothing about me." She willed the tears filling her eyes not to fall.

His eyes widened. "Is what you've told me about yourself a lie?" he asked in a dangerously soft voice.

Averting her head, she stared out the windshield. The rapid pumping of her heart echoed in her ears, the roaring sound deafening. "When you introduced me to your high-born *friends* why didn't you give my full name? I'm not on the FBI's Most Wanted list. I'm also not one of those women who make their living as Amber or Bambi for 1-900-talk-dirty-to-me."

Sheldon shook his head. "It's not like that, darling."

"Oh, really? Let me tell you what it's like. I'm not going out with you again."

Sheldon gave Renee a long, penetrating stare. She did not understand, couldn't understand her impact on those who'd met her. The men were awed by her lush beauty, the women envious because she claimed what most of them hadn't had in a long time—natural beauty. He would not refute her accusations. Not now. Not when she was so visibly upset. He shifted into gear, then rejoined the flow of traffic.

He didn't know whether Renee had lied to him about her ex, but he was certain of one thing: he hadn't been entirely forthcoming when he admitted adoring her. The truth was that he *had* fallen in *love* with her. It was only the second time in his life that he'd found himself in love with a woman.

Renee sat at the workstation, staring out the window instead of printing an inventory schedule. She hadn't been able to concentrate for days. Her confrontation with Sheldon had caused a shift in her emotional equilibrium.

They'd returned home Saturday night, climbed the staircase and gone to bed—alone. She hadn't seen or heard from him in days, and it was over breakfast she overheard Ryan tell Jeremy that they would have to wait for Sheldon to return from his mountain retreat.

He had gone without her, and his promise to teach her to fish had been an empty one.

She felt a familiar flutter, closed her eyes and smiled. Her expanding waistline, viewing sonogram pictures and listening to the rapidly beating heartbeat with Doppler had all become insignificant since the first time she felt her baby move.

"Renee."

She swiveled on her chair. Jeremy stood in the doorway. He had come for his report. "Please come in. I just have to print out the schedule for you."

Jeremy sat in a chair near a desk, draping one leg over the opposite knee and studied Renee from under lowered lids. She'd changed since coming to the farm, and it wasn't only the changes in her body. She had become less reclusive, more open with the other farm residents.

He'd told himself to mind his own business; what went on between Sheldon and Renee was no concern of his. The responsibility of running the horse farm, being a husband and impending fatherhood left little time for him to indulge in gossip.

Leaning forward, Jeremy studied the printed list Renee had tacked to a corkboard. It was a schedule of tasks and projected dates for completion. So far, it appeared as if she was ahead of schedule.

While Renee waited for the printer to complete printing more than thirty sheets, her cell phone rang. The sound startled her. It wasn't often her phone rang, and if it did it was usually her mother, brother or sister-in-law.

Reaching for the tiny instrument, she pushed the talk button. "Hello."

"Hey, Rennie."

She smiled. It was her brother. "Hey, yourself. What's up, Teddy?"

There was a pause before Edward Wilson's voice came through the earpiece. "This is not a social call, Rennie."

Knees shaking, she sank down to her chair and closed her eyes. "Is it Mama?" She had just spoken to her mother the week before.

"No," came his quick reply. "It's about Donald."

Renee sat up straighter, opened her eyes. "What about him?"

"He called here looking for you. He said he just got a divorce and he wants to marry you."

"What did you tell him?"

"I told him that I didn't know where you were."

"Thanks, Teddy."

"Don't thank me yet, Rennie. He says he knows you always spend Thanksgiving with us, so he plans to stop by to see if he can run into you."

"I can't come, Teddy. If he sees me then he'll know that I'm carrying his baby." Her voice had lowered when a pair of smoky gray eyes studied her.

"Then, don't come. Let me handle Mr. Rush. If he decides to get funky with me, then I'll just have to lock him up. I'll come up with a charge after I cuff the lying bastard."

Renee smiled. Her brother, a Kentucky state trooper, flew into a rage after she'd told him of Donald's duplicity.

"I'm going to miss you guys."

"We'll miss you, too. Let's plan to get together for Christmas. I have a lot of time coming to me, so we'll come to Virginia. The kids have been bugging me about visiting Williamsburg."

"I would like to see it, too."

"Then that does it. We'll come by and pick you up Friday afternoon, and bring you back Monday night."

"Okay, Teddy."

"I'll call and let you know if the clown shows up here."

Renee pulled her lower lip between her teeth. "Please be careful. I've seen Donald lose his temper a few times and he was unbelievably rude."

"Don't worry about me. You just stay put."

"Okay. Love you, Teddy."

"Love you back, Rennie."

Renee ended the call, gathering the pages from the printer. She stapled and handed them to Jeremy, mindful her hands were shaking.

Jeremy took the papers without dropping his gaze. "Do you want to get together when you're feeling better?"

"I'm all right," she said a little too quickly.

"You're shaking."

"I'll be okay in a few minutes." She made her way over to her chair and sat down. Meeting her boss's questioning gaze, Renee drew in a deep breath before letting it out slowly. "The first page is an analysis covering the past three years."

Jeremy half listened to what Renee was saying, his mind recalling her telephone conversation. He knew Teddy was her brother, because when he'd called the Louisville area code and exchange, Teddy Wilson had answered the call, telling him he would give his sister the message.

He hadn't intended to eavesdrop on her conversation, but once she said, *"If he sees me then he'll know that I'm carrying his baby,"* all of his senses were on full alert. It was obvious Renee did not want the father of her baby to know her whereabouts.

There came a light knock against the door frame. "I'm sorry for interrupting." Jeremy and Renee turned to find Sheldon's broad shoulders filling out the doorway. He nodded to her. "Good afternoon."

Renee hadn't realized how much she'd missed Sheldon until now. She missed his drawling voice, deep sensual laugh and most of all the warmth of his embrace. She had come to depend on him more than she'd wanted to.

Tilting her chin, she smiled up at him. "Good afternoon, Sheldon."

Jeremy studied the myriad of emotions crossing Sheldon's face. His mother had died the year he turned ten; however, he'd been old enough to recognize the surreptitious glances between his parents. Unspoken glances that precipitated retiring to bed before their sons. And the look his father and Renee shared was one usually reserved for lovers.

Sheldon reluctantly pulled his gaze away from Renee and nodded at his son. "Jeremy."

"Hey, Pop. I'm glad you're back because I need to talk to you."

"I'll be in the den when you're finished here."

Jeremy turned to Renee. "Can we finish this another time?"

She blinked as if coming out of a trance. "Of course."

Jeremy stood up and followed Sheldon, the remnants of Renee's conversation with her brother lingering in his head.

Sheldon entered the den and sat in his favorite chair, while Jeremy took a facing love seat. "What's up?"

Jeremy studied his father, seeing what he would look like in another twenty years, while hoping he would age as elegantly.

"Ryan and Kevin want to race Jahan at Santa Anita and Kentucky Oaks."

Leaning forward and clasping his hands between his knees, Sheldon caught and held Jeremy's gaze. "You don't trust their decision?"

"It's not that I don't trust them, Pop. It's just that I—"

"You don't trust them, Jeremy," Sheldon repeated emphatically, interrupting his younger son. "If you did then we wouldn't be having this conversation. Once I retired and turned complete control of running the farm to you, I'd hoped you wouldn't second-guess Ryan or Kevin's decision whether a horse is ready for a race.

"When you and Ryan decided to race Jahan for the International Gold Cup, I conceded because you, Kevin and Ryan overruled me by three-to-one. You've been overruled, Jeremy, so leave it at that."

For a long moment, Jeremy stared back at Sheldon. "Okay, Pop. I won't oppose them. But, there is something else I should tell you."

He repeated what he'd heard of Renee's conversation with her brother, watching Sheldon change before his eyes like a snake shedding its skin. An expression of hardness had transformed his father into someone he did not know—a stranger.

It was Jeremy's turn to lean forward. "Talk to me, Pop."

Sheldon's voice was low, quiet as he told his son what Renee had disclosed about her relationship with Donald Rush. "Are you familiar with the slug?" he asked.

"I know he is a pioneer in the computer game industry."

"Like those games Sean plays with?"

Jeremy nodded. "Yes. She doesn't want him to find her, Pop."

"And he won't. At least not here. If he steps one foot on Blackstone property he'll be shot on sight."

"What are you going to do? Hold her hostage?"

Sheldon shook his head. "No. I'll protect her. I want you to increase security around the property."

"Can you actually protect Renee from a man who might sue for joint custody of a child he can prove is his?"

"No," Sheldon admitted.

"I know another way you can protect Renee without becoming her bodyguard or shooting her ex-boyfriend."

"How?"

Jeremy watched his father with hooded eyes that resembled a hawk. "Marry her." The instant the two words were uttered, he girded himself for a violent outburst, but when Sheldon sat staring at him with eyes filled with raw, unspoken pain he regretted the suggestion.

Lowering his head, Sheldon stared at the toes of his boots. "I can't do that."

"Why not, Pop?"

His head came up. "Why not?" he repeated. "Because I wouldn't be a good husband for her."

"Is it because she's carrying another man's baby?"

"No. I wouldn't have a problem raising her child as my own."

"Then, what is it?"

A melancholy frown flitted across Sheldon's taut features. "I wasn't there for Julia when she needed me. Your mother found a lump in her breast, and had a biopsy without my knowledge; when she discovered it was malignant she swore her doctor to secrecy."

Jeremy's eyes widened. "Why wouldn't she tell you?"

"Because she knew I never would've completed the circuit for Boo-yaw's Derby eligibility. She knew how much I wanted a Derby win."

"But, Pop. You can't blame yourself for something you couldn't control."

Sheldon buried his face in his hands. "The signs were there, son, but I was too caught up in my own world to notice them."

Moving to the opposite end of the love seat, Jeremy rested a hand on his father's shoulder. "What happened with my mother is over, and can't be undone. But now you have a second chance to make things right."

Sheldon's head jerked up. "What are you talking about?"

Rising to his feet, Jeremy turned to walk out of the room. He hesitated, but didn't turn around. "Look at what you have, and what you could hope to have."

Sheldon repeated Jeremy's cryptic statement to himself, refusing to accept the obvious. The minutes ticked off, the afternoon shadows lengthened, the sun dipped lower on the horizon. Dusk had fallen when he finally left the den.

Chapter Nine

Renee did not see the shadowy figure sitting on the top stair until she was practically on top of him. If she hadn't been daydreaming then she would have detected the familiar fragrance of sandalwood aftershave.

The telephone call from her brother had continued to haunt her although she'd told herself over and over that Donald wouldn't come after her. After all, she was just one in a string of many women he had dated or lived with—one of a lot of foolish women who thought they could hope to become Mrs. Donald Rush.

The only difference between her and Donald's other women was that it had taken him more than a year to get her to agree to go out with him. And once she did, it was another six months before she agreed to sleep with him. She thought he would give up his pursuit, but he kept coming back. After eighteen months Renee believed he was truly serious about wanting a future together. She hadn't known that during a wild, uninhibited week in Vegas he'd married a long-legged dancer.

"What are you doing here?" Her query came out in a breathless whisper.

"I live here."

Renee felt heat sweep over her face and neck. "I know you live here, Sheldon, but I didn't expect you to be sitting on the steps." Light from hallway sconces did not permit her to see his expression.

"I was waiting to talk to you." He patted his knees. "Please sit down."

She shook her head. "I can't. I need to change for dinner." His right hand snaked out, caught her wrist and pulled her down onto his lap. Renee squirmed, but she couldn't free herself. "Please let me go."

He buried his hair in her hair. "Indulge me, Renee. Just for a few minutes."

Relaxing in his embrace, Renee luxuriated in the muscled thighs under her hips and the unyielding strength in the arms holding her in a protective embrace. Oh, she'd missed those arms around her; she'd missed Sheldon.

"What do you want to talk about?"

"About what happened two weeks ago."

She stiffened before relaxing again. "What about it?"

Sheldon pressed a kiss to her fragrant hair. "I want to apologize if you feel I was not supportive of you."

"All I asked of you was to be a friend, to support

me during the good and bad times, but I got a lover instead."

"I am your friend, darling—friend, lover *and* protector. I wanted to tell you to forget about Susanna and Valerie, but you were too upset for me to reason with you. They said what they said because they're jealous."

"They can't be jealous of me, Sheldon."

He pressed a kiss along the column of her neck. "They are, sweetheart. We have no control over what another person says or thinks, but if any of what they said about you in that bathroom gets back to me, then there's going to be hell to pay."

Covering the hands cradling her belly, Renee shook her head. "I didn't tell you so that you could fight with someone. I just wanted to let you know why I don't want to attend any more soirees with you."

"You don't have…" Whatever he intended to say died on Sheldon's lips when he felt movement under his hand. His expression changed, features softening. "When did she start kicking you?"

Renee smiled at Sheldon over her shoulder. "Last week. At first they were flutters, but they're much stronger now."

"She's a frisky little thing," he said with a broad smile.

"She sleeps all day, then wakes up and performs somersaults half the night."

"Does she keep you up?"

"Sometimes." Renee eased Sheldon's hands away

from her belly. "I have to go get ready for dinner." She moved off his lap; he also rose to his feet.

"I'll wait downstairs for you."

"I'm not eating at the dining hall."

"You're going out?"

"Yes."

"Off the farm?"

"Why?"

Sheldon crossed his arms over his chest, deciding on honesty. "Jeremy told me about your telephone call."

"He had no right to tell you about a personal conversation."

"If it was so personal, then you could've either called your party back or asked Jeremy to leave the room."

Renee rolled her eyes at Sheldon. "One does not ask one's boss to leave the room to indulge in a personal telephone conversation during work hours. Besides, he shouldn't have told you my business."

"Jeremy told me because as long as you live and work here you *are* his business. You, thirty-five others, thirty-six including the child you're carrying, and half a billion dollars in horseflesh. Don't ever forget that, Renee.

"If you leave the farm, then you will be accompanied either by me or an armed escort. Security has already been tightened around the property. Now, I'm going to ask you again, Renee. Are you leaving the farm tonight?" He had enunciated each word.

There was a long, brittle silence as Renee struggled to keep her raw emotions in check. After ending the call with her brother she'd forced herself not to think about Donald. If he had divorced his wife in order to propose marriage, did he actually believe she would marry him now?

No. She could not and would not even if she were carrying quintuplets. Not when she had fallen in love with another man, a man who had become her friend, lover and protector.

"No, Sheldon. I'm not leaving the farm tonight."

Moving closer, he cradled her face and brushed a kiss at the corners of her mouth. "Shall I wait up for you?"

Renee wanted to tell Sheldon he was being controlling, but offered him a saucy smile instead. There was no doubt he wanted to make certain she was safe.

"Only if you wish. Perhaps when I return we can have a sleepover."

Throwing back his head, Sheldon laughed, the sound rich and full-throated. "I'm looking forward to it, princess."

Rising on tiptoe, she kissed his clean-shaven cheek, then made her way down the hallway to her bedroom. She had been invited to share dinner with Kelly, Tricia and Beatrice Miller, followed by a game of bidwhist.

Renee rang the doorbell to Kelly and Ryan's home, pushed open the door and walked into bright light, heat and mouthwatering smells.

Tricia appeared from the rear of the house, a bright

smile softening her round face. "Hi. Come on back to the kitchen."

Renee noticed Tricia's curly hair was longer than when she'd been introduced to her. Thick black shiny curls fell over her ears and the nape of her neck. Tricia Blackstone was blooming—all over.

She walked into the kitchen and into a flurry of activity. Beatrice Miller stood at the cooking island slicing an avocado, while Kelly browned chicken cutlets in a frying pan. Kelly's daughter, four-month-old Vivienne, sat in a high chair, patting the chair's table as Tricia resumed spooning food into her birdlike mouth.

Beatrice, a petite woman with salt-and-pepper hair and smooth dark brown skin had a slender body that rivaled women half her age. A quick smile, soft drawling voice and a gentle manner made her the perfect companion for Gus Parker.

The four women, ranging in age from sixty to mid-thirties, shared a warm smile. "Thank you for coming," Kelly said.

Renee nodded. "Thank you for inviting me. Can I help with something?"

Kelly shook her head. "Not this time. The first time you're a guest. The next time you can do something more strenuous like set the table."

Renee could not stop the rush of heat flooding her face. "I'm pregnant, not physically challenged."

"Not yet," chorused Kelly and Tricia.

Kelly stared at Renee's belly. "By the time you're

ready to deliver you won't be able to bend over to tie your own shoes."

"Stop teasing the child," Beatrice chided softly. "She's carrying rather nicely."

"When are you due, Renee?" Tricia asked.

"March third."

Tricia sucked her teeth. "I'm due the beginning of July and already I can't fit into my slacks."

Kelly stared at her sister-in-law. "I told you even before you knew you were pregnant that I dreamt you were holding three fish. And that means you're going to have triplets."

Tricia sucked her teeth again, this time rolling her eyes at Kelly. "You and your lying dreams."

Beatrice nodded. "You know the old folks say when you dream of fish you're going to hear of a pregnancy."

"I know for certain I'm having one," Renee said quietly.

"Girl or boy?" Beatrice asked as she sliced a ripe mango.

"Girl."

Kelly pressed her hands together. "Wonderful. Now Vivienne will have someone close to her age to play with."

"May I feed her?" The question was out before Renee could censor herself.

Tricia looked at Renee and smiled. "Sure."

"Where can I wash my hands?"

Tricia pointed to a door at the opposite end of the kitchen. "A bathroom is over there."

The three women exchanged knowing glances as Renee went into the bathroom. "She's going to need the practice before you, Tricia," Kelly whispered to her sister-in-law.

Renee returned, exchanging seats with Tricia. Vivienne Blackstone was a beautiful little girl. She'd inherited her mother's looks and her father's curly black hair; her eye color had compromised. It was gunmetal-gray.

Over a dinner of chicken piccata, linguine with roasted garlic and oil, a tropical salad of smoked chicken with avocados and mangoes, toasted Italian bread and lemon sorbet, followed by a lively card game, Kelly and Tricia became the girlfriends Renee had left behind in Miami. Beatrice provided the sage advice she occasionally sought from her mother.

Ryan and Sean had returned from the dining hall in time to put Vivienne to bed; they retreated to the family room to watch a movie, leaving the women to their card game.

"Where did you learn to play bidwhist?" Kelly asked Renee.

"I used to watch my mother and aunts. How did you learn?"

Kelly smiled. "From my mother. She and her sorority sisters used to get together and play Sunday afternoons when they were in college."

"How about you?" Renee asked Tricia.

"My grandmother taught me."

Beatrice stared across the table at Renee. "Do young people still play?"

"I don't think so. Some of the college students who worked part-time at the law firm where I worked talked about playing spades."

Tricia laid down a card. "That's too bad. I suppose we're going to have to keep the tradition going."

"You're right," Kelly concurred. "If Sheldon and his wild bunch can hang out at his cabin to play poker, smoke cigars and drink beer for their annual fall camping weekend, then I suggest we get together every other month for a bidwhist party."

Tricia stared at her grandfather's fiancée. "Did you smell cigar smoke on my grandfather when he got back this afternoon?"

Beatrice shook her head. "No. Gus swore he didn't take one puff and neither did Sheldon, who told the other two guys that they couldn't smoke inside the cabin."

"They need to give up the cigars *and* the beer. It takes them two days to empty a keg," Tricia grumbled.

"Get out!" Renee gasped. "That's a lot of beer."

Kelly put down her cards and placed a hand on her hip. "Why don't you talk to your man?"

Renee's eyes widened. "Sheldon's not my man!"

Kelly lifted an eyebrow. "I didn't mention Sheldon's name. Gotcha!" she teased, pointing a finger at Renee.

Tricia peered over the top of her cards. "Is my father-in-law your man-n-n-n, Renee?" she drawled singsong.

"I'm not telling," Renee teased back, flashing a dimpled grin.

Leaning across the table, Kelly and Tricia exchanged high-five handshakes. "Boo-yaw!" they chorused in unison.

Renee laughed until her sides hurt.

She was still chuckling under her breath as she climbed the porch steps and found Sheldon sitting on a rocker waiting for her. He rose to his feet, extended his arms and she moved into his embrace.

Burying her face in the soft fibers of his sweater, Renee felt safe, safer than she had ever been in her life. Even safer than when she'd slept in the Miami Beach mansion surrounded by gates, guard dogs and high-tech electronic surveillance equipment.

Easing back, she smiled up at Sheldon. "Are you ready for our sleepover?"

He returned her smile. "Yes, I am."

Renee did not have time to catch her breath as he lifted her off her feet and carried her into the house. Sheldon shifted her body, locked the door and then headed for the staircase.

Sheldon did not walk to the end of hallway, but stopped before they reached his bedroom, lifting a questioning eyebrow. Every time he and Renee made love he had come to her. The only exception had been their first encounter at the cabin. However, the day of reckoning could not be postponed forever. He had to know whether she wanted him in her life as much as he wanted her.

"Yours or mine?"

Renee did not know how, but she knew what Sheldon was feeling at that moment. The doubts, questions as to where they and their relationship were heading, and if what they shared went beyond sharing a bed and their passion.

Closing her eyes, she affected a secret smile. "Yours."

Sheldon lowered his head and pressed a kiss to the top of her head. In that instant all that made Renee Wilson who she was seeped into him, becoming a part of him.

It had taken three days away from her, three days where he and three of his best friends had gotten together for their annual fall camping weekend, to remind him what had been missing in his life.

The wild bunch, as they'd called themselves, had become longtime friends who left the farm to kick back for several days of male bonding. They fished, hunted, cooked, smoked cigars, drank beer, swapped war stories and talked about the women they'd loved and lost. These men had become the brothers Sheldon always wanted, but never had. They were his confidants and his conscience.

However, this year it was different, different because although he had brought women to the cabin, none of them had touched the part of him that ached for more than a physical release. None of them were able to make him look beyond the basic human need of food, shelter and clothes for the one thing every human being needed for ultimate survival and perpetuation of oneself: love.

He'd stopped trying to rationalize why Renee had come to him carrying another man's child beneath her heart. Why her and not some other woman, unencumbered by her past. And why did he feel so completely helpless whenever he thought about what she needed most: a husband. Jeremy's parting cryptic statement was imprinted on his brain: "look at what you have, and what you could hope to have."

He had enough money to last him well into old age, had transferred a horse-racing legacy to the next generation and had set aside ten thousand acres of prime property for his grandchildren. He had everything a man could ever hope for—everything but a woman to share his future and the dreams he had for the second half of his life. Every time he opened his mouth to say the two most blissful words a woman yearned to hear, they died on his lips.

He remembered his mother on her deathbed begging his father to "marry" her before she drew her last painful breath. And, although James Blackstone knew he was breaking the law and could have been sent to jail, he had married the woman whom he had loved.

Let go of the fear, his inner voice whispered. Renee wasn't Julia and he was no longer a thirty-two-year-old single father with two young sons who depended on him for their daily needs. *Marry her,* the voice continued. And if he did marry, Renee and her daughter would become Virginia Blackstones, a name with clout and influence.

Walking into the bedroom, he placed her on the king-size bed. The side of the mattress dipped with his weight as he sat beside Renee. A loud pop, followed by a brilliant shower of burning embers behind a decorative fireplace screen threw macabre shadows on the whitewashed ceiling and walls.

Leaning over, Sheldon quietly, seductively removed and then placed Renee's clothing on the bench at the foot of the large bed.

Renee did not open her eyes as she luxuriated in the gossamer touch of Sheldon's fingertips as he sculpted the roundness of her swollen belly before moving up to trace the outline of her engorged breasts. One hand slipped between her knees, moving upward and parting her thighs as it traveled toward the source of heat and the soft throbbing making it almost impossible for her to lie motionless.

Reaching for his hand, she held it against her moist, pulsing warmth, unable to stop the moans coming from her constricted throat. If Sheldon did not take her— quickly—it would be over within seconds. His finger searched and found her. It was his turn to groan when her flesh convulsed around his digit.

Pulling back, he sat on his heels and pulled the sweater over his head. Within seconds his slacks and underwear were pooled on the floor. Gently, he shifted Renee until her buttocks were pressed to his groin. He rested her top leg over his, then eased his swollen flesh into her, both moaning in satisfaction as their bodies melded as one.

I'm home, the scalding blood in Renee's veins sang. It wasn't the modest house where she'd grown up in a Miami suburb; it wasn't the shabby apartment where she'd lived with her mother and brother after her father's untimely death; it wasn't the small condominium apartment she'd bought after working two jobs to save enough money for the down payment; and it certainly wasn't the palatial beachfront mansion with views of the Atlantic Ocean and passing luxury yachts and cruise ships in the distance. Sheldon Blackstone was home and everything the word represented: love, safety, comfort and protection.

Closing her eyes, she tried concentrating on anything but the hardness sliding in and out of her body. Her heart rate skyrocketed along with the uneven rhythm of her breathing. She experienced extreme heat, then bone-chilling cold that made her teeth chatter. Sheldon had set a pace that quickened, slowed, then quickened again until she was mindless with an ecstasy that had become a mind-altering trip shattering her into millions of pieces before lulling her back to a euphoric state that left her weak and mewling as a newborn.

Sheldon clenched his teeth as he fought a hopeless battle. He did not want to let go—release the passion streaking along the edges of sanity. He wanted the whirling, swirling sensations to last—forever if possible. The passion Renee wrung from him hurtled him to heights of erotic pleasure he had never experienced before—not with any woman. He quickened his movements, mindful of the child kicking vigorously in her womb, then went completely still as he moaned and poured out his passions in a flood tide that made him forget everything.

They lay joined, waiting until their hearts resumed a normal rate. Sheldon moved once to pull the sheet and blanket up and over their moist bodies, then as one they fell into a deep sated sleep.

Chapter Ten

Renee slipped out of Sheldon's bed early Thanksgiving morning, retreating to her old bedroom to shower. She hadn't slept there since the night of her bidwhist party with Kelly, Tricia and Beatrice.

Her daily routine had changed since she'd begun sleeping in Sheldon's bedroom. She retired earlier and woke up earlier. Weather permitting she usually took a morning walk. And what Sheldon had told her about additional security around the perimeter of the farm had become apparent whenever she spied a man sitting on horseback with a rifle resting in the crook of an arm or slung across his chest.

Dressed in a bulky sweater, stretch pants, boots and a baseball cap, she set out on her walk. A haze hung over the valley like a diaphanous blue-gray veil. Although a national holiday it was not a farm holiday. Horses had to be washed, groomed and turned out into the paddocks for daily exercise.

Her early morning walks were now a part of her daily exercise regimen. The added weight had put pressure on her lower back, but since she'd begun walking it eased.

Forty minutes and a mile later, she stood in front of one of four barns where the Thoroughbreds were stabled. Several grooms were hosing down horses. She spied Shah Jahan as he stood motionless under the stream of water sluicing over his ebony coat. She couldn't pull her gaze away from the long arching neck, noble head and the sleek powerful lines in half a ton of regal horseflesh. Jahan had raced twice since the International Gold Cup, and had come in first both times. The scorecard with Jahan's racing statistics read:

Owner: Blackstone Farms
Trainer: Kevin Manning
Sire: Ali Jahir Dam: Jane's Way
Starts: 3 Wins: 3 Earnings: $1.2 million

What had most people in the world of Thoroughbred racing wagging their heads was the fact that Shah Jahan had yet to celebrate his second birthday.

Nodding to the grooms, Renee walked into the barn. The sounds of stalls being swept out reverberated in the large space. The sweet smell of hay masked the odor of sweat, manure and urine.

She stepped aside just in time to avoid a ball of black and white fur scampering around her feet. Leaning down, she picked up a tiny puppy. It wiggled and yelped as it struggled to free itself.

"To whom do you belong?"

"No one, Miss Renee."

Turning on her heel, Renee stared at Peter McCann, a teenager whose pleasant looks were neutralized by an outbreak of acne.

"Is he a stray?" she asked.

Peter nodded. "His mama whelped a litter about six weeks ago. Dr. Blackstone has already given away four. He's the only one left. Doc already gave him his shots."

Renee smiled at the large black eyes staring back at her. "What breed is he?"

"Mutt," Peter replied, deadpan. "His mama is part lab and sheepdog. Don't know about his papa. Lady Day must have snuck off the farm when she was in heat and found herself a man. She didn't come back until she was ready to whelp. Now that she's weaned this last one Dr. Blackstone plans to neuter her. He claims we have enough dogs to keep the horses company."

Sheldon had explained to Renee that most horse farms kept either dogs or goats as pets to keep the stabled horses, which are by nature social animals, company. She did not know why, but she felt an instant kinship with the puppy.

"I think I'm going to take him home with me."

"He's going to be a big one, Miss Renee. Take a look at his paws."

She looked at his paws. They were rather large for a small puppy. "If he's part sheepdog, then he'll adapt to staying outdoors."

"None of the farm dogs come inside, except when it snows. If you're going to take him home, then I'll get a leash for you. I'll also bring over some food after I finish up with my chores."

Renee gave him a warm smile. "Thank you."

It wasn't until after she had attached the leash to the collar around the puppy's neck that she thought about Sheldon. Would he even want a dog in his house? Had his sons grown up with pets?

She hadn't had a pet of her own since her mother was forced to sell their house and move into an apartment where the landlord had posted a sign prohibiting pets of any kind.

The puppy tired, stopped and sat down. Squatting, she picked up the dog, cradling it against her jacket. She'd just walked past Jeremy and Tricia's house when she saw Sheldon striding toward her. A sensual smile curved her mouth. He had a sexy walk. His back ramrod-straight, he swaggered, broad shoulders swaying from side to side.

Slowing her pace, she smiled, stopped and waited for him to approach her. He'd elected to wear a flannel shirt with jeans and a pair of worn boots.

She'd seen him dressed in a tailored suit, a tuxedo and jeans with a pullover sweater or cotton shirt, and she liked him dressed down best. The casual attire seemed to enhance his rugged handsomeness.

Her smile faded the moment she noticed his stern-faced expression. "Good morning."

Sheldon's gray eyes swept over Renee, lingering momentarily on the puppy cradled against her chest. "I thought because it wasn't a work day you'd stay in bed beyond daybreak."

"I enjoy getting up early and walking."

"Why don't you wait for me to walk with you." His tone was softer, almost conciliatory.

"I don't want to wake you up."

"Wake me up, Renee."

"Okay, Sheldon. I'll wake you up."

He pointed to the puppy. "What do you have there?"

"A pet."

He lifted both eyebrows. "A pet?"

"Our pet, Sheldon."

He crossed his arms over his chest. "Did I say I wanted or needed a pet?"

Renee shook her head. "No. But, if I'm going to live with you then he will become *our* pet." She peered up at him. "Don't you like animals?"

Sheldon gave Renee an incredulous look. "If I didn't like animals why would I own a horse farm? I'm not opposed to you having a dog, but who's going to take care of him when we go away?"

"When are we going away?"

"I'd planned to take you to the cabin this weekend. You said you wanted to learn how to fish."

"Can't we take him with us, Sheldon? Please," she added when a frown appeared between his eyes.

The corners of his mouth twitched then inched upward as he tried and failed to bite back a grin. "Yes, princess. You can bring *our* pet to the cabin."

Moving closer, she wound her free arm around his waist, encountering a bulge in the small of his back. "Sheldon." His name was a weak whisper. He was carrying a handgun.

Grasping her hand, he pulled it away from his body. "It's all right, baby."

"It's not all right. I don't like guns."

"Neither do I," he countered. "But sometimes they are a necessary evil."

She took a step backward. "I don't want to see it."

"Walk ahead of me and you won't see it."

Renee moved in front of Sheldon. She could feel his gaze boring into her back. "I need a name for the puppy."

"Is it a boy?" She nodded. "How about Patch?"

"How did you come up with that one?"

"Because he looks as if he's wearing a black patch over one eye."

Renee stared at the sleeping puppy. So much for her being observant.

"Patch Blackstone. I like the sound of that," she said, peering at Sheldon over her shoulder.

"He's going to need food."

"Peter promised to bring some to the house."

Sheldon shook his head. Three months ago he lived alone. Now he had not only a woman but also a dog sharing his home. "Try to paper train him as soon as possible, because I don't want more work for Claire."

"I'll clean up after him."

"No, you won't."

"Why not, Sheldon? He's my pet and therefore my responsibility."

"You don't need to be on your knees cleaning up dog crap. I'll do it."

Renee's back stiffened. "No, you won't."

"If that's the case, then get rid of the damn dog." She stopped, spun around and walked back to face him. "I'm not going to argue with you, Renee," he warned in a deceptively soft voice.

There was something about Sheldon's expression that stilled Renee's tongue. His implacable expression was unnerving. "Nor I you," she said quietly.

Turning on her heel, she bit down on her lower lip until it pulsed between her teeth. How could she prove her point with a man who refused to debate?

The answer was she couldn't.

Renee sat next to Sheldon at a table in the dining hall. Each table's centerpiece was representative of the season: tiny pumpkins, gourds, sprigs of pine and pine cones. Orange and yellow tablecloths had replaced the usual white. Prerecorded taped music provided a nice backdrop for the various conversations from the diners.

She'd had a light breakfast because she wanted to save her appetite for Thanksgiving dinner. Within minutes Kevin Manning, his wife and their niece, Cheryl, joined them.

Nineteen-year-old Cheryl had become a racing celebrity. Barely five feet in height, she topped the scales at an even one hundred pounds.

Ryan Blackstone stood up, waiting for conversations to fade. He smiled, flashing sparkling white teeth under a neatly barbered mustache. "Good afternoon. Unlike my esteemed father and brother, I'll make this speech short and sweet, because I don't know about you but I'm hungry enough to eat a horse."

There came a round of hisses and boos when he mentioned horse. "Not any of our horses, of course." This was followed with applause. Ryan sobered. "But on a more serious note, I'd like to give thanks for so many things this year. I'm thankful for our families, immediate and extended. We also have to thank Kevin and Cheryl for their incredible successes. We are thankful and grateful for the new members of our farm family." He smiled at Renee and Beatrice.

"I'd also like to thank my brother for his hard work and unwavering support as we prepare for another generation of Blackstone Farms achievements. I'd like to thank my father for always being here not only for me but also for all of us. He's sacrificed a lot to make Blackstone Farms what it is today, and for that I'm certain he will be rewarded in ways he cannot imagine.

"Last year our mothers came to Sheldon because they wanted a safe environment for their children. That request gave birth to the Blackstone Farm Day School and Infant Center. This year some of you have asked for a place of worship, and your request has been taken under advisement. Sheldon has offered to give up five acres of land in the north end for the construction of an interdenominational church. The contractor laid the foundation two days ago, and we hope to have the project completed before spring."

Ryan paused as applause and whistles rent the air. He held up a hand. "Some of you may not be aware of it, but in another life one of our grooms served as an assistant pastor in a little church in Texas." He motioned to a table to his right. "Reverend Jimmy Merrell, I'd like for you to meet your flock and bless the food." There were gasps of surprise intermingled with applause.

Jimmy stood up and clasped his hands, everyone following suit. Renee folded her hands in her lap. She gave Sheldon a sidelong glance when his hand covered hers.

There were so many things to be thankful for this year: the child kicking vigorously inside her; the love of the man cradling her hand; the love and happiness her mother had found after so many years of pain and despair, and her brother for his love and support after she'd come to him when she needed him most.

The invocation concluded and the feasting began. Renee ate so much that she had to refuse dessert. She'd wanted to sample the pastry chef's renowned sweet potato pie, and in the end she had a slice wrapped up to take with her before she and Sheldon left for their weekend at the cabin.

* * *

Sheldon cradled Renee to his chest, staring into the flickering flames in the fireplace. A gentle smile touched his mouth. It was a perfect scenario: a man and woman in bed together while their dog slept on a rug in front of the fireplace.

He'd come to the cabin with Renee because he needed to be away from the farm…and alone with her. Here he hoped he would be able to face his fear and come to terms with his feelings for her. He had known there was something special about her from the very beginning, yet he could not have imagined he would fall in love with a woman carrying the fruit of her love for another man inside her.

Once he'd recovered from the shock that she was pregnant it had become insignificant. Kelly had married Ryan and had become mother to Sean, his son from a prior marriage. Kelly had legally adopted Sean the year before.

Sheldon closed his eyes, sighing softly. If he married Renee before the birth of her daughter, then she would automatically become a Blackstone.

"Have you thought of a name for the baby?"

Renee snuggled closer and wiggled her nose when the hair on Sheldon's chest tickled her. "I've thought of a few."

"Do you want to tell me, or it is a secret?"

"It's not a secret. I'm considering Virginia, because it was my grandmother's name. I also like Sonya and Hannah."

"They're all strong, traditional feminine names. Have you picked out ones for a boy, just in case?"

Pulling out of his embrace, Renee sat up. "I can't have a boy."

Sheldon noted the look of distress on her face. "Why not? Sonograms aren't always that accurate."

Tunneling her fingers through her hair, Renee held it off her face. "I don't want a boy, because…" Her words trailed off, locked in her throat.

Reaching for her, Sheldon pulled her up to sit on his lap. "Why not, Renee?"

She stared at him in the wavering light from the fireplace fire. "A boy needs a mother *and* a father. I know I can raise my daughter by myself, but not my son."

"I'll help you, darling."

She froze. "What?"

"I'll help you raise your son. I've made mistakes with Ryan and Jeremy, yet they've turned out all right. I'm very proud of them."

Renee shook her head. "No, Sheldon. I can't ask you to do that."

"Didn't you ask me to protect you and your baby?"

"Protect, not assume responsibility for raising it."

A weighted heaviness settled in Sheldon's chest as he digested Renee's statement. She would permit him in her life but not to share in it.

His life had come full circle. Julia had married him, borne his two sons, yet she had withheld a part of herself from him, had concealed her illness until it was too late.

Was he destined to repeat the same mistake? Had he fallen in love with a woman like Julia?

Now it was his turn to hide, hide his true feelings from Renee. He had fallen in love with her, would probably always love her, but it was something he would never reveal to her or anyone else.

He squeezed her shoulder. "Let's get some sleep because we're going to have to get up early tomorrow to go fishing."

"Let's go, sleepyhead. Time to get up." Renee mumbled in her sleep, but did not wake up. Sheldon shook her harder. "Renee."

Her lids fluttered wildly as she opened her eyes. Where was she? She heard a soft yelping and came awake. Rolling over on her back she saw Sheldon leaning over her.

"What time is it?"

"Four," he whispered.

"Four o'clock in the freaking morning?"

Grinning, he nodded. "Let's go while the fish are biting." He nuzzled her ear. "Okay, princess. If I catch the fish you'll have to clean them."

Renee sat straight up. She hated cleaning fish. "No. Give me a few minutes and I'll be ready."

Sheldon sat down on the side of the bed, watching her as she walked to the bathroom. She was moving more slowly now. Cupping a hand over his mouth, he closed his eyes.

He had spent a restless night wondering whether he'd

coerced Renee into living with him. Renovations on her bungalow were nearing completion, and he thought about giving her the option of moving out of his house and into her own.

But seeing her waddle across the room while massaging her lower back squeezed his heart. He couldn't leave her—not now. Not until after she delivered the baby.

Renee lay on a wooden bench in the bathroom, her legs covered with foam. Sheldon straddled the bench, razor in hand. He had offered to shave her legs.

He raised her foot to his thigh. "Relax, baby. I'm not going to cut you."

"I've always shaved my own legs."

Leaning forward, he laid a hand over her distended belly. "That was before, when you could bend down or lift your leg. Right now, you're at my mercy."

Staring up at the recessed lights, Renee nodded. "That's what I'm afraid of."

His right hand moved up her thighs and covered the furred mound. "You know I wouldn't take advantage of you."

She slapped at his hand. "I know nothing of the sort."

"Maybe if I shave a little higher the hospital won't charge you for that particular procedure once you go into labor."

"Stop it, Sheldon!" She laughed so hard that her stomach muscles contracted. "Now, I'm hurting," she said between guffaws.

"Where?"

"My sides and back."

Hovering over her, Sheldon smiled. "I'll give you a massage after I finish your legs."

Renee calmed down enough to remain still as he drew the blade over her legs.

Sheldon finished one leg, then did the other. Gathering her off the bench, he cradled her to his chest.

"I think you've gained a few pounds since yesterday."

Renee met his gaze. "Did you see how much I ate for Thanksgiving?"

He shook his head. "No, because I was too busy stuffing my own face."

"I hope the doctor won't put me on a diet after I weigh in."

"How much have you gained overall?"

"Twelve pounds." She'd doubled her weight gain since coming to the farm.

"That's not much."

"I know. But there are times when I feel like a beached whale."

"You look beautiful."

Tightening her hold on his neck, Renee kissed his stubbly jaw. "You're so good for a woman's ego."

He angled his head. "You are beautiful, Renee."

"Thank you. I'd like to cook for you tonight, Sheldon."

"Are you sure you know how to cook?"

She remembered another time when he'd doubted

her culinary skills. "Stay out of the kitchen, and you'll see if I can. I'm going to check your refrigerator and freezer, and if you don't have what I need then you're going to have to drive me to the nearest supermarket."

He placed her on her side on a table in a steam room. "There are no supermarkets around here."

"Where do you buy your food?"

"I usually bring it from the farm."

"Like the keg of beer you and your buddies drink during your annual fall frolic."

"If I tell you something, will you promise not to tell anyone?"

Sheldon's expression was so serious Renee felt her heart stop before starting up again. "Yes."

"We usually drink a couple of six-packs, not a keg."

"Tricia said her grandfather brags about you guys emptying a keg in a couple of days."

Pulling over a stool, Sheldon sat down and gently kneaded the muscles in Renee's lower back. "The first year we got together we bought a keg. We emptied the keg by pouring out more than three quarters of the beer. I'm lucky if I can drink two beers in one sitting."

"Then it's all a lie?"

He pressed his mouth to her bare shoulder. "It wasn't a lie. When I said we emptied a keg everyone assumed we had actually drunk a keg of beer. We never bothered to clarify the misconception because that would destroy the wild bunch's mystique. Do you know how many guys want in our elite organization?"

Renee laughed again. "You guys are a fraud."

"And you better not tell," Sheldon threatened.

"I'll think about it."

"Renee!"

"Okay, Sheldon. I'll keep your secret."

Rounding the table, he hunkered down and kissed her until her lips parted to his probing tongue. The kiss claimed a dreamy intimacy that hinted of more as Sheldon gathered Renee off the table and carried her into one of the downstairs bedrooms. He lowered her to the bed, his body following; he supported his weight on his elbows.

Reversing their positions, Sheldon pressed his back to the headboard and brought Renee to straddle him, her back against his chest. Lifting her slightly, he entered her, covering her breasts with his hands. The coupling lasted minutes, but when they climaxed simultaneously it was to offer the other the sweetest ecstasy either had ever experienced.

Chapter Eleven

Renee stood at the cooking island, adding chopped fresh rosemary to a lemon marinade for the trout she'd planned to cook on the stovetop grill.

"Do you need me for anything before I go upstairs and wash my hair?" Sheldon asked as he walked into the kitchen. He had taken Sean with him to Staunton for a haircut.

She smiled at Sheldon. "No. I'm good here."

After sharing cooking duties over the Thanksgiving weekend, she and Sheldon continued the ritual once they returned to the farm. He had been so impressed with her cooking skills that he had begun making special requests.

He left the bed when she did, accompanying her on early morning walks, and returning to the house after stopping for breakfast at the dining hall. She had adjusted her work hours from nine-to-five to eight-to-four. Although she no longer required a nap during the day, she rarely slept soundly through the night. As soon as she got into bed the baby began her nightly aerobic workout.

She concentrated on whisking the marinade, then placed it on a shelf in the refrigerator. Removing a platter with two cleaned and filleted trout, she lightly salted them, added freshly ground pepper, wrapped two slices of bacon around each fish and tucked bay leaves inside the fold close to the skin of the fish.

Sheldon entered the kitchen as Renee was putting the finishing touches on the meal.

Renee took several steps, stopping inches from the man whom she had fallen in love with and rested her head over his heart. It was pounding a runaway rhythm. "Talk to me, Sheldon."

Reaching out and pulling her to his body, he rocked her gently. "I love you, Renee. I love you, yet I'm afraid of losing you."

Tilting her chin, she saw pain in his eyes before he shuttered his gaze. "Why on earth would you lose me?" she whispered. "I plan to be around for a long time."

He released her shoulders, cradling her face between his hands. "I want you in my life not for a few months or for a few years, but for always. I know I can be a good father to your baby, but I doubt whether I can be a good husband to you."

"Why, Sheldon?"

Lowering his head, he pressed his mouth to her ear, telling Renee about Julia, her illness and his selfish pursuit to make horse-racing history.

"I saw her grow weaker and weaker, but whenever I asked if she was all right she reassured me she was okay. And like a fool I believed her."

"It's not as if you didn't ask her, darling. She just chose not to tell you the truth."

"I should've insisted."

Renee shook her head. "That wouldn't have changed a thing. Not when you live with someone who chooses to conceal the truth."

Sheldon pulled himself from his past and back to the present. *Not when you live with someone who chooses to conceal the truth.*

Julia had deceived him, and Donald had deceived Renee. The difference was Julia was gone and Renee was here. He should ask her to marry him and claim her child as his own.

But could he risk it?

"Yes," he said softly.

Renee stared at Sheldon. "Yes, what?"

He blinked as if coming out of a trance. "Do you love me, Renee?"

A flicker of apprehension coursed through her. Was Sheldon losing his mind? "What's going on with you?"

"Do you love me, Renee Wilson?" He'd enunciated each word as if she were hard of hearing.

Her lids fluttered wildly, keeping time with her runaway pulse. "Yes, I do, Sheldon Blackstone. I do love you."

"Will you do me the honor of becoming my wife?" She hesitated. "Yes or no, Renee?"

"Yes."

"And will you also permit me the honor to be a father to your daughter?"

As their gazes met, Renee felt a shock run through her. Sheldon was offering her what she had wanted all of her life: a man she could love *and* trust, a man who would protect her *and* her baby.

She bit down on her lower lip to still its trembling. "Yes, Sheldon." A delicious shudder heated her body when he dipped his head and kissed her. "Will this arrangement be strictly business?" she whispered against his mouth.

Lines fanned out around his incredible eyes. "Oh, it will be business, all right. I want to marry you before the end of year, turn one of the upstairs bedrooms into a nursery, then when Virginia, Sonya or Hannah Blackstone is at least six months old we're going to go on a belated honeymoon to somewhere exotic and make mad, passionate love to each other."

Giggling and snuggling as close as her belly would allow her, Renee curved her arms under his shoulders. "We don't have to go away to make mad, passionate love to each other."

Sheldon placed a hand over her middle. "Just once I'd like to make love to you without our daughter coming between us."

"Three months, then another six weeks. It's not that far off."

"You're right. I think I'm going to like having a daughter."

"I'm sure she's going to love having you for her father."

His hands moving up and down her back in a soothing motion, Sheldon rested his chin on the top of Renee's head. "I'm going to tell you now that I'm going to spoil her, Renee."

"That's okay as long as she doesn't become a brat."

"Let's have dinner, then we'll call Jeremy and Ryan and let them in on our good news. After that we'll call your folks."

"I think I'd like to have a Christmas Eve wedding."

"And you will, princess. You can have any and everything you want."

Renee knew there was something special about Sheldon Blackstone the instant she stepped out of her car to find him staring down at her. So special that she fell in love with him despite her vow never to trust another man.

Christmas Eve

White damask tablecloths, delicate china, crystal stemware, sterling silver, beeswax tapers in sterling holders and large pine wreaths decorated with white satin bows and white rosebuds at Blackstone Farms' dining hall set the stage for the nuptials between Renee Anna Wilson and Sheldon James Blackstone.

Rumors were circulating throughout Virginia's horse country that there was to be a wedding at Blackstone Farms, and for the first time in farm history no one deigned to confirm or deny the rumor.

Sheldon had selected Jeremy as his best man, Ryan and Sean as his groomsmen. Renee had asked her brother to give her away, her sister-in-law had agreed to be her maid-of-honor and Kelly and Tricia were her bridesmaids.

The farms' employees began filing into the dining hall at seven forty-five, sitting at assigned tables. A string quartet played Mozart concertos, then at exactly eight o'clock, the lights dimmed. Jeremy and Sheldon, dressed in formalwear, entered the dining hall. An eerie hush fell over the room as groomsmen with burgundy silk ties and bridesmaids in floor-length matching gowns followed the procession.

The distinctive strains of the wedding march began and Renee, clinging to her brother's arm, concentrated on putting one foot in front of the other as she made her way over the white carpet leading to where Sheldon waited in front of the stained-glass window. Her dress, an off-white, long-sleeved satin gown with an empire waist, was designed to artfully camouflage her swollen belly. She looked at her mother and smiled.

Edward Wilson tightened his hold on his sister's hand. "We're almost there, Rennie."

Edward had contacted Donald Rush after Renee informed him that she was marrying Sheldon, and told him that his sister had married. Donald offered his best wishes for her happiness, then abruptly hung up. The telephone call had closed the door on Renee and Donald's past.

Renee let out a soft gasp as she felt a strong kick. Her baby had awakened in time to celebrate her parents' wedding. She focused her attention on the Reverend Jimmy Merrell, who waited to perform his first wedding as the farm's resident minister.

After midnight, when Renee lay in the warmth of her husband's embrace, she recalled her wedding and the reception dinner that followed. The resident chefs had outdone themselves with a reception that included passed hors d'oeuvres, seafood, carving and Asian stations. A seated dinner menu offered soup, salad, blue lump crab cakes and entrées of rib-eye steak and free-range chicken breast.

Shifting to her right side, she placed her left hand over her husband's chest, the light from a table lamp glinting off the precious stones in her wedding band.

Sheldon squeezed the tiny hand, whispering a silent prayer of thanksgiving for his wife and the child kicking in her womb. He had been given a second chance to be a good husband. This time he was certain he would get it right.

"Do you want to know something, Sheldon?"

"What, darling?"

"I just realized how lucky I am."

"Why?"

"I get to have a sleepover with my best friend every single night."

Chuckling softly, Sheldon kissed her forehead. "Merry Christmas, princess."

Renee kissed his shoulder. "Merry Christmas, my love."

This Christmas they would celebrate as husband and wife.

The next one would be as husband, wife, mother and father.

Epilogue

Eighteen months later

The photographer checked his light meter, then changed the lens on his camera.

"Renee, please move closer to your husband. Jeremy, you're going to have to hold two of your daughters."

The Blackstones had gathered in Renee and Sheldon's living room for a formal family photo session. In only a year and a half the family had increased by five.

Renee had given birth to a daughter whom she'd named Virginia.

Tricia and Jeremy had become the parents of identical triplet daughters who were feminine miniatures of their father.

Ryan and Kelly had welcomed their third child, a

son, who was named for his grandfather, Sheldon James Blackstone the second.

Virginia squirmed to free herself from Renee's arms. "Poppa."

Sheldon reached over and took his daughter, bouncing her on his knee. The chubby little girl had become his pride and joy from the moment she came into the world, crying at the top of her tiny lungs. He'd kissed her, cut the umbilical cord and had claimed her as his own within seconds of her birth. Virginia may have looked like her mother, but there was no doubt she was his daughter.

"Let's do this now," Sheldon ordered the photographer.

The man held up a hand. "One, two, three. Hold it." A flash of light went off, startling the children. They'd barely recovered when another flash followed. This time they laughed, trying to catch the tiny white circles floating in front of their eyes.

The photographer got off one more shot, capturing the lively smiles and bright-eyed stares of the next generation of Virginia Blackstones.

* * * * *

A YOUNGER MAN

Chapter One

"Do you need help?"

Veronica Johnson-Hamlin stared at the large man sitting astride a motorcycle. He removed a black shiny helmet, tucking it under one arm. "No, thanks. I've already called road service." Raising her right hand, she showed him her cellular telephone.

"How long have you been waiting?"

"Not too long."

"How long is not too long?"

She glanced at her watch. "About twenty minutes."

Kumi shook his head. "That's a long time to be stranded here."

His protective instincts had surfaced without warning. She was a lone female, stuck along a stretch of road that was not heavily trafficked, in an expensive vehicle.

Swinging a denim-covered leg over the bike, he pushed it off the road, propping it against a tree. Looping the strap of his helmet over one of the handlebars, he made his way around to the back of the Lexus SUV, peering into the cargo area before returning to the driver's side again.

"Do you have a jack and a spare?"

Vertical lines appeared between Veronica's large clear brown eyes. "I told you that I've called for road service."

Kumi moved closer, staring directly at her for the first time. He hadn't realized he was holding his breath until he felt tightness in his chest. The woman staring back at him had the most delicately feminine features he'd ever seen. A slender face claimed a pair of high cheekbones that afforded her an exotic appearance. Her slanting eyes, a light brown with flecks of amber-gold, were clear—clear enough for him to see his own reflection in their mysterious depths, and they were the perfect foil for her flawless umber-brown skin. Her nose was short, the bridge straight, the nostrils flaring slightly as she pressed her full, generously curved lips together. He wasn't able to discern the color or texture of the hair concealed under a navy blue cotton bandana. His gaze slipped lower to a white man-tailored shirt she'd tucked into a pair of jeans.

"Do you have any perishable items in the back?" he asked, gesturing with his thumb.

Veronica's eyelids fluttered. There was no doubt some of her frozen purchases had begun defrosting when she'd turned off the engine. She forced a smile. "They should keep until the service station sends someone."

Kumi rested his hand on the door. "Look, miss, I'm just trying to help you. You're stuck here in a very expensive truck. I'd hate to read about someone coming along and jacking you for your ride. And you'd be lucky if they only took your vehicle."

She registered his warning as she studied his face— feature by feature. His black hair was cropped close to his scalp, and she suspected the stubble covering his perfectly shaped head was new growth from what recently had been a shaved dark brown pate. He had a strong face with prominent cheekbones, a bold nose and a lush full mouth. She couldn't see his eyes behind his mirrored sunglasses, but she still felt their intense heat. He was tall, no doubt several inches above six feet, and built like a professional athlete. She estimated that he was somewhere in his midthirties. Her gaze lowered to his powerful arms. There was a small tattoo on the left bicep, but she couldn't quite make out the design.

"What's it going to be, miss? Do you want to wait here by yourself, or do you want me to fix your flat?"

Veronica took another glance at her watch. It was at least half an hour since she'd dialed the number to her automobile club. Reaching over, she removed the key.

"I have a spare and a jack in the cargo area."

Kumi took the key from her outstretched fingers. By the time he'd rounded the truck and opened the rear door, she'd stepped out and stood alongside the Harley.

He glanced over at her, silently admiring the way her jeans clung to her curvy waist and hips. She wasn't tall, but then she couldn't be called short, either. There was a mature lushness about her body that epitomized her femininity. His sensitive nose caught a whiff of the perfume on her body and clothing and a muscle quivered in his jaw. The fragrance was perfect for her, reminding him of an overripe lush peach bursting with thick, sweet juice.

Moving several bags, he found the jack and spare tire. He bounced the tire on the asphalt, making certain it was inflated. Working quickly, Kumi removed the flat, replacing it with the spare. His biceps bulged under his suntanned skin as he tightened lug nuts. It had taken him less than fifteen minutes to change the tire and store the flat behind the front seats.

"I suggest you get this one repaired as soon as possible, because it's not safe to ride around without a spare."

Veronica nodded at the same time she reached into the front pocket of her jeans. She withdrew two twenties. "Thank you for your help."

He stared at the money as if it were a venomous reptile. "I don't want *that*."

"It's the least I can do," she countered.

Turning on his heel, Kumi walked over to his bike and swung a leg over it. "I didn't help you because I expected to be paid."

A flush swept over her face. "If you won't take any money, then how can I repay you?"

Behind his sunglasses, his gaze moved leisurely over

her body. He smiled for the first time and displayed large, straight and startling white teeth. "How about a home-cooked meal?"

Veronica's jaw dropped at the same time her eyes narrowed. "What?"

His smile widened. "I've been out of the country for ten years, and what I've missed most is a home-cooked Southern meal."

She arched dark eyebrows. "What if I can't cook?"

It was his turn to lift his eyebrows. "You sure bought a lot of food for someone who can't cook."

She smiled, her eyes crinkling attractively. Veronica didn't know why, but there was something quite charming about the young man sitting on the Harley. He had gone out of his way to help her. If he hadn't come along, she still would be waiting for road service.

He angled his head. "Well?"

"Well what?" The two words were layered with a thread of annoyance.

"Are you going to fix that meal?"

What Veronica wanted to do was jump in her truck, drive away and leave him sitting on his bike watching her taillights.

"What do you want?"

His gaze shifted to her Georgia license plate. "Surprise me, Miss Georgia Peach."

"What if I met you at a restaurant?"

Kumi wagged a finger. "No fair. I want home-cooked."

Her temper flared without warning. "If you think

I'm going to invite you—a stranger to my home—then you're crazy."

Folding massive arms over a broad chest, he glared at her behind the lenses of his sunglasses. "What do you think I'm going to do to you? Rape you? If I was going to assault you I would've done that already."

Heat stole into her cheeks. "Don't put words in my mouth! I didn't say anything about rape."

"Speaking of mouths—I still want a home-cooked meal."

Folding her hands on her hips, Veronica glared back at him. "Do you ride around looking for hapless women to rescue in exchange for food?"

Throwing back his head, Kumi laughed loudly, the sound coming from deep within his wide chest. "I kind of like that idea."

"Look, Mr...."

"Walker," he supplied. "The name is Kumi Walker."

"Mr. Walker."

"Yes, miss?" He lifted his thick black curving eyebrows in a questioning expression.

"It's Ms. Johnson." She'd given him her maiden name. "Okay," she said, deciding to concede.

What harm would there be in cooking a meal for him? And he was right about attacking her. If he'd wanted to attack her and take her vehicle, he could've done it easily.

Kumi flashed a victorious grin. "How about Sunday around four?"

"Sunday at four," she repeated, holding out her hand. "I need my key."

He removed the car key from the back pocket of his jeans and dangled it in front of her. "Where do you live?" She grabbed for the key, but he pulled it away from her grasp. "Your address, Ms. Johnson."

Swallowing back the curses threatening to spill from her lips, Veronica counted slowly to three. "Do you know Trace Road?" He nodded. "I live at the top of the hill." She held out her hand, palm upward. "Now give me my damn key."

Kumi dropped the key in her hand, then picked up his helmet and placed it on his head. He waited, watching the gentle sway of her hips as she walked over to the SUV and got into the driver's seat. He was still waiting when she slammed the door to the Lexus, started up the engine and sped away. As she disappeared from view he glanced at his watch. He would have to exceed the speed limit if he were to make it back to his cottage to shower and change his clothes in time.

Twenty minutes later he stood under the spray of a cool shower, recalling his interaction with Ms. Johnson. He didn't know what had drawn him to her, but he intended to find out.

It wasn't until later that night when he lay in bed that he thought perhaps there could be a Mr. Johnson. Even though she hadn't worn a ring, he knew instinctively she would've mentioned a husband—if he did indeed exist.

Closing his eyes, Kumi tried recalling her incredible face and body, and much to his chagrin he couldn't.

Veronica left the warmth of her bed, walking across the smooth, hardwood parquet floor on bare feet to a set of double French doors. Daybreak had begun to breathe a blush over the night sky, depositing feathery streaks of pinks, blues, violet and mauve. Rays from the rising sun cut a widening swath across the navy blue canvas, as ribbons of light crisscrossed the Great Smoky Mountains and painted the verdant valley with delicate hues from a painter's palette. With a trained eye, Veronica witnessed the breathtaking splendor.

Opening the doors, she stepped out onto the second-story veranda and leaned against the waist-high wooden railing. She closed her eyes, shivering slightly against the early morning chill sweeping over her exposed flesh. Her revealing nightgown was better suited for sultry Atlanta, not the cooler temperatures of the western North Carolina mountain region. Despite the softly blowing wind molding the delicate silken garment to her curvy body, she felt the invisible healing fingers massaging the tension in her temples, dissolving the lump under her heart and easing the tight muscles in her neck and shoulders.

Breathing in the crisp mountain air, she watched the sun inch higher—high above the haze rising from the deep gorges. The sight was more calming and healing than any prescribed tranquilizer.

Why had it taken her so long to return to this mountain retreat? Why hadn't she returned after burying her husband Dr. Bramwell Hamlin? Why had she lingered in Atlanta, Georgia, a year after defending her legal claim to his estate?

She knew the answers even before she'd formed the questions in her mind. She hadn't wanted to leave Atlanta—leave a way of life that had become as necessary to her as breathing. It was where she'd been born, raised and had set up a successfully thriving art gallery; it was also where she'd married and had been widowed.

It hadn't mattered that Bram had been old enough to be her father. In fact, he'd been several years older than her own father, but she'd come to love him—not as a father figure but as a husband. She'd married Bram at thirty-four, was widowed at forty and now at forty-two had to determine whether she truly wanted to leave the glamour of Atlanta and relocate to her vacation retreat in the North Carolina mountains.

Pushing away from the railing, she stepped back into the bedroom and closed the doors. It was Sunday and she had to decide what she was going to prepare for dinner. It was the first time in two years that she would cook for a man. Cooking dinner for Kumi Walker would be a unique and singular experience. After she fed the arrogant young man his requested home-cooked meal, she would show him the door. And that was certain to be an easy task, because since becoming a wealthy widow, she had become quite adept at rejecting men.

Easing the narrow straps of the nightgown off her

shoulders, she let it float to the floor. She stepped out of it, bending down and picking up the black silk garment. Straightening gracefully, she headed for the bathroom.

The sun had shifted behind the house, leaving the kitchen cooler. Overhead track lighting cast a warm gold glow on stark white cabinets and black-hued appliances. Veronica had adjusted the air conditioner to counter the buildup of heat from the oven. She'd spent nearly four hours preparing oven-fried chicken, smothered cabbage with pieces of smoked turkey, candied sweet potatoes, savory white rice, cornbread and a flavorful chicken giblet gravy. Dessert was homemade strawberry shortcake.

Glancing up at the clock on the built-in microwave oven, she noted the time. Kumi was expected to arrive within forty-five minutes. All she had to do was set the table in the dining area off the kitchen, take another shower and select something appropriate to wear.

Kumi hung his jacket on a hook behind his seat and placed a bouquet of flowers on the passenger seat alongside a bottle of champagne. Slipping behind the wheel of his brother-in-law's car, he turned the key in the ignition and headed in the direction of Trace Road.

Warm air flowing through the open vents feathered over his freshly shaven face. He wanted to enjoy the smell of his home state. He hadn't realized how much he'd missed Asheville and North Carolina until he'd sat on the bike and rode through towns and cities he'd remembered from his childhood. Memories—good and bad—had assailed him.

He'd left the States at twenty-two, returning a decade later as a stranger.

He'd been back for eight days, yet had not seen or spoken to his two older brothers or his parents. His sister Deborah had disclosed that the elder Walkers were vacationing abroad, and were expected to return to the States for the Memorial Day weekend. And that meant he had ten days before he would come face-to-face with his father—Dr. Lawrence Walker—a man who was as tyrannical as he was unforgiving. A man who'd hung up on him whenever he called home. A man who had symbolically buried his last-born because Kumi would not follow his edict. After a while, Kumi had stopped calling.

Concentrating on his driving, he turned off the local road and onto a narrowed one identified by a sign as Trace. He reached the top of the hill, slowing and searching for Ms. Johnson's house. He saw one house, and then another.

He swallowed an expletive. He hadn't asked her the house number. His frustration escalated as he steered with one hand, driving slowly, while peering to his right at structures set several hundred feet back from the winding road. There were a total of six along the half-mile stretch of Trace Road. He drove another quarter of a mile into a wooded area before reversing direction. As soon as the houses came into view again, he saw her Lexus.

Kumi turned into the driveway behind her SUV, shifted into Park and turned off the engine. He retrieved his jacket, the flowers and the champagne.

He felt her presence seconds before he saw her, and when he turned to stare at the woman who'd promised to cook for him, he almost dropped the flowers and the wine.

She stood in the open doorway dressed in off-white. His gaze was fused to the outline of her body in a sheer organdy blouse she'd paired with tailored linen slacks. A delicate lacy camisole dotted with tiny pearls showed through the fabric of the airy shirt. Her feet were pushed into a pair of low-heeled mules in a matching pale linenlike fabric covering.

Kumi forced himself to place one foot in front of the other as he approached her, mouth gaping. Her hair—it was thick, chemically straightened, and worn in a blunt-cut pageboy that curved under her delicate jawline. It wasn't the style that held his rapt attention, but the color. It was completely gray! A shimmering silver that blended perfectly with her flawless golden-brown face.

Chapter Two

Veronica knew she'd shocked the arrogant young man when he wouldn't meet her amused gaze. He'd come on to her thinking she was only a few years older than he was. But it was her gray hair that had left this swaggering mahogany Adonis gaping, slack-jawed.

"Good afternoon, Kumi."

The sound of her voice shattered his entrancement. He smiled. "Good afternoon, Ms. Johnson."

Veronica returned his smile, capturing his gaze with her brilliant amber one. His eyes were large, alert, deep-set and a mysterious glossy black.

"You may call me Veronica." She stepped back, permitting him entrance to her home.

He walked into the living room, staring up at the towering cathedral ceiling and winding wrought-iron staircase leading to a loft. Streams of sunlight from floor-to-ceiling windows highlighted the highly waxed bleached pine floors with a parquetry border of alternating pine and rosewood inlay.

Shifting slightly, he turned and stared down at Veronica Johnson staring up at him. The fragrance of Oriental spice clinging to her flesh, hair and clothes swept around him, making him a prisoner of her startling beauty and femininity.

Veronica's eyes crinkled in a smile. "I think you'd better give me the flowers before you shred them."

He looked at the bouquet he'd clutched savagely in his right hand. The petals from some of the roses and lilies had fallen off the stems within the cellophane covering.

"I'm—I'm sorry. But…these are for you." He handed her the flowers and the bottle of champagne, chiding himself for stuttering like a starstruck adolescent. What he did not want to admit was that seeing Veronica Johnson again had left him more shaken than he wanted to be.

"Thank you. The flowers are beautiful." Her gaze shifted from the bouquet to Kumi. "Is something wrong?" Her voice was soft, comforting.

"No…I mean yes." He decided to be honest with her and himself. "You surprised me."

She arched a questioning eyebrow. "How?"

"Your hair. The color shocked me. I didn't expect the gray."

Her expression was impassive. "In other words, you didn't expect me to be *that* old."

His mouth tightened slightly before he said, "I was talking about your hair color, not your age."

"I'm gray because I'm old enough to claim gray hair." She knew she didn't owe him an explanation, but decided to teach him a lesson. The next time he met a woman, he would be less apt to flirt with her. "I began graying prematurely at twenty-eight," she continued, "and by the time I was thirty-eight I was completely gray."

"There's no need for you to address me as if I were a child," he retorted sharply.

"I did not call you a child, Kumi. But if you feel that way, then I can't help it."

Closing his eyes briefly, Kumi struggled to control his temper. It had begun all wrong. He hadn't come to Veronica Johnson's house to debate age differences. He'd come because there was something about her that drew him to her. She was older than he was, but that didn't bother him as much as it appeared to disturb her.

"The flowers need water, the champagne should be chilled and I'd like to eat. The only thing I've eaten all day is a slice of toast and a cup of coffee. Meanwhile, you seem out of sorts because you're a few years older than me."

It was Veronica's turn for her delicate jaw to drop. Kumi was beyond arrogant. "I'm not out of sorts."

Kumi flashed a sensual smile, disarming her immediately. She returned his smile.

"Can we discuss age after we've eaten?" he asked.

"No," she said quickly. "There's no need to discuss it at all, except to say that I'll turn forty-three on September 29." To her surprise he showed no reaction.

"And I'll celebrate my thirty-third birthday next January, which means there's only a ten-year difference in our ages," he countered in a lower, huskier tone.

Which makes you too young to be my mother, he added silently.

Veronica wanted to yell at him, *Only ten years.* Ten years was a decade; a lot of things, people and events changed within a decade. Her life was a perfect example.

She displayed a bright polite smile—one Atlanta residents recognized whenever she and Bramwell Hamlin—African-American plastic surgeon to the rich and famous—had entertained in their opulent home.

"Everything is ready. If you follow me I'll show you where you can wash up before we dine."

Kumi noticed that she'd said "dine" instead of "eat." He liked that. Following her, he admired her hips as she walked across the yawning space of a living and dining room, to a screened-in room off the corner of the expansive kitchen. A delicate pewter chandelier lit up a large table with seating for six. Two place settings were set with fine china, silver, crystal stemware and damask napkins. Water goblets filled with sparkling water were positioned next to wineglasses.

Attractive lines fanned out around his dark eyes. "You set a beautiful table."

She nodded, acknowledging his compliment. "Thank you. The bathroom is over there." She pointed to a door several feet from the dining space.

Kumi walked over, opened the door and stepped into a small half bath. Potted plants lined a ledge under a tall, narrow window, a profusion of green matching the tiny green vines decorating the pale pink wallpaper. The room was delightful and feminine with its dusky rose furnishings and leaf-green accessories. He washed and dried his hands, then left the bathroom.

Returning to the table, he braced his hands on the back of a chair, staring openly at Veronica's back as she bent from the waist and peered into a kitchen cabinet.

"Is there anything I can help you with?"

"No. Everything's done. Please sit down."

He complied, watching as she retrieved a vase and crystal ice bucket from a cabinet under a countertop. She half filled the bucket with ice from the ice maker in the refrigerator door, then inserted the bottle of champagne. Her movements were fluid as she unwrapped the flowers and arranged them in the vase, filling it with water.

Rising quickly to his feet, Kumi closed the space between them, grasping the vase and the bucket. He placed them on the table. Ignoring her warning look, he carried several platters and covered dishes from the countertop to the table. After Veronica had placed a gravy boat on the table, he came around and pulled out a chair for his hostess. She sat, and he lingered over her head, inhaling the scent emanating from her body.

Curbing the urge to press a kiss on her luminous silvery hair, he took his seat.

Staring at her hands, he noted their fragility. And like the rest of her they were beautifully formed. She uncovered several dishes, halting when she glanced up and caught him staring at her.

Veronica knew she intrigued Kumi. There was something in his gaze that communicated that her being older than him was not an issue. She shrugged a shoulder, thinking perhaps he just liked older women. Dropping her gaze, she returned her attention to uncovering the platter of chicken.

"You are incredible," Kumi crooned when he saw the cabbage, fluffy white rice, sweet potatoes and the thick slices of buttery cornbread.

"Voilà, a home-cooked meal." Veronica handed him several serving pieces. "Please help yourself."

Reaching across the table, he picked up her plate. "What do you want?"

A smile trembled over her lips. She was clearly surprised that he'd offered to serve her. "A little bit of everything, thank you."

"White or dark meat?"

"I eat both."

Kumi speared a leg, and then spooned a portion of rice, cabbage and sweet potato onto her plate. He rose slightly and placed it in front of her before serving himself.

Placing a napkin over her lap, Veronica gestured to

the bottle of chilled white wine already on the table. "Would you like wine or the champagne?"

"Is there another alternative?"

She gave him a direct stare. "*Homemade* lemonade."

His dark gaze roamed leisurely over her features, lingering on the tempting curve of her lower lip before returning to fuse with the amber orbs with flecks of darker lights. He marveled at her brilliant eyes, her sexy mouth and her flawless skin.

He forced his gaze not to linger below her throat where the outline of full breasts pushed against the silk under the gossamer material of her blouse. Within seconds his body betrayed him; a rush of desire hardened the flesh pulsing between his thighs. Clenching his fists tightly, he clamped his teeth together. He couldn't speak or move as he waited in erotic agony for the swelling to ease.

"Wine, champagne or lemonade?" Veronica asked again.

Kumi shifted uncomfortably on his chair, praying she wouldn't ask him to get up. The pressure of his engorged flesh throbbing against the fabric of his briefs was akin to a pleasurable pain he did not want to go away.

"Wine," he gasped, eliciting a questionable look from her.

Noting his pained expression, she asked, "Are you all right?"

"Yes," he replied a little too quickly. Reaching for

the bottle of wine and a nearby corkscrew, he uncorked the bottle with a minimum of effort.

Leaning against the cane-back chair, Veronica gave him a critical squint. "How did you do that so quickly?"

"I've had a lot of experience."

"How?"

"Working in restaurants."

And he had. After leaving the Marine Corps, instead of returning to Asheville, he'd traveled to Paris and fell in love with the City of Lights on sight. A monthlong vacation became two months, then three, and after a while he discovered he didn't want to leave. His decision to live in France had changed him and his life forever.

Veronica studied the impassive expression of the man sitting opposite her. His face was a work of art. High cheekbones, a chiseled jaw, a dark brown complexion with rich red undertones and large deep-set black eyes made for an arresting visage.

"Do you still work in restaurants?" Her tone was soft, but layered with sarcasm.

Kumi filled her wineglass and then his own, a slight smile tugging at the corners of his mouth. He'd picked up on her disdain. It was the same question his mother had asked the last time he'd spoken to her.

Jerome, darling, are you still working in restaurants?

And his response had been, *Yes, Mother, I'm still working in restaurants.*

What he hadn't disclosed to anyone was that he

hoped to open his own restaurant within the next eighteen months. He'd worked hard, saved his money and now looked forward to running his own business.

He knew Jeanette Walker wanted him to return to the States, go to college and apply to medical school. This had been his parents' dream after their two older sons had not exhibited the aptitude for a career in medicine. Their focus then shifted to their last-born, hoping and praying that Jerome Kumi Walker would follow the Walker tradition of becoming a doctor like his father, grandfather and great-grandfather had been.

Capturing the questioning amber gaze and holding it with his own, he nodded. "Yes, I still work in restaurants. Right now I'm helping out my sister and brother-in-law."

Veronica picked up a fork. "Do they own a restaurant?"

He shook his head. "No. They're setting up a bed-and-breakfast."

This disclosure intrigued her. "Where?"

"It's about five or six miles outside of Asheville. Two years ago Debbie and Orrin bought a run-down seventeen-room Victorian and began restoring it to its original state."

"Are they doing all the work themselves?"

He nodded. "Yes. Debbie's an interior decorator and my brother-in-law is a general contractor. The project has become a labor of love for them, and they expect to be fully operational by mid-July."

Veronica's gaze narrowed slightly. "And are you going to work in their kitchen?"

It was the second time within a minute he'd picked up the censure in her voice. He stared at her through half-lowered lids, gorging on her blatant feminine beauty. Her white attire made her appear innocent, almost virginal. But he knew Veronica Johnson was not a virgin. She couldn't be. Not with her face and body. She was lush, ripe, like a piece of fruit bursting with thick, sweet juices.

He wanted to taste her, lick her until satiated. He'd lived in Europe for the past decade, traveling to every country, while taking side trips to Asia and Africa. But never had he ever seen or encountered a woman whose femininity cried out to his masculinity the way Veronica Johnson's did. The wild, uninhibited part of him wanted her!

"Yes, *Veronica*. I'm going to work in their kitchen." He'd planned to remain in North Carolina long enough to hire and train the chefs for the elegant bed-and-breakfast.

Her name on his lips became a caress, one that sent a shiver of warning up Veronica's spine. Kumi was flirting with her. He was very subtle, but she sensed that he was coming on to her.

And she had to admit it. She was flattered. Older *and* younger men still found her attractive. Lowering her head slightly, she said a silent grace, and then began eating.

Kumi also blessed his food, then reaching for his

wineglass he held it aloft. "I'd like to make a toast." He waited for Veronica to raise her glass, touching his to hers, a clear chime echoing in the awaiting silence. "It's a quote from Ecclesiastes." She nodded. "Everything that happens in this world happens at the time God chooses. He has set the right time for everything. He has given us a desire to know the future, but never gives us the satisfaction of fully understanding what He does. All of us should eat and drink and enjoy what we have worked for. It's God's gift."

Staring wordlessly across the table, Veronica's expression mirrored her shock. *Who was Kumi Walker?* she asked herself. Who was the young man who rode a Harley and quoted Bible verses?

"Amen," she whispered softly after recovering her voice. She sipped her wine, savoring its dry fruity taste. Her dinner guest was much more complex than she'd originally thought. Veronica smiled. This Sunday dinner was certain to be a very interesting encounter.

Kumi cut a small portion of chicken breast, biting into the moist succulent meat. Chewing slowly, he savored the distinctive taste of buttermilk with a hint of chili, cumin and oregano. He took another bite. The chicken had been dredged in finely ground cornmeal instead of flour.

Closing his eyes, he shook his head. "Unbelievable," he said after opening them.

Veronica shrugged a shoulder, smiling. "It's different."

"No, it's wonderful," he argued laughingly. "You fried it in the oven?"

"Yes."

She watched the play of emotions on his face. There was no doubt he was pleased and surprised with her recipe for spicy oven-fried chicken. It was only one of many recipes she'd inherited from her paternal grandmother.

Kumi took a sip of wine, his eyebrows lifting slightly. Even the wine was excellent. "Would you mind sharing the recipe?" He probably could duplicate the recipe on his own, but only after several exhaustive taste tests.

"Not at all," she replied after swallowing a mouthful of sweet potato.

"I'm certain it would be a favorite if Debbie added it as one of the selections on her menu."

"You said they're opening a bed-and-breakfast. Do they intend to serve dinner also?"

He nodded. "They're calling it a B and B, but I see it more like a country inn. Of course they'll offer the customary breakfasts during the week, brunch on the weekends and dinner every night."

A smile softened her mouth. "It sounds very exciting."

His smile matched hers in liveliness. "It is."

The liquid gold in Veronica's eyes flickered with interest. Suddenly she wanted to know more about the man sharing her table. "You said you've been out of the country for ten years. Where were you living?"

For a long moment, he looked back at her. "France."

She sat up straighter. "Where in France?"

"Paris."

Her lids lowered at the same time a soft gasp escaped her. "What a wonderful city."

He leaned forward. "You've been there?"

It was her turn to nod. "I spent two summers there studying art."

Kumi stared, complete surprise on his handsome face. "You're an artist?" he asked in French.

"No. I always wanted to be an artist, but what I lacked in talent I made up in enthusiasm. I studied drawing for two years, but abandoned it to become an art history teacher," she replied in English.

She'd taught art history at a college level for five years before she left academia to open her gallery in Atlanta. She'd specialized in showing the work of up-and-coming African-American artists. Two weeks ago she'd sold the gallery to a consortium of artists who'd pooled their meager earnings to display their work.

"Do you paint?" he asked, again speaking French.

"The closest I get to painting is sketching. I must have dozens of pads filled with incomplete sketches."

"Which medium?"

"Charcoal, pastels and colored pencils."

Excitement shimmered in his dark gaze. "Do you have anything to show? Because Debbie hasn't decided what type of art she wants to display in some of the rooms."

"Parlez plus lentement, s'il vous plaît," she said,

speaking French for the first time. It had been years since she'd spoken the language and Kumi was speaking it too quickly for her to understand every word.

He chuckled softly. "I'll try to speak more slowly."

"Your French is flawless. You speak it like a native."

Inclining his head, he said, "Thank you. I've come to believe that it is the most beautiful language in the world."

Veronica had to agree with him. "I'd studied the language in high school and college, but it wasn't until I lived in Paris that first summer that I truly came to understand the intricacies of the spoken language. I once overheard two men screaming at each other on a street corner, not realizing they were insulting each other's mothers with references to them being donkeys and camel dung. But to me it was just a passionate heated exchange until my mentor translated the profanity for me."

Kumi laughed, the deep warm sound bubbling up from his broad chest. "It's the only language in which curses sound like words of love."

"You're right," she agreed. "After all, it is called the language of love."

Sobering, he thought of the city he now called home. He lived in the City of Lights, spoke the language of love, yet had never been in love. But, on the other hand, he hadn't lived a monkish existence, either. There were women in his past, but none he liked or loved enough to make a permanent part of his life. Most of the women he'd been involved with claimed he was too aloof and moody. What they hadn't understood was his driving ambition. He'd spent the past six years working and saving his money because he was committed to establishing his own unique dining establishment in a city that boasted hundreds of restaurants, bistros and cafés.

"Who did you study with?" he asked, lapsing fluidly into English.

"Garland Bayless."

"The Garland Bayless who passed away four years ago?"

Attractive lines appeared at the corners of her eyes with her broad smile. "The same."

"The man has become a legend in France."

"I doubt whether he would've become a legend if he'd remained in the States. As a college freshman, I went to his first showing at a gallery in New York, absolutely stunned by his genius. Several noted critics panned his work as amateurish. Their attack was so scathing that Garland packed up and left the country two days after the show closed. He moved to Paris and began selling his work at a fraction of what it was worth at that time.

"I wrote to him once I completed my sophomore year, asking if I could study with him for a summer. Much to my surprise, he wrote back, encouraging me to come to Paris and stay with him at his flat. My father threw a fit."

Kumi swallowed a forkful of cabbage. "Did your father know Bayless was gay?"

"No. And I didn't tell him until after I returned home," she said.

Anyway her father needn't have worried. It wouldn't have mattered what Garland Bayless's sexual preference had been, she thought. At that time Veronica had been so traumatized by a near date-rape episode that she wouldn't permit any man to touch *any* part of her body. She'd been too embarrassed to report the incident and for years she'd lived with the disturbing fear of being raped. It wasn't until later, after she'd married Bramwell, that she knew her reason for marrying a man thirty years her senior was because he was safe. Her husband had been impotent. She wasn't a virgin, but she hadn't had sex with a man in more than twenty years.

"Garland taught me the language, how to choose an inexpensive quality wine and the differences in cheese. I wore my hair in cornrows before they became fashionable in the United States, dressed in funky clothes and shoes, and soaked up everything he taught me."

Kumi didn't know why, but suddenly he envied the time Garland Bayless had spent with Veronica Johnson.

"How many summers did you spend with him?"

"My junior and senior years. I went back to visit him once after I got married."

Here it comes, Kumi groaned inwardly. Now it was time for her to talk about her husband. At first it hadn't bothered him if there was a Mr. Johnson, but after interacting with Veronica, he now resented the man.

He sat across the table from a woman, enjoying an

exquisitely prepared meal by another man's wife, a woman who'd turned him on just because she existed. And despite the ten-year age difference, they shared many things in common: both had lived in Paris, spoke French and were devotees of an expatriate African-American artist who had become an icon in his adopted homeland.

"Garland no longer lived in the loft, but had purchased a pied-à-terre in the heart of the city," Veronica continued. "His work hung in museums, were part of private collections, and he managed to find happiness with a sensitive and devoted lover. He threw a lavish party in my honor, telling everyone that I was the only woman that he'd ever considered making love to."

"What did your husband say when he heard this?" Kumi asked with a staid calmness. He didn't think he would appreciate *any* man—gay or straight—openly admitting that he'd wanted to sleep with *his* wife.

Veronica registered a change in Kumi. His tone was coolly disapproving. "Bram couldn't say anything because he'd hadn't gone with me."

Momentarily speechless in his surprise, Kumi finally said, "You traveled to Europe without your husband?"

She bristled noticeably. He had no right to be critical or disapproving. After all, he knew nothing about her or her relationship with her late husband. "There were several occasions when we did not travel together."

Vertical lines appeared between Kumi's eyes. "Were or are?"

A tense silence enveloped the room and Veronica and Kumi stared at each other. The silence loomed between them like a heavy fog.

He waited, half in anticipation and half in dread. He wanted—no needed—to know if this encounter with Veronica Johnson would be his last. If she was actually married, then he would retreat honorably. It had never been his style to pursue a married woman.

"I am a widow," Veronica said in a voice so soft, he had to strain his ears to hear her. "My husband died two years ago."

Slumping back on his chair, Kumi's eyelids fluttered wildly. She *wasn't* married. That meant he could court her. That is, if she didn't rebuff his advances.

"I'm sorry," he said, quickly regaining his composure.

"Are you really sorry?"

Sitting up straighter, he met her direct stare. A frown furrowed his smooth forehead as his long fingers toyed with the stem of his wineglass.

"Do you really want to know the truth?"

Her expression did not change. "Yes."

His gaze bore into hers. "The truth is that I'm not sorry, because I didn't know your husband. What I am sorry about is that you had to go through the loss."

Veronica stared at a spot over his broad shoulder. She liked Kumi Walker. In fact, she liked him a lot, especially his straightforward manner. Unlike a lot of men she'd met over the years, he was not afraid to speak his mind.

She shifted her gaze to his perfectly symmetrical features. "Thank you for your honesty."

Lowering his gaze, he smiled. "I know no other way to be."

"Then you're truly exceptional."

Long lashes that touched the ridge of his high cheekbones swept up, and his black eyes impaled her, not permitting her to move or breathe. He shook his head slowly.

"I'm not worthy of the compliment."

"I beg to differ with you," she argued softly. "Honesty is something I value and admire in a human being." What she didn't say was *especially in a man.*

He noticed she'd said "human being" and not "a man." Picking up the bottle of wine, he said, "Would you like more wine?"

Running the tip of her tongue over her lower lip, Veronica smiled. "Yes, please."

Kumi wanted to put the bottle down and pull Veronica across the table and kiss her lush mouth. Didn't she know what she was doing to him? What he did instead was fill her glass, then his own. He concentrated on eating the food on his plate, and then took a second helping of everything. She could've easily become a chef. Her cooking skills were exceptional. Everything he'd observed and she'd shown him thus far was exceptional.

"I hope you left room for dessert," she said as Kumi touched the corners of his mouth with his napkin.

Groaning audibly, he shook his head. "Why didn't you mention dessert before I had seconds?"

"I know you haven't been gone so long that you've forgotten that a Southern Sunday dinner is not complete until there's pecan pie, lemon pound cake, strawberry shortcake, the ubiquitous sweet potato pie or jelly-roll cake."

Reaching across the table, Kumi caught her hand, holding it firmly within his larger, stronger grip. "Which one did you make?"

She felt a jolt of energy snake up her arm, and wanted to extract her fingers from his, but the sensations were much too pleasurable. What was it about this younger man that touched her the way no other man had ever been able to do? What was happening to her at forty-two that hadn't been there at twenty-two or thirty-two?

Her last gynecological visit revealed that there hadn't been a drastic drop in her estrogen level, so she wasn't what doctors had referred to as perimenopausal. What the doctor hadn't known was that she hadn't experienced any sexual desire since a college student attempted to rape her after she'd rebuffed his advances. In other words, there never had been a sexual pinnacle for her.

A teasing smile played at the corners of her mouth, bringing Kumi's gaze to linger on the spot. "It's a wonderful complement for champagne."

"It has to be the strawberry shortcake."

"Did you peek in the refrigerator?"

"When did I get the opportunity to peek in your re-frigerator?" She gave him a skeptical look, her eyes narrowing slightly. "Don't tell me you don't like to lose?"

Veronica wrinkled her delicate nose. "I hate losing."

"Then I'll let you win the next time."

Her expression stilled, becoming serious. "What next time?"

Releasing her hand, Kumi crossed his arms over his chest. "I want to return the favor and cook for you."

She shook her head, the silvery strands sweeping around her delicate jaw. "That's not necessary."

"I want to."

"Kumi…"

"When was the last time you ate authentic French cuisine?" he said, interrupting her. "I could prepare chicken with Calvados, chicken paillard or a succulent saffron chicken with capers. If you don't want poultry, then I'll make something with lamb, beef or fish." He would agree to cook anything just to see her again.

"Stop!" There was a hint of laughter in the command.

He affected a hopeful look. "Will you let me cook for you?"

"Yes. But…" Her words trailed off.

"But what?"

"Only if you let me assist you. I'd like to learn to perfect a few dishes."

She'd totally ignored her own vow to share only one meal with the man. That was before she'd found him so charming. Besides, he was someone with whom she could practice her French.

"Agreed." His smile was dazzling. "Next Sunday?" She nodded. "What time should I come over? Unless you wouldn't mind coming to my place."

A wave of apprehension swept through her. She'd once gone to a man's home alone and had been sexually assaulted. "You can cook here."

"At what time?"

"Anytime. I'm always up early."

Pushing back her chair, she stood and reached for Kumi's plate and silverware, but was thwarted when his fingers curved around her wrist. "I'll clear the table."

"That's not necessary," she said.

"You cooked, so I'll clean up." He gave her a warning look. "Sit and relax."

Veronica pretended not to understand his look. "But you're a guest in my home."

He refused to relent. "That may be true, but I was raised to show my appreciation for anyone who has gone out of their way to offer kindness. And that translates into my clearing the table."

A wave of heat flooded her cheeks. "And I repaid your kindness for changing my tire with dinner."

Kumi recognized willfulness in Veronica's personality—a trait that was so apparent in his own. "You offered to repay me by offering me money. Therefore, dinner wasn't your first choice."

Her eyes darkening, she struggled to control her

temper. "Then you should've taken the money, *Mr. Walker*."

He let go of her wrist, gathering the silverware and placing it on his plate. Kumi felt the heat from Veronica's angry gaze as he stacked the plates and carried them to the sink. She was still glaring at him, hands folded on her hips, as he returned to the table to retrieve the serving dishes. What would've taken her three or four trips, he'd accomplished in only two.

Standing in front of the refrigerator, he smiled sweetly. "May I open it and get dessert?"

Taking a half-dozen steps, she moved over to stand near Kumi. She tilted her chin, staring up at him staring down at her. His body's heat intensified the scent of his aftershave. It was as potent and intoxicating as the man who wore it. Her heart fluttered wildly in her breast as her dormant senses leapt to life.

What was it about this boy-man that quickened her pulse and made her heart pound an erratic rhythm?

Clearing her throat, she pretended not to be affected by his presence. "You may open the champagne."

Kumi went completely still as he held his breath. She stood close enough for him to feel the feminine heat and smell of her body. A warming shiver of desire skipped along his nerve endings as he counted the beats of the pulse in her throat. Time stood still as they shared an intense physical awareness of each other.

"Do you have a towel?" His request broke the spell.

Veronica moved to her right, making certain no part of her body touched his, and opened a drawer under the countertop. She withdrew a black-and-white striped terry-cloth towel, and handed it to him.

He mumbled a thank-you, walking back to the table while she opened the refrigerator to remove a dish with a whipped-cream-covered cake topped with fresh strawberries. By the time she reached the table, he'd opened the bottle of champagne without spilling a drop. The only sound in the silence had been the soft popping sound of the cork as it was removed from the bottle.

Chapter Three

Veronica squared her shoulders and turned to face Kumi.

"Would you mind sitting on the patio now that the sun is on the other side of the house?"

Turning his head slightly, he smiled at her, and he wasn't disappointed when she returned his smile. The tense encounter was behind them.

"I'd like that very much."

"Please come with me."

He followed her out of the kitchen, through a narrow hallway and into a screened-in, glass-enclosed room spanning the length of the rear of the house. He was completely stunned by the panorama unfolding before his gaze. Hanging, flowering and potted plants, a large portable waterfall, rattan furniture covered with colorful kente-cloth cushions and a rug made of woven straw fibers were reminiscent of a rain forest. The soothing sound of the gurgling water blended with the relaxing strains of music flowing from a stereo system discreetly hidden under a table.

Nodding his approval, Kumi said, "I feel as if I'm in a jungle."

"That's the effect I wanted to create."

He turned slowly, his gaze sweeping over the meticulously chosen furnishings. "How long does it take for you to water all the plants?"

She placed the cake on a small round glass-topped rattan table with two pull-up matching chairs. "I don't know yet. They were delivered yesterday."

"You just moved here?"

Meeting his questioning gaze, she shook her head. "No. We purchased this house three years ago, ordered the furniture, but I hadn't added the touches that would make it feel like home. I've been away for two years."

He clutched the towel-covered champagne bottle tighter to his chest. "Do you plan to live here permanently?"

"I'm not certain," she replied honestly. "What I plan to do is stay the summer and relax."

What she did not tell him was that she needed to put some distance between herself, the Atlanta gossipmongers and her late husband's adult children. They'd challenged their father's will, accusing her of manipulation. Dr. Hamlin hadn't disinherited his two sons and daughter, but had divided his estate with: one-fourth to be divided between his three children, one-fourth to Veronica and the final half to establish a scholarship foundation bearing his name for exceptional African-American undergraduate students who planned for careers in medicine.

There had been no mention of Martha Hamlin, the first Mrs. Hamlin. After the divorce, Bramwell had given Martha a generous settlement, which should've permitted her to continue the comfortable lifestyle she'd established as the wife of the most prominent black plastic surgeon in the country. Bramwell had established his reputation and vast wealth whenever a superstar athlete or entertainer of color sought out his specialized cosmetic or corrective surgical procedures.

However, within six months of her separation and eventual divorce, Martha found solace in her prized vodka cocktails, losing herself in a drunken haze that usually lasted for days. And whenever she was under the influence, she wrote countless checks in staggering amounts to her overindulged children.

Less than a year after Veronica married Bramwell, Martha came to her gallery, sobbing uncontrollably that she was going to lose her million-dollar home because she hadn't paid property taxes for two years. Veronica wrote the woman a check from her own personal account. Both had sworn an oath that no one would ever know of their private business transaction.

Martha had kept her word, but of course her children hadn't known that their father's second wife had kept their mother from becoming homeless. None of that mattered when they verbally attacked her after the reading of Bram's will.

Yes—she had made the right decision to close her home and leave Atlanta for North Carolina. She'd had enough of the Hamlins, their lies, harassment and assaults on her character.

Kumi stared at the thickly forested area in the distance. "This is the perfect setting for relaxation."

"That it is," she concurred. "We can sit over there." She motioned to the table with the cake. "Make yourself comfortable while I get the flutes, plates and forks."

He removed his jacket and placed it over the back of one chair. He was still standing in the same spot when she returned. A vaguely sensuous current passed between them as she moved closer. He took the flutes from her loose grip, then the dessert plates and forks. She gasped when his right arm curved around her waist, pulling her against his middle.

With a minimum of effort, he led her to the center of the room. Her startled gaze reminded him of a deer frozen by an automobile's headlights. "Dance with me," he whispered close to her ear. "This song is a favorite of mine."

Veronica forced herself to relax as she sank into his comforting protective embrace. The runaway beating of her heart slowed. She recognized the instrumental version of "I Can't Make You Love Me."

She felt a flicker of something so frightening that she wanted to pull away. It had been twenty years since a man had held her to his body. Twenty years ago it had been an act of violence, unlike the gentle touch of the hands caressing her back through the delicate fabric of her blouse. She was frightened and curious at the same time when she felt Kumi's hardness pressing against her thighs. She realized the strange feeling was desire. It had taken her two decades to feel desire again. And she wanted to cry because it was with a man ten years her junior.

Why now? Why not with some of the other men she'd met before or after her marriage?

Pressing her face against his solid shoulder, Veronica breathed in the masculine scent. The motion caused Kumi's arm to tighten around her waist, pulling her even closer. Dropping his hand, she wound her arms around his neck, certain he felt her trembling.

This time it wasn't from fear, but from a need—a desperate need to experience the passion she hadn't felt in a very long time. The musical piece ended, and they still swayed to their own private song. She finally found the strength to lower her arms and push firmly against his chest.

Lowering his head, Kumi breathed a kiss under her ear. "Thank you for the dance."

She smiled shyly. "You're welcome." She should've been the one thanking him. Raising her chin, she looked up at him as he stared down at her under lowered lids. She wanted to see his eyes. "Kumi?" His name was a breathless whisper.

"Oui?"

"The champagne is getting warm and the cream on the cake is melting."

He blinked as if coming out of a trance. Cradling her hand in his, he led her over to the table, pulled out a chair and seated her. He sat down, silently cursing himself for not kissing her. He'd been provided with the perfect opportunity to taste the confection of her generously curved mouth.

The next time, he mused. And there would be a next time. That she'd promised.

Veronica lay in bed Monday morning, staring up at the sheer mosquito netting flowing sensuously around the massive four-poster, loathing getting up. The feeling of being wrapped in a silken cocoon of bottomless peace persisted. She closed her eyes and smiled. The person who'd helped her achieve that feeling was Kumi Walker.

They'd lingered over dessert, drinking champagne and talking for hours about Paris, she experiencing an overwhelming nostalgia for Le Marais, Champs-Élysées, St. Germain-des-Prés, and the Chaillot, Latin, Luxembourg and Jardin des Plantes Quarters. And it was the first time in a very long time that she truly missed Paris—a city wherein each section claimed its own charm and artistic enclave.

She'd recalled restaurants, cafés, art galleries and museums she'd visited while Kumi offered her an update on each. What had surprised her was that he exhibited an exhaustive knowledge of art and architecture. Later he admitted he'd spent hundreds of hours in many of the museums his first year in Paris.

The sun had set and the late-spring night sky was painted with thousands of stars when Kumi finally prepared to leave, and at that moment Veronica hadn't wanted him to go. She'd wanted him to stay and talk— about anything. After he left she realized she was lonely—lonely for male companionship. Lonely because she missed her husband and their nightly chats. There had never been a time when she and Bram weren't able to bare their souls to each other. She'd been able to discuss anything with him—all except for the sexual assault that made it impossible for her to share her body with a man.

She'd met the elegant older man when he'd come into the tiny gallery she'd opened only six months before, looking for a gift for a colleague's birthday. She'd suggested a watercolor of a seascape. Dr. Bramwell Hamlin was more than satisfied with his purchase and quite taken with the woman who'd recommended the painting.

He returned to the gallery the following month, this time to ask her assistance in helping him select artwork for his new home. She'd selected several landscapes and a magnificent still life, and a year later shock waves swept through Atlanta, Georgia's black privileged class when Dr. Hamlin married Veronica Johnson, a woman thirty years his junior.

Veronica opened her eyes, rolling over on her side and peering at the face of the clock on a bedside table.

It was ten-thirty. She hadn't slept that late in years. Throwing off the sheet, she sat up, parted the netting and swung her legs over the side of the bed. Her feet hadn't touched the floor when the telephone rang. She picked up the receiver before the second ring.

"Hello."

"Why did I have to hear it from our mother that you now live in the sticks?"

Veronica cradled the cordless instrument under her chin, smiling. "You wouldn't have to hear it secondhand if you stopped stalking your husband."

Candace Johnson-Yarborough's husky laugh came through the earpiece. "Bite your tongue, big sis. You know I wouldn't permit Ivan to go away on a three-day business trip without making him check in every hour, so what makes you think I'd be apart from him for three months?"

It was Veronica's turn to laugh. Candace had married, what she and thousands of other Georgia black women had referred to, as the "world's sexiest brother." And she had to agree with her sister—Ivan Yarborough was not only good-looking but also a brilliant businessman. Ivan headed a consulting firm whose focus was setting up consortiums of small businesses in predominately African-American communities. He was always a much-sought-after speaker at corporate seminars, colleges and high schools. Candace, a former schoolteacher, had resigned her position to homeschool their two sons while they all traveled together as a family.

"Bite your tongue, little sis. I'll have you know that I don't live in the sticks."

"Yeah, right. Your closest neighbor is at least a mile away."

Veronica wasn't going to argue with Candace, who had always said she preferred living in the middle of a thriving metropolis. Her younger sister craved bright lights, honking automobile horns and blaring music. Besides, she wanted to tell Candace that Trace Road was only half a mile long.

"When are you coming to visit me and see for yourself that it's quite civilized here? There's even a shopping mall less than three miles away."

"I can't now. I have to prepare the kids for final exams. I'm calling for two reasons. One to say hello and let you know we're back, and the other is to let you know the family reunion has been confirmed for the second weekend in August. Aunt Bette is hosting it this time."

She wanted to tell her sister that she was going to conveniently come down with a strange illness for that particular weekend. Their mother's sister was the most annoying and exasperating woman in the entire state of Georgia.

Instead, Veronica agreed to mark the calendar and then asked about her preteen nephews, telling Candace to give them her love.

Kumi showed the middle-aged cook to the door.

"Thank you so much for applying, Mr. Sherman.

You'll be informed of our decision before the end of the month."

Waiting until the man walked out of the office his sister and brother-in-law had set up as their office, Kumi shook his head. He'd spent the past two days interviewing applicants, all who were more suited to cooking for a roadside café, than a full-service kitchen offering gourmet meals.

Deborah Walker-Maxwell entered the office seconds later, a pained expression distorting her attractive features. She sat down on a love seat and closed her eyes. "How many does that make?" she asked.

Kumi stared at his sister. The strain of trying to get the B and B ready for opening was beginning to wear on her. The puffiness under her large dark eyes was the most obvious sign. Deborah, the only daughter of Lawrence and Jeanette Walker, was also the most ambitious.

A very successful interior decorator, Deborah had resigned her position at one of the country's leading design firms to go into business for herself. At thirty-eight, she'd taken her life savings, purchased the abandoned dilapidated property and with her contractor-husband, Orrin Maxwell, had begun renovating the former showplace to its original elegance.

Orrin had replaced the floors, walls, hung wallpaper and installed light fixtures, while his wife visited estate sales, antique shops and the many North Carolina furniture makers for furnishings. Each room now had its own name and personality.

"He was the eighth one." Kumi's tone mirrored his disappointment. He shook his head. "You advertised for chefs, yet you're getting cooks. There's a big difference in a short-order cook and a graduate from a culinary school." So far he'd filled one position—pastry chef.

Tears filled Deborah's eyes. "What am I going to do? We're opening in eight weeks."

Rising to his feet, Kumi moved to sit beside her. Dropping an arm over her shoulder, he cradled her head to his chest. "I'm going to contact several culinary schools and ask for their recommendations. A recent graduate would be provided the perfect opportunity to showcase their talent and training. If you're not fully staffed by the time you open, then I'll act as executive chef."

Deborah smiled up at her brother through her tears. Large dark eyes so much like Kumi's crinkled in a smile. "How can I thank you? I know you're losing millions of francs—"

"Euros," he corrected, interrupting her.

"Okay." She laughed. "Euros. You're still losing tons of money not working because you're here helping me out. I'm going to make it up to you, Kumi. I swear I will."

He placed a forefinger over her lips. "No swearing, Debbie." Lowering his head, he removed his finger and brushed a light kiss on her cheek. "If I was worried about losing money I never would've agreed to help you and Orrin."

He'd taken a four-month leave from his position as

executive chef at a five-star Parisian hotel to help his sister. He loved Debbie enough to put his own plans on hold for her. She'd always been there for him when they were children. She was the only one who'd protected him from Dr. Lawrence Walker, who punished her for her insubordination, but it hadn't seemed to matter to her. She simply spent the time in her room either building dollhouses or reading.

Kumi stared down at Debbie. She'd been a pretty girl, but she was a beautiful woman. She looked just like their mother: petite and delicate with cinnamon-colored skin, large dark eyes and a quick smile. In marrying Orrin Maxwell, she'd rebelled against her parents' wishes. Orrin hadn't been the college graduate their parents hoped she would marry. When Debbie decided to devote herself to her career rather than start a family, she once again shocked her parents.

"When are you going to settle down?" Deborah asked Kumi.

"I have settled down. I have a career and I own a home."

"Not that settling down. When are you going to get married?"

He glanced over her head, his gaze fixed on a massive armoire concealing a television and stereo components. "I don't know, Debbie. Perhaps I'm not cut out for marriage."

"Are you seeing someone?"

He shook his head. "No."

"Don't you ever get lonely? Don't you miss home?"

"I work too many hours to get lonely." Four days of the week he worked at the hotel. On his days off he often catered private parties. "And don't forget that France is my home now."

Her fingertips grazed his smooth-shaven jaw. "Have you ever considered moving back to the States?"

He exhaled audibly. "The first two years I spent in Paris I thought about it a lot. I used to wander the streets all night, while spending my days in museums staring at the same painting for hours. When the money I'd earned in the marines began to run out, I got a job in a restaurant. I waited tables and eventually found myself helping out in the kitchen. I discovered I had a knack for cooking, so I enrolled in a culinary school. The rest is history."

A slight frown furrowed Deborah's smooth forehead. "Why didn't you tell me this in your letters? You always wrote that life in Paris was perfect, and that you were wonderful."

"It was and still is wonderful, Debbie." What he wouldn't say was that anything was wonderful as long as he didn't have to interact with his father. At that time exile was preferable to exclusion.

Removing his arm, he pushed to his feet and extended his hand. She placed her hand in his and he pulled Deborah up in one strong motion. "I'm going out. I'll see you later."

She stared at his broad back under an expertly tailored jacket. "Are you coming back for dinner?"

Smiling at her over his shoulder, he said, "I don't know."

And he didn't know. Right now he felt as jumpy and finicky as a cat. It was a restlessness he hadn't felt in a long time, and he knew it had something to do with Veronica Johnson. They weren't scheduled to see each other again until Sunday, but he did not want to wait another three days.

He was scheduled to interview two more candidates the following day, and he shuddered at the thought. His only confirmed hire was a pastry chef, and he still needed someone to oversee the sautéed items, and one who would be responsible for pasta and accompanying sauces. The B and B was designed to have a full-service kitchen for dinner, which meant it would need at least four assistant chefs.

He walked back to his cottage, his arms swinging loosely at his sides. He was bored out of his skull. If he hadn't been in the States, either he would be working at the hotel's restaurant, catering a private party or relaxing in the courtyard of his modest home in the Luxembourg Quarter. In his spare time he usually prowled the corridors of a museum. And it was on an even rarer occasion that he entertained women in his home.

He covered the distance between the B and B and his cottage in less than fifteen minutes. Unlocking the door, he walked into the parlor, past a tiny kitchen and into his bedroom and changed out of the shirt, tie, jacket and slacks and into a pair of jeans, T-shirt and boots. Returning to the parlor, he picked up the keys to his bike from a table near the front door. Closing the door behind him, he headed for the Harley parked under a carport. Within minutes he was astride the large motorcycle, the wind whipping the shirt on his back as trees, cars and telephone poles became a blur.

His body pulsed with pleasure—a delightful excitement similar to what he'd felt when he'd cradled Veronica Johnson to his chest. He wanted to see her once more before their scheduled Sunday encounter.

Downshifting, he maneuvered up the steep hill to Trace Road. Once at the top he slowed until he came to Veronica's house. The Lexus was parked in the driveway.

She was home!

Chapter Four

He came to a complete stop behind her truck, shutting off the engine. The front door stood open, and as he neared the screen door he saw the outline of Veronica's body as she came closer.

His steady gaze bore into her in silent expectation. *Come to me, Veronica. Open the door,* his inner voiced implored. What he didn't want was for her to send him away.

Kumi had registered the expression of surprise freezing Veronica's features before it was replaced by indecision. Had he made a mistake in stopping by without calling her? Had he felt so comfortable with her that he'd assumed that she would open her door and her arms, welcoming him into her home and her life?

Veronica saw him, and a shiver of awareness raced through her body. She'd been thinking about Kumi, and suddenly there he was at her door as if she'd conjured him up.

She felt the heat of his gaze on her face as he watched her intently through the finely woven mesh. She felt the tingling in the pit of stomach because as she watched Kumi staring at her she saw something so maddeningly arrogant in the man standing at her front door that it rendered her motionless and speechless for several long seconds.

Struggling to maintain her composure, her eyelids fluttered. She'd wanted to see him again, but on her terms. She'd spent most of the morning working in her garden and had just come in to shower and change her clothes when she heard the roar of his Harley.

Here she was standing less than a foot away from him, only a screen door separating them, dressed in a pair of shorts, a revealing tank top and a pair of tattered running shoes.

"Good afternoon, Kumi." Her voice was low, husky, sounding strange even to her ears.

He inclined his head, a half smile tilting the corners of his mobile mouth. "Afternoon, Veronica. I just came by to see if you wanted to go for a ride in the country."

Her gaze narrowed. "On your bike?"

Placing his left hand over his heart, he bowed from the waist, the motion incredibly graceful for a man his height and size. "Yes. I apologize for showing up unannounced, but it would be a shame to waste this beautiful day indoors. Besides, I didn't have your telephone number, so I couldn't call you."

She wanted to tell him that she'd just spent more than two hours working outdoors in her flower garden, but did not want to hurt his feelings. Despite his arrogance, there was something in Kumi Walker's gaze that hinted of vulnerability. It was as if he was waiting for her to reject him. And she wondered if someone he cared for had rejected him, wounding him deeply.

"I'd like to go, but I'm afraid of motorcycles," she admitted honestly.

He lifted a thick black eyebrow. "Have you ever ridden before?"

"No."

"Then how do you know you're afraid?"

"It's too open. I need something around me to make me feel safe, protected."

He stood a step closer—close enough for her to feel his moist breath whisper over her forehead through the barrier of mesh separating them. "I'll protect you, Veronica. I promise I won't let anything happen to you." Her golden gaze widened, and for a long moment she stared at him, giving him the advantage he sought. "Go change your clothes," he ordered softly. "I'll be here waiting for you." The sight of her wearing the revealing attire tested his self-control. Seeing so much of her flesh made him feel as randy as an adolescent boy.

She blinked once. "I don't have a helmet."

"You can use mine."

"What will you use?"

"Nothing."

Veronica shook her head, a silver ponytail swaying gently with the motion. "No. I'm not going if you're not going to wear a helmet. I don't want to be responsible for you cracking your skull if we have an accident."

"I've never had an accident."

"There's always the first time, Mr. Walker."

He glared at her. "Are you using my not wearing a helmet as an excuse not to go?"

"If I didn't want to go, then I'd just come out and say so. Go get another helmet, Kumi Walker, or get lost."

His eyes darkened dangerously as he returned her hostile glare. He knew it was useless to argue with her. If she were afraid for herself, then it probably would go without saying that she'd be afraid for him to ride without protective headgear.

"Okay. But I'll be back."

Veronica watched him as he returned to the motorcycle, swinging his right leg over the bike in one, smooth motion. Straddling the bike, he placed the shiny black helmet over his head. Raising his chin in a gesture of challenge and defiance, he started up the engine. It took only seconds for him to go from zero to forty as he took off down Trace Road, the roar of the powerful engine fading quickly as man and bike disappeared from view.

Veronica had showered, changed into a pair of jeans, white camp shirt and a pair of low-heeled leather boots by the time Kumi returned with a smaller helmet painted in vivid shades of reds and pinks. He placed the helmet on her head, adjusted the strap and helped her straddle the seat behind him. She curved her arms loosely around his waist.

"Hold me tighter," he said over his shoulder.

She tightened her grip, her breasts pressing against the wide expanse of his back. She wasn't given the opportunity to inhale once he shifted into gear and maneuvered out of the driveway.

Closing her eyes, Veronica pressed her cheek to Kumi's shoulder, certain he could feel the pounding of her heart through the shirt on his back. Her fright and fear eased as he turned off onto a two-lane highway. Five minutes into the ride she felt what he experienced each time he rode his bike—absolute and total freedom.

She was flying, soaring unfettered as the world whizzed by. Suddenly there was only Veronica, Kumi and the steady humming of the powerful machine under their bodies. A rising heat penetrated the layer of cotton covering his upper body; her sensitive nostrils inhaled the natural scent of his skin and that of the sensual cologne that complemented his blatant masculinity. She savored the feel of lean hard muscle under her cheek. There wasn't an ounce of excess flesh on his hard body.

A contented smile curved Kumi's mouth as he peered through the protective shield of his helmet. The soft crush of Veronica's breasts against his back had aroused him. Shifting into higher gear, he increased his speed. Riding with Veronica was like making love. It had begun slowly, tentatively at first, but as the speed accelerated so did his passion.

Veronica Johnson had become the Harley; he'd straddled her, riding faster, harder and deeper. They seemed to leap off the asphalt, the machine eating up the road in voracious gulps. The vibration of the engine had become her body, pulsing faster and faster until he found himself sucked into a vortex of ecstasy from which he never wanted to escape.

Is that how it would be? Would making love to her be slow, methodical, parochial, then wild, frenzied and completely uninhibited?

They'd gone about fifteen miles when he slowed and left the highway, heading up a steep hill to a wooded clearing. It was where he'd learned to ride a motorcycle for the first time; he'd begun racing dirt bikes at twelve, then graduated to motorized bikes before he finally learned to handle the larger, more powerful Harley-Davidson.

He reached the top of the hill and came to a complete stop. Removing his helmet, he stared down at the countryside dotted with trees, houses and narrow, winding streams, breathing deeply. Reaching behind him, he caressed Veronica's arm as she slid off.

Supporting the bike on its stand, he unbuckled her helmet and pulled it gently from her head. Her gleaming hair was pressed against her moist scalp. Anchoring the helmets on the handlebars, he cradled her face between his hands, his fingers curving around the column of her slender neck. He saw a shimmer of excitement in her sun-lit eyes.

Smiling, he asked, "How did you like it?"

"Fantastic." She shrugged a shoulder. "That is once I got over the fright of going so fast."

He tightened his grip along her delicate jawline.

"Didn't I tell you that I wouldn't let anything happen to you?"

Her fingers closed around his thick wrists as she sought to pull his hands away from her face. A rising panic wouldn't permit her to breathe. The image of the student seizing her throat, while pressing her against a wall as he fumbled with the zipper to his slacks, came rushing back with vivid clarity, and she panicked.

"No, Kumi. Don't—don't touch me."

He stared at her, baffled as vertical lines appeared between his eyes. "What?"

Closing her eyes against his intense stare, she shook her head. "Please, don't hurt me," she pleaded in a shivery whisper.

Kumi felt as if someone had just doused him with cold water as his hands fell, at the same time his fingers curling into tight fists.

Why would Veronica plead with him not to hurt her? He'd only touched her once before, and that was to dance with her.

He moved closer, this time making certain not to touch her. Leaning down, he whispered close to her ear, "I would never hurt you, Ronnie."

Her breasts trembled above her rib cage, her chest rising and falling heavily under her blouse. She'd made a fool of herself; her greatest fear had surfaced the instant Kumi touched her throat—a chilling, paralyzing fear she'd lived with for more than twenty years, a fear she'd successfully repressed until now.

She wrapped her arms around her body in a protective gesture. Closing her eyes, she shook her head. "It's not you, Kumi."

"Who is it, Veronica?"

She opened her eyes, seeing concern and tenderness in his midnight gaze. Everything that was Kumi Walker communicated itself to her: strong, protective and trusting. But could she trust him? Would she be able to tell him what she hadn't been able to disclose to anyone in two decades? That it had been her fault that she was almost raped?

Tell him, the inner voice whispered, but she ignored it.

"I can't tell you."

He came closer without moving. "Do you think you'll ever be able to tell me?"

Shaking her head, she whispered even though there was no one else around to hear them, "I don't know."

A sad smile touched Kumi's strong mouth. "It's okay, Ronnie."

What he wanted to tell her was that it wasn't okay, not when he wanted to touch her, make love to her. The realization that he wanted to make love to Veronica Johnson had shaken him to the core earlier that morning. It had been years since he'd awakened, hard and throbbing from an erotic dream. The dream had been so vivid that he'd sat up gasping, his body moist and her name on his lips.

And he had yet to discover what had drawn him to Veronica other than her startling natural beauty. She was older than he was, yet he didn't view her as a mother figure. In fact, she was nothing like the other women he'd been attracted to in the past. There was a strength about her that did not lessen her femininity.

He'd found her composed, confident—until now.

"Are you ready to go back?"

Veronica forced a smile she did not feel. She wasn't ready to get back on the bike—not until she was back in control. "Not yet. I'd like to stay and enjoy the scenery."

Kumi nodded, extending his right hand. He watched Veronica staring at his outstretched fingers for a long moment, then trustingly placed her smaller hand in his. He closed his fingers around hers, tightening slightly before he floated down to the grass, gently pulling her down to sit beside him. They sat, shoulders only inches apart, staring out at the picturesque panorama of the Great Smoky Mountains rising in the background. A massive oak tree provided a canopy of natural protection from the fiery rays of the sun.

Pulling his knees to his chest, Kumi wrapped his arms around his denim-covered legs as he replayed the eerie scene they'd just experienced over and over in his head. He could still hear the fear in her voice when she'd pleaded with him not to hurt her. Had he held her that tightly? Had he not known his own strength?

He stood six-two, weighed two hundred and ten pounds and had been trained to bring a man to his knees with a single blow. But each time he'd touched Veronica it had only been in gentleness and protection.

His expression hardened as he considered another

possibility. Had she ever been hit by a man, been a victim of domestic violence? And had that man been a boyfriend, or even her late husband?

Why, he wondered, had she waited two years after her husband's death to take up residence in North Carolina? Whom or what in Georgia prompted her to spend the summer in another state? What or whom was she running from?

He'd asked her to tell him of her fear and she had refused. That meant he had to wait—wait for her to feel comfortable or trusted him enough to perhaps open up to him. He wanted and needed her to trust him, because he knew he couldn't continue to see her and not touch her. Not when all of his sleeping and waking moments were filled with the images of her shimmering silver hair, delicately defined feminine face and her temptingly lush body.

He would give himself three months. It was now late May, and he had secured reservations to return to Paris mid-September. If his relationship with Veronica Johnson remained the same, he would return to Paris—with memories of her and what might have been.

Veronica turned her head slightly, staring at Kumi's profile. His expression was impassive; he was so still he could've been carved out of stone.

A refreshing mountain breeze filtered through the leaves of the tree, cooling her moist face. Her gaze swung back to the valley. The view was magnificent. She wished she'd had a sketch pad. Even though some of her art instructors had labeled her drawings as immature and amateurish, that hadn't stopped her from attempting to capture images on a blank sheet of paper. Pulling her knees to her chest, she executed a pose similar to Kumi's, willing her mind blank.

They sat side by side in silence for more than twenty minutes until Veronica raised her hand, trailing her fingertips over his forearm. Kumi jumped as if she'd burned him and placed his hand over hers, tightening his grip when she attempted to pull away from him.

"I'm ready to go back now."

She was ready and he wasn't. He'd enjoyed sitting with her, her closeness, while marveling in the panorama of the landscape. At no time had he felt the need to initiate conversation. Veronica offered him what he'd sought most of his life—a quiet, healing, calming peace that made him want to stay with her forever.

Releasing her hand, he stared at her, his eyes dark and unfathomable. "Are you certain you're ready?" *Are you ready for me?* his inner voice asked.

Veronica's gaze lingered on the curve of his beautifully shaped mouth. "Yes."

Kumi went completely still. There was something about his expression that made it impossible for her to look away. Something undeniably magnetic was building between them and binding them together. She felt drugged by his clean and manly scent as he lowered his head.

He came closer and closer; she was unable to move because she did not want to. Shivering despite the heat, she inhaled his moist breath the instant his lips brushed against hers, the touch as soft as a butterfly's gossamer wings.

He kissed her without touching any other part of her body. The warmth of his mouth, the slight pressure of his lips pressing against hers ignited spirals of ecstasy throughout her body. The fingers of her left hand grasped long blades of thick grass, pulling them from their roots. Kumi's kiss sang through her veins, heating her blood.

As quickly as it had begun it was over. Kumi pulled back, leaving her mouth burning with a lingering, smoldering fire. Her eyes were dark, pupils dilated with a rising passion as she stared at the man sitting inches from her.

Kumi smiled once he noted her soft, moist, parted lips. She hadn't kissed him back, but more importantly she hadn't pulled away or panicked, either. He'd risked everything, kissing her when less than half an hour before she'd pleaded with him not to touch her.

"You asked me not to touch you, and I didn't. But you never said I couldn't kiss you."

Veronica studied the lean dark-skinned face, entranced by what she saw. What was it about Kumi Walker that made her feel like a breathless girl of sixteen? She thought him charming *and* arrogant—an arrogance that was compelling and exciting.

"You're right, Kumi." Her voice was soft, seductive. "I never said you couldn't kiss me."

He stared at her and then burst out laughing. Curving an arm around her waist, he stood, pulling her up with him. He did not drop his arm as he led her back to the bike. Three minutes later the wind tore at their clothes, caressed their moist flesh and sang a nameless song in their ears as man, woman and machine became one.

Chapter Five

Images of Kumi and the kiss they'd shared lingered with Veronica over the next two days. She'd given him her telephone number while he had insisted she keep the brightly colored helmet for their next outing. She hung the helmet on a hook in the mudroom at the rear of the house, and each time she saw it she was reminded of his broad back, trim waist and the wildly intoxicating fragrance of sandalwood mingling with his body's natural scent.

She'd established a habit of rising early and slipping outside for a morning walk. By the time she'd walked the length of Trace Road, the sun had risen above the peaks of the mountains, the rays penetrating the haze hovering over the deep gorges and valleys. After showering and a light breakfast of fruit, raisin toast and a cup of decaffeinated coffee, she slipped behind the wheel of her SUV, touring the mountain region and stopping in Cherokee and other small towns in the High Country.

She spent hours in the Museum of the Cherokee Indian, studying artifacts in the art gallery and the outdoor living exhibit depicting Cherokee life in several eras, returning home with a handmade basket, mask and a wood carving from the Qualla Arts and Crafts Mutual, the cooperative set up across the street from the museum.

The last day she lingered at the Oconaluftee Indian Village, observing demonstrations of traditional skills such as weaving, pottery making, canoe construction and hunting techniques.

The tiny town of Dillsboro was added to her itinerary once she boarded a steam locomotive for a ride on the Great Smoky Mountains Railway, berating herself for not bringing a camera once she realized the open-side cars were ideal for taking pictures of the mountain scenery. She returned home late Saturday afternoon, and unlocked the door to the sound of the ringing telephone. By the time she picked up the receiver, the caller had hung up before the answering machine switched on. Too exhausted to think about who may have been calling, she headed for the staircase leading to her bedroom, showered and lay across her bed completely nude, falling asleep as soon as her head touched the pillow.

Veronica woke up Sunday morning, completely rejuvenated. She'd left the French doors open and crisp mountain air filled the room with the scent of pine and rain. Stretching her bare arms above her head, she stared up at the mosquito netting covering the bed. Bram had hated sleeping with the netting, claiming it had reminded him of a burial shroud.

However, she loved the drapery. It provided the protective cloaking she sought whenever she lay in bed. It made her feel as if she'd retreated to a shadowy fairy-tale world, a make-believe world in which she could sleep and shut out her fear.

Parting the sheer fabric, she swung her legs over the side of the antique bed and headed for the adjoining bathroom. Despite the rain, she would take her walk, then return home to shower and shampoo her hair.

If she'd been in Atlanta she would've worked out at a downtown sports club where she'd been a member for years. However, she found the Trace Road walk a lot more peaceful and invigorating. The solitude provided her with time to think and reflect on what she wanted to do with her life. She hadn't decided whether she would teach again, only because earning a salary wasn't a factor because Bram had left her with enough money to last her well into old age, providing she did not squander it.

She owned the house her late husband had bequeathed her in Buckhead, Atlanta's wealthiest neighborhood, and the three-bedroom, two-and-a-half bath mountain retreat in North Carolina. She'd invested the proceeds from the sale of the gallery in a risk-free mutual fund based upon the recommendation of her family's longtime investment banker.

Even without the money Bram had left her, Veronica Johnson was a wealthy woman. She was old Atlanta, fourth-generation and had grown up in the right neighborhood, earned the right degrees, she had held a prestigious position as an assistant college professor and had married into the right family.

Two priceless Garland Bayless paintings, one she'd purchased and the other a gift from the talented artist, along with a velvet pouch filled with precious baubles she'd inherited from her paternal grandmother lay in an Atlanta bank vault. She'd removed the jewelry and paintings from the Buckhead residence a week before she'd closed the house.

Despite her prestigious pedigree, a few of her more conservative relatives thought her less than proper because she'd expressed a desire to become an artist, had lived with a gay man then married another man, older than her own father. There had been a few occasions when her mother, Irma Johnson, had thrown up her hands saying Veronica was going to be the death of her. Irma had recently celebrated her seventieth birthday and was healthier and more attractive than she'd ever been.

Veronica brushed her teeth, splashed water on her face and slipped into her workout attire. Heavy fog and a falling mist greeted her as she stepped out the back door. She doubted whether the sun would put in an appearance during the daylight hours but that was okay.

She hadn't planned any outdoor activities today because Kumi had promised to cook for her.

"I'm coming," Veronica called out seconds after the doorbell echoed through the house, while simultaneously, the clock on the fireplace mantel chimed twelve noon.

Approaching the door, she spied Kumi cradling two plastic crates to his chest, smiling.

After her walk she'd showered, shampooed her hair, blown it out and then curled it in tiny spiral curls that fell in seductive disarray around her face. In deference to the cloudy day, she'd elected to wear a simple linen sheath in a sunny yellow color. On her feet she wore a pair of black ballet-type slippers.

Pushing open and holding the door, she smiled at Kumi. He wore the type of loose-fitting tunic worn by the chefs she'd viewed on the Food Network channel. He'd exchanged his jeans for a pair of sharply creased khakis.

"Please come in."

He hesitated, leaning down to press a kiss to her velvety cheek. "*Bonjour.* I like your hair," he said in French.

Veronica wrinkled her pert nose. "*Merci.*" She peered into the crates, trying to discern what they contained. "What on earth did you bring?" she asked in English.

His eyes crinkled attractively. Not seeing him for two days made him more attractive than she'd remembered. He looked different, and as she stared at him she realized his hair was growing out. It was a glossy black, curling softly over his scalp.

"Lunch and dinner are in one crate, and some of my pots are in the other." He continued to speak French, but slow enough for Veronica to understand.

"Some?"

He stared at her over his shoulder. "The rest are in the trunk of the car."

Veronica stared at his retreating back as he walked in the direction of the kitchen. He returned within minutes, going back to the late-model sedan parked behind her vehicle. He retrieved another plastic crate, shutting the trunk with a solid thunk.

He walked back into the house. "That does it."

She closed the screen door and locked it, then joined Kumi in the kitchen where he'd begun emptying the crates. She stood, stunned, as he set a variety of pots and pans on the countertop. Soon every inch of counter space was taken up with cooking utensils and food-stuffs: a large aluminum bowl was filled with live lobsters, crab, clams and mussels; there was a platter of assorted cheeses; bottles of cooking and drinking wine; champagne; the ingredients for a salad; a container of bright green asparagus; and last but certainly not least a large uncooked duck. Her shock was complete when he turned out a mound of dough sealed in plastic wrap into a large ceramic bowl.

Folding her hands on her hips, she shook her head. "Do you really expect the two of us to eat all of *that?*"

"Oui, madame."

Kumi withdrew two aprons from the last crate, tying one around his waist. He motioned to Veronica. "Come here, and turn around."

She walked over and presented him with her back, suffering his closeness as he looped a strap around her neck, then wrapped the apron around her waist, tying it securely.

Kumi wanted to take her in his arms and kiss her until she pleaded with him to stop. His need to taste the sweetness of her lush mouth again was overwhelming. Resisting the urge to press his mouth to the nape of her neck, he turned and walked into the half bath to wash his hands.

Veronica spent the next two hours exchanging French phrases with Kumi while he washed the clams and mussels, ground dried lavender blossoms, savory thyme, peppercorns and salt together to season the duck before he rolled out dough for two loaves of French bread.

It was only after she saw him wield a knife with rapid precision as he sliced lardoons into tiny pieces before frying them in a skillet for a salad that she realized Kumi Walker couldn't be a waiter or a busboy in a restaurant, he must be a trained chef. Moving the skillet rhythmically up and down, and then back and forth over a flame, he flipped the diced bacon, turning it with a quick flip of his wrist.

He threw Veronica a knowing glance, winking and

offering her a wicked grin. "Please check to see if the bread dough has doubled in size."

She rolled her eyes at him. "'I've been out of the country for ten years, and what I've missed most is a home-cooked Southern meal,'" she mumbled, repeating what he'd said to her after he'd fixed her flat.

Blowing her a kiss, he said, "Don't be such a sore loser."

"Why didn't you tell me you were a chef?"

He shrugged a broad shoulder. "You didn't ask."

He was right. She hadn't asked. She'd just assumed he was a waiter. She'd misjudged him, believing he was a cocky young man who was so aware of his virility that he flaunted it like a badge of honor. And riding the Harley had only served to reinforce the macho image.

She was guilty of what so many in Atlanta had done to her—misjudged her when she married Dr. Bramwell Hamlin. But she'd loved Bram—loved him enough to marry him. It had nothing to do with his social standing or his wealth.

After checking on the fragrant-smelling dough under a towel, she returned to the stove. "It's ready."

Curving an arm around Veronica's waist, Kumi pulled her closer, handing her the skillet. "Try flipping it."

She took the pan, attempting to shake and turn the lardoons at the same time and failed.

Standing behind her, Kumi grasped her right wrist. "Loosen your grip on the handle," he said close to her ear. "That's it. Now move the skillet back and forward over the flame while tossing the contents so that they move toward you."

A brilliant smile lit up her golden eyes. "I did it!"

"Yes, you did," he crooned, kissing the side of her neck. She went completely still for several seconds before the tense moment vanished. "When they're golden brown, strain them and then let them drain on some paper towels. We'll warm them up slightly before topping off the salad."

Veronica and Kumi moved comfortably around the large functional kitchen, baking bread and tearing leaves for a salad. He mixed herbs and spices for a dressing, while she unwrapped a square of creamy goat cheese from a layer of cheesecloth. She watched as he dropped two small lobsters, two crabs, half a dozen clams and the same number of mussels into a large pot of boiling water.

It was two-thirty when they sat down at the table in the dining area off the kitchen to enjoy a lunch of freshly baked French bread, a country salad with goat cheese and diced crispy lardoons in a vinaigrette dressing, and the lobster, mussels, crabs and clams in a sauce flavored with wine, butter, garlic and parsley.

Veronica had turned off the overhead recessed lights and the chandelier, lit several votives, turned on a radio on a countertop and enjoyed the exquisitely prepared meal and the man responsible for its creation. The soft sounds of a muted trumpet punctuated the comfortable silence.

She'd suggested Bram buy the North Carolina property so they could come and spend time there and relax from their Atlanta social obligations, but doubted whether she and her late husband had come to the house more than four times since they'd purchased it. What she was sharing with Kumi was what she'd wanted to experience with Bram.

It had taken less than a week for Veronica to realize that she was attracted to Kumi. What she would not permit herself to do was fantasize about sleeping with him, even though she wanted to see him—every day.

Her eyes widened as she stared at her dining partner staring back at her. The flickering light from the votives threw flattering shadows over his dark brown face, accentuating the curve of his strong jaw and chin. Her gaze moved to his mouth, remembering how hers had burned in the aftermath of his brief possession.

Resting an elbow on the table, she cradled her chin in the heel of her left hand. "What made you decide to become a chef?"

His lids came down as he flashed a sensual smile. "I sort of fell into it?"

"How?"

Kumi's expression changed, becoming almost somber. "It's a long story. Are you certain you want to hear it?"

"Of course." She wanted to tell Kumi that she wanted to know everything about him, hoping she would be able to identify what it was about him that drew her to him.

"I enlisted in the marines and—"

"At what age did you enlist?" she asked, interrupting him.

"Eighteen. This really ticked my parents off because I was scheduled to enter Morehouse that September. My father and I did not get along well, so I saw the marines as an escape."

"Didn't you see leaving North Carolina for Georgia as an escape?"

He shook his head. "No. I still would've been under my father's thumb. And there was no doubt that he would've constantly reminded me that it was his money that kept a roof over my head, clothes on my back and food in my belly. What I did was shift that responsibility from Lawrence Walker to the United States Marine Corps.

"I served four years, then instead of coming back here I went to Europe. I'd planned to spend about three months touring and visiting most European capitals, but something happened to me my first day in Paris."

Leaning forward, Veronica gave him an expectant look. "What happened?" Her voice was a velvety whisper.

His expression brightened as he flashed a warm smile. "I fell in love."

She recoiled as if he'd slapped her. Her breath quickened, her cheeks becoming warm. He had a woman—perhaps a wife. While she wasn't quite lusting after him, what Veronica was beginning to feel for Kumi Walker was quickly approaching that.

"Did you marry her?" she asked, recovering her composure.

"Every Parisian is married to the City of Lights."

She was almost embarrassed at how happy his statement made her. He was talking about Paris, not a woman.

"Once I recovered I realized I needed a job, and because the money I'd saved wasn't going to last more than another month I secured a position working in a restaurant's kitchen. I washed dishes and bused tables before moving up to waiter. One of the chefs befriended me, suggesting I should try cooking. He eventually became my mentor. I attended classes during the day and worked at the restaurant at night." What he didn't tell Veronica was that he'd created several dishes that had won numerous awards.

"How about you, Veronica?" Kumi asked, "What did you feel when you visited Paris for the first time?"

"It took me a week to stop walking around with my mouth gaping. I found it hard to believe everything looked so old yet so incredibly beautiful. The photographs in my art textbooks did not prepare me for the magnificence of Notre Dame or the Jardin des Tuileries. It was if I'd stepped back in time, while at the same time I had every modern convenience at my fingertips."

Kumi took a sip of a dry white wine. "What made you decide to study art?"

The animation left her face. "For as long I could remember I wanted to be an artist. As a child I always had a pad and pencil, drawing everything I saw. My parents were pleased with my artistic talent, but freaked when I told them I wanted to become an artist. They believed a career in law, medicine or education was a more respectable profession, but in the end they supported me.

"My work was good enough for me to be accepted into Parsons School of Art and Design in New York. I'd earned an A in studio drawing and a B in landscape and still-life drawing my freshman year. I knew I'd never be a Picasso, Henry Tanner or Romare Bearden, but I was quite secure with my talent. Everything changed when…"

Her words dropped off; she couldn't continue. It was halfway through her sophomore year that everything changed—she and her life had changed with a single act attributed to poor judgment.

Kumi saw fear—wild and naked—fill Veronica's eyes. "What happened, Ronnie?" She closed her eyes, shaking her head. Glistening silver curls bounced around her cheeks and over her forehead with the motion.

"I can't," she gasped.

Wiping his mouth with a linen napkin, he pushed back his chair and rounded the table. She gasped a second time. She was sitting, and then without warning she was swept up in Kumi's arms as he cradled her effortlessly to his chest.

"It's all right," he crooned over and over in her ear, walking out of the kitchen and making his way to the patio. "I am not going to hurt you."

Panic rendered Veronica motionless and speechless. She wanted to believe Kumi, but the fear she'd repressed for two decades would not permit her to trust him completely.

Kumi carried Veronica into the comforting space. The overcast day and steadily falling rain cast dusky shadows over all of the furnishings. He sat on a rattan sofa covered in dark-green-and-orange kente-cloth cushions, still cradling her to his chest. The pressure of her hips against his groin failed to arouse him. He wanted to comfort Veronica, not seduce her. He held her, his chest rising and falling in unison with hers. Closing his eyes, he smiled. She'd begun to relax.

Veronica lay in Kumi's arms, absorbing his warmth and strength. She counted the strong steady beats of his heart under her cheek. Inhaling deeply, she breathed in the scent of his aftershave. The sandalwood was the perfect complement for his body's natural scent. Kumi Walker was perfect from his beautiful masculine face, to his perfectly proportioned physique.

Her left arm moved up and curved around his neck the way she'd done to her father when she was a young child. It was a gesture that indicated trust.

Her eyelids fluttered wildly before closing. Could she trust Kumi—trust him enough to tell him of her fear? Tell him that she'd almost been raped and that it had been her own fault?

Swallowing, she drew in a deep breath and said, "I stopped drawing because something happened to me."

Kumi held his breath before he let it out in an audible sigh. Cradling her chin in his hand, he stared down into her wounded gaze. "What happened, Ronnie?"

"I was… Someone tried to rape me."

He blinked once, completely freezing his features. The shock of what she'd disclosed caused the words to wedge in his throat. What was she talking about? His sharp mind recalled her saying that she'd switched her major from drawing to art history. And she hadn't been married when she spent the two summers in Paris living with Garland Bayless. Did someone attempt to rape her before she left for Paris, or had it happened years later?

Lowering his head, he pressed his lips to hers, caressing her mouth more than kissing it. "Tell me about it, sweetheart," he crooned softly.

Chapter Six

Veronica opened her mouth and the words came pouring out, words she had never uttered to another human being.

"My college roommate introduced me to this guy, and he eventually became my first serious boyfriend. I was eighteen and he was twenty-two. He was born and raised in New York, so he took me everywhere, showing me places that I never would've visited on my own.

"We talked about what we wanted for our futures— places and things we wanted to see and do together. One weekend he canceled a date, claiming he didn't feel well. Being young, impulsive and very much in love I decided to cook dinner. I wanted to surprise him.

"I was the surprised one, because when he opened the door there was another woman in his apartment with him. He'd tried to explain that she was just a friend, but I didn't want to hear it. He'd thrown on a robe, but his *friend* came out of the bedroom butt naked. Within seconds he wore the robe *and* the dinner.

"I left, tears streaming down my face. I'd trusted him. I'd slept with him because I truly loved him. Not wanting to go back to my apartment and explain everything to my roommate, I decided to go to a bar frequented by students who attended New York University.

"Three drinks later I found myself in a stranger's dorm room with his hands around my throat and my skirt up around my waist." She ignored Kumi's gasp of horror. "I thought he was going to strangle me until he had to release my throat to tear off my panties while he fumbled to pull his pants down. That gave me the advantage I needed. I kneed him in the groan, punched him in an eye and then made my escape. I took a taxi back to my apartment, snuck in quietly so I wouldn't wake my roommate and spent the night in the bathroom.

"The next day my neck was swollen and so bruised that I couldn't talk above a whisper. A colorful scarf concealed the bruises and I told everyone I had laryngitis. Jeff called, but I wouldn't talk to him. He waited for me after class, but I ignored him. After a while he took the hint and left me alone.

"After the attack I discovered I couldn't draw. Something in my head just shut down. That's when I decided to go to Paris—to get away, and to study with Garland. I was desperate to see if I could recapture my muse."

Tilting her chin, she stared up at the man holding her so protectively in his strong embrace. "I'd just turned twenty and I was old enough to know better. It was all my fault. I should've never gone anywhere with a stranger, especially if my reasoning was impaired by alcohol."

"Don't beat up on yourself."

"Who do I blame? Certainly not the student who tried to rape me."

"It wasn't your fault, Veronica. No man has a right to force a woman to have sex with him if she doesn't want it. I don't care how intoxicated she is."

Her chin quivered as she fought back tears. "He ruined me, Kumi. He ruined me for any man."

Kumi stared at her, baffled. What was she talking about? She hadn't been raped. "How did he ruin you? You're perfect. You're so incredibly beautiful that you take my breath away whenever I look at you."

Her mind refused to register the significance of his words. She wasn't talking about her looks. It was the inside that mattered. What she didn't feel.

"I don't feel anything when a man touches me. Something inside of me died that night."

Kumi struggled with his inner thoughts. "But…" His words trailed off. A pregnant silence ensued, engulfing them. "You married."

She forced a smile when she saw blatant confusion cross his features. "Yes. I did marry. It was a marriage in name only. And before you ask, yes, I did love my husband. If I hadn't I wouldn't have married him."

Kumi's expression darkened with an unreadable emotion. How ironic. It had taken him years to find a woman he wanted in *and* out of bed, and he doubted whether she would ever offer him the intimacy he sought from her.

He knew he had to make a decision—quickly. Would he continue to see Veronica Johnson after today, or would he walk away from her, leaving her to confront her fears—alone?

His eyes moved slowly over her face as lovingly as a caress, seeing what she could not see. She was beautiful and sexy. Sexier than any woman he'd ever met.

Something greater than Jerome Kumi Walker had forced him to ride along that deserted road almost two weeks ago, something that made him stop and help Veronica Johnson. And that something had put the words in his mouth when he'd asked her to cook for him when he knew he could cook for himself. And he also believed and treasured the verse from Ecclesiastes: a time for making love and a time for *not* making love.

He was falling in love with Veronica, and if he did love her then he would have to accept whatever she was able to offer him. At thirty-two he wasn't ready to become a monk, but there were ways a man could relieve himself without benefit of a woman.

Burying his face in her luminous curls, he breathed a kiss on her scalp. "You may believe he ruined you for all of the other men in your life, but actually you were saving yourself for me."

The heavy lashes that shadowed her eyes flew up. "What are you saying?"

"I'm saying that I like you, Veronica Johnson. I want to see you and not just for Sunday dinner."

"No, Kumi. That's not a good idea."

"That's your opinion. I happen to think it's a wonderful idea."

"I don't know what you want from me, but whatever it is I can't give it to you."

His hand moved over her breast, measuring its shape and firmness. "Do I want your body? Yes. I'd be a liar if I said I didn't. But I'd never ask or take from you what you're not willing to give me."

Veronica's body pulsed with new life with his touch, her breast swelling under the fabric of her bra. The sensation was so exquisitely pleasurable she gasped.

"But I'm older than you, Kumi," she whispered.

He smiled, shaking his head. "I thought we settled that last week."

"It's not going to work."

"Why not?"

"I know nothing about you."

"I'm not married, if that's bothering you. I'm neither an absent or deadbeat dad because I don't have any children."

"That's not what's bothering me."

"Then what is it?" When she didn't answer him, he decided to press his assault. "You're the first woman I've met that I can talk to without censoring my thoughts or my words."

Veronica fought the dynamic vitality he exuded and failed miserably. Kumi exhibited a calm and self-confidence men twice his age hadn't acquired. And she'd felt comfortable enough with him that she'd revealed a secret she'd hidden away from everyone—including her sister *and* her parents.

"Why is that, Kumi?"

Tilting his head, he regarded her for a long moment, his near-black eyes peering into her soul. "I believe it's because I'm falling in love with you."

She shook her head. "You don't know me."

"I know what I see and what I like," he said, showing no signs of relenting in his pursuit of her. "Your first lover may have screwed up when you caught him with another woman, but he also screwed up a second time when he didn't get you to forgive him for his indiscretion. You're not going to worry about me screwing up, Veronica Johnson, because there's not going to be another woman."

And there's nothing you can do or say to make me stay away from you, he added silently.

Placing her fingertips over his mouth, Veronica leaned in closer and her mouth replaced her fingers. She kissed him, tentatively at first, then became bolder as she parted her lips, capturing his breath and drinking in his nearness.

Shifting her on his lap, Kumi cradled her face between his large hands. He returned her kiss, resisting the urge to push his tongue into her mouth. What they shared was too new, too frightening to rush.

He wanted to press her down to the cushions, remove her dress and undergarments. The urge to feast on her lush beauty, to run his tongue over her body until she begged him to take her was so strong it frightened him. If ever he claimed her body, he knew he was capable of taking her with all of the gentleness and love she deserved. But he would wait—for another time and when she was ready for him.

Pulling back, he brushed a kiss over her forehead and eyelids, before returning to her moist parted lips.

The kiss ended with both of them breathing heavily. Resting her head on his solid shoulder, Veronica closed her eyes, smiling. She'd believed she was unable to give herself completely to any man. Kumi had proven her wrong. She knew she wasn't ready to take off her clothes and lie with him, because she couldn't forget the ordeal that had happened twenty-two years earlier.

Her unexpected response to the man holding her to his heart was as shocking as the depth of his feelings for her. He was falling in love with her and what he didn't know was that she also was falling in love with him.

The fingers of Kumi's right hand toyed with the buttons of her dress, and one by one he undid the buttons until he bared an expanse of flesh to her waist. She froze as he caressed the silken flesh over her ribs, her breathing quickening.

He eased her onto her back, his hand working its magic, and leaned over her. For a moment he studied her intently, searching for a sign of the fear. A slight smile tilted the corners of his strong mouth.

"Are you all right?"

Veronica's chest rose and fell under the sensual assault on her bare flesh. She nodded rather than speak. His fingers burned her breasts through the sheer fabric of her bra. Her flesh was on fire; she was on fire. It was all she could do not to squirm and writhe under his touch.

Lowering his body, Kumi supported his greater weight on his elbows as he buried his face against the side of her neck, inhaling the distinctive scent that was Veronica's.

"I won't do anything you don't want me to do," he crooned in her ear, when all he wanted was to touch, kiss and taste her.

Veronica felt as if she were standing outside of herself looking on as a spectator. This wasn't happening to her. She'd permitted a man, a stranger she'd known less than two weeks, to touch and kiss her, and she'd kissed him in return.

This stranger had come into her home and into her life to make her feel something she'd thought long dead—desire. She met his gaze. His eyes alone betrayed his ardor. In the raven gaze there was an open invitation she recognized immediately. He was waiting—waiting for her to grant him permission to make love to her.

He pressed closer, her soft curves molding to the contours of his hard body. Her hands slipped up his arms, curling around his strong neck. Closing her eyes, she smiled. "What am I going to do with you?" she whispered.

Kumi laughed deep in his chest. "You can start by permitting me to call on you, Miss Johnson."

Her soft laugher joined his. "You sound so proper, Mr. Walker."

"That's because I was brought up proper," he said truthfully.

It hadn't escaped her notice that Kumi was an absolute gentleman. He always made certain to seat her, and when she stood up, he also rose to his feet. His mother had done a fine job raising him. And if she did agree to go out with him publicly, she knew Kumi would never embarrass her.

Wrapping his arms around her midriff, he held her close—close enough for her to feel the outline of his extraordinary arousal. Her blood warmed and raced through her veins. Suddenly her body was alive, throbbing with a need that resulted in a gush of wetness between her thighs. She lay panting, her chest heaving as she surrendered to the raw sensations pulsing throughout her lower body.

Kumi watched the play of emotions cross Veronica's face as she breathed through parted lips. He wanted to take her, easing his hardened flesh into her celibate body. But he knew that would not become a reality— not yet. He wanted her to get used to him, the weight of his body. He wanted to be able to touch her and not have her pull away. They had time—at least three full months to get to know each other—in and out of bed.

He reversed their positions, settling her over his chest. "I'm going to keep you prisoner until you grant my wish, princess."

"You are most arrogant, Sir Knight."

"Aye, mistress," he countered, "that I am."

"If I grant your wish, then what can I expect?"

"Grant the wish, princess, and you'll find out."

She punched him softly on the shoulder. "That's not fair, Kumi."

"Yes, it is, because I'm willing to give you all of myself while asking nothing in return." She sobered, a slight frown furrowing her smooth forehead. He brushed a kiss over her lips. "By the time the summer's over you'll know exactly what I mean."

Veronica hummed along with the sultry voice of Lena Horne singing "Stormy Weather." Veronica had left North Carolina at eight, hoping to make it to Atlanta within four hours, because she'd promised her parents she would arrive in time to share lunch with them.

She hadn't planned to return to Atlanta until her family reunion weekend, but the board of the Bramwell Hamlin Scholarship Foundation had requested she present a check to an impoverished Atlanta high school senior at an awards dinner. The young woman had been accepted into an historically black college's premed program. The check would underwrite the cost of four years of tuition, books and room and board.

The fact that half of Bram's estate had been set aside for the foundation further angered his children. Clinton, the eldest son felt that Veronica had deliberately talked his father into endowing the scholarship fund to cut him out of his rightful inheritance. In a heated discussion with the enraged man, she had quietly reminded Clinton that his father did not owe him one copper penny, and if he'd received anything from the estate then he should've considered it a gift. It was only after the surrogate court had upheld the contents of Bramwell Hamlin's last will and testament that Veronica had become aware of more Hamlin addictions: Clinton's gambling and Norman's drinking. Cordelia seemed to be the only one of Bram's children that was free of the addictive personality of her mother and brothers.

The haunting image of Kumi penetrated her musings. *By the time the summer's over you'll know exactly what I mean.* She would be the last to openly admit it, but she was looking forward to the summer. She wanted to share with Kumi what she should've experienced in her twenties and thirties.

After her Sunday afternoon confessional, she had consented to seeing him. Over the next three days, they'd taken in a movie, and then ate the most delicious chiliburgers in the state at a small roadside café that boasted sawdust floors and loud music blaring from a colorful jukebox. They'd sat in a booth in the back, laughing uncontrollably when she attempted to drink beer from a longneck bottle for the first time in her life, spilling some of the rich brew down her chin. Kumi had moved from sitting opposite her to next to her and surreptitiously used the tip of his tongue to lick the beer from her chin. She'd sat motionless, glorying in the erotic gesture.

She'd ridden home on the back of the Harley, her face pressed against his back, her body tingling from a heightened sexual awareness that had never been there before—not even with her first lover.

She didn't know how, but Jerome Kumi Walker had overwhelmed her with his sexy, compelling personality, leaving her off balance and gasping whenever he touched or kissed her. She'd been able to keep every man at a distance—all except for the motorcycle-riding master chef.

A sensual smile softened her mouth as she thought of how much she'd come to like Kumi. He was even-tempered and generous, and more importantly he was a good listener and very easy to talk to. His above-average intelligence was more than apparent by his fluent French and his vast knowledge of art and architecture. He'd reluctantly admitted he'd been valedictorian of his high school graduating class.

How ironic, she thought, as the skyline of downtown Atlanta came into view. She was scheduled to present a scholarship to a deserving high school graduating senior, a student who planned for a career in medicine, while Kumi, who had been given the opportunity to become a doctor, had deliberately rejected it.

* * *

Veronica sat at the lace-covered table on the patio of the home where she'd grown up, enjoying her second glass of iced tea. She had to admit that Irma Johnson brewed the best pitcher of iced, or sweet, as Southerners referred to it, tea in the state.

Smiling, Irma's gold eyes sparkled like citrines. "I must admit you look wonderful, darling." She called everyone darling, and no one took offense because of the way the word rolled off her tongue like watered silk.

She returned her mother's smile. "Thank you, Mother."

Harold Johnson, two years his wife's senior, reached over and patted his daughter's hand. "I have to agree with your mother. You do look wonderful."

Leaning over, she kissed her father's smooth cheek. "Thank you, Daddy."

A tall, spare man, Harold still claimed a head filled with softly curling white hair that contrasted beautifully with a complexion that always reminded Veronica of a sweet potato. Her genes had compromised when she'd inherited her mother's eyes, and body, and her father's hair, coloring and height. Petite, seventy-year-old Irma Wardlaw-Johnson's thick black hair was streaked with only a few silver strands. A former schoolteacher, Irma had met Harold at a fund-raiser for the NAACP and had fallen madly in love on sight. Irma's parents had thought widely traveled Harold too urbane for their twenty-two-year old daughter, but reconsidered once they discovered Harold was heir to an insurance company that sold policies to Georgia's Negro populace. Harold and Irma had recently celebrated their forty-eighth wedding anniversary.

"How long do you intend to live in that godforsaken place, darling?"

Veronica rolled her eyes at her mother. "You make it sound as if I live hundreds of miles from civilization."

"You live at the top of a mountain where, if you screamed, your so-called neighbor would never hear you. For heaven's sake, Veronica, you could be dead for a month before someone discovered your body."

"Don't be so melodramatic, Irma." There was obvious censure in Harold's tone.

"Thank you, Daddy," Veronica crooned, winking at Harold.

Veronica did not intend to argue *again* with her mother about where she'd chosen to live. But then, for as long as she could remember, Irma had always been critical of her lifestyle. It was her mother who had dissented loudly about her becoming an artist and spending the summers in Paris. It was Irma who protested vocally when Veronica had announced her intent to marry Bramwell—a man older than her own father.

She was forty-two, independent and capable of running her life and making her own decisions, despite Irma's objections. She'd been labeled a rebel and a renegade, while her younger sister, Candace, had been the good daughter.

Staring at a pair of eyes that were an exact match for her own, Veronica wondered how Irma would react if she saw her daughter riding on the back of the Harley—or if Veronica invited Kumi to accompany her to their annual family reunion celebration? A mysterious smile lifted her corners of her mouth. Perhaps she would invite him and find out.

Candace Yarborough's expression spoke volumes as she opened the door to Veronica's ring. "You look absolutely fabulous. Why, you're practically glowing." Throwing her arms around her older sister's neck, she kissed her cheek.

Veronica pressed her cheek to Candace's, feeling blissfully happy and wonderfully alive. The awards dinner had been a rousing success. The first recipient of the Bramwell Hamlin Scholarship Foundation award hadn't been able to deliver her prepared speech because she hadn't been able to stop sobbing out her joy. The emotional moment had most in attendance crying, as well—Veronica included.

Candace pulled her into the entryway. "Come in and make yourself comfortable."

Following her sister into an expansive living room, Veronica said, "Where are the boys?" She'd been in Atlanta for two days, but had yet to reconnect with her brother-in-law and her nephews.

"They went with Ivan to see his mother. She's not doing too well after her hip-replacement surgery, because she refuses to listen to her orthopedist. I keep reminding Ivan that his sons are as hardheaded as his mother." Glancing at her watch, Candace, said, "They should return sometime around eleven."

Sitting down on an off-white silk club chair, Veronica silently admired the furnishings in the Yarborough living room. Candace had employed the services of a professional interior decorator to make her home a magazine layout designer showplace.

"How did Bobby and Will do on their final exams?"

Candace ran a manicured hand through her short coiffed hair. "They aced them. I initially had my doubts about them being homeschooled, but after seeing their grades this year I'm glad I decided to go through with it."

Veronica studied Candace's round face. She claimed a pair of large, dark eyes, bright smile and a flawless golden complexion; she saw the serenity that had become so apparent in her sister's life. Candace had taken one look at Ivan Yarborough, declared herself in love and embarked on a relentless crusade to become his wife and the mother of his children. She'd loved teaching school, but loved being a wife and mother more. She homeschooled her children and the family traveled together whenever Ivan spent more than three weeks away from home. Candace was determined not to raise her sons alone because of an absentee father.

"Do you want anything?"

Veronica waved her hand. "No, thank you." She'd eaten at the awards dinner.

"Are you sure?"

"Yes, I'm sure."

"When are you going back to North Carolina?"

"Tomorrow."

"What time tomorrow?"

Veronica paused for several seconds. "Probably around noon. Why?"

"Come shopping with me. I need to replenish my lingerie."

"Where do you want to go?"

"To your favorite boutique in Buckhead. I love their selections."

"You or Ivan?"

A rush of color suffused Candace's golden skin. "Well, I do get to model them before he undresses me."

"Be careful, little sis, before you make me an aunt for a third time."

"Bite your tongue, Veronica. At thirty-eight I'm through making babies. It's your turn."

"Bite your tongue back. At forty-two I'm much too old to think about having a baby."

Candace lifted her eyebrows, shaking her head. "Not! Remember Helene had her first one last year, and she was older than you."

"Didn't Andy James say that his son was born with a gray beard?"

"Andy was drunk as a skunk for a week after celebrating his son's birth, so he could've said anything. You need to find a man, get married, settle down and have at least one baby."

"What if I have a baby without getting married?" Veronica teased. She'd given up all hope of ever having a child. At first it had bothered her when her sister and girls she'd grown up with had married and became mothers. But after a while she conceded herself that she was still a woman even if she never bore a child.

Candace groaned. "Don't let Mother hear you say that. It would kill her if her daughter was to become an unwed mother."

"I wouldn't be an unwed mother—I'd be a single mother."

"Is there a difference?"

"Big difference, Candace. What if I'd had a child with Bram? I wouldn't be an unwed mother, but a widow and a single mother."

Candace gave her a skeptical look before changing the subject.

The two sisters talked for hours, stopping only when Ivan called Candace to inform her he and their sons had planned to spend the night in Athens and would return the following morning. Veronica left minutes after midnight, promising to meet Candace at the mall in downtown Atlanta at ten that morning.

Chapter Seven

The afternoon sun had shifted, sending pinpoints of gold through the leaves of trees flanking Trace Road. The cargo area of Veronica's truck was crowded with shopping bags from several of the boutiques she and Candace had visited. Much to her surprise she'd purchased quite a few sheer and lace-trimmed undergarments. On a dare from her sister, she had bought a lacy black thong panty and matching bra. She would wear the bra, but doubted whether she'd ever wear the thong. The cooler mountain air flowing through the vents of the Lexus was refreshing, unlike the humidity smothering Atlanta like a weighted blanket.

She pulled into the driveway to her home, smiling. Shutting off the engine, she left the SUV, retrieving the shopping bags from the rear; a minute later she unlocked the front door. She'd been away for three days, and it felt good to be back.

Walking up the staircase to her bedroom, she dropped her purchases on a chair in her sitting room, checked the messages on the telephone on the bedside table, listening while undressing.

She raised an eyebrow when Kumi's voice came through the speaker, greeting her in French and telling her that he'd enjoyed spending time with her. The next message was also from him. In this one he confessed to missing her, hoping she would return his call. He left a number. The third and final message stunned her with his intensity. "I miss you, Veronica. Please call me when you get this message." Then there was a pause before he spoke again. "I love you."

Sinking to the bed, clad only in her bra and panties, she stared at the French doors. Each time she saw Kumi, her feelings for him intensified. She was totally entranced whenever he was near and she ached for the protectiveness of his strong embrace. Her eyelids fluttered wildly as she reached for the telephone.

Kumi paced the floor in the small cottage like a caged cat. His initial reunion with his father hadn't gone well. While his mother clung to him weeping inconsolably, his father had stood off to the side glaring. He'd acknowledged Dr. Lawrence Walker's presence with a nod, and then walked out.

He had expected the reunion to be strained, but thought his father would have at least said something—

even if he were to just yell at him, proving that his relationship with his father would never change, not even after a fourteen-year separation. Kumi had ridden back to his cabin saddened, tears not for himself but for his mother, because she'd always ended each of her letters to him with a prayer of reconciliation for him and his father. It was apparent that all of her prayers were in vain.

He stopped pacing long enough for his thoughts to stray to Veronica. He hadn't seen her in three days, although he'd left several messages on her answering machine for her to call him. When she hadn't his frustration level had gone off the chart. After the third message he thought perhaps she had taken ill or injured herself and he had ridden over to her house. When he didn't see her truck he knew she had gone away.

He refused to believe that she'd returned to Atlanta. She'd said she planned to spend the summer in North Carolina. He could handle any disappointment—his father's alienation and his mother's tears as long as he had Veronica in his life.

When, he mused, had he become so dependent on her? What was there about her that sent his emotions into overdrive? Why had he fallen in love with her and not some other woman in his past?

The phone on a table in the parlor chimed softly. Turning slowly, he stared at it as if it were a foreign object as it rang again. It rang a third time and he was galvanized into action. Taking three long strides, he picked up the receiver.

"Hello."

"*Bonjour,* Kumi."

His smile matched the warm glow flowing through his body. "How are you, darling?"

"A little tired, but glad to be home. If you're not busy tomorrow evening I'd like to take you out to dinner. My treat."

"I can't."

"You can't what?"

"I can't permit you to pay."

"Why not? Every time we go out you pay for everything."

"I'm an old-fashioned Southern guy—"

"You're more French than Southern and you know it," Veronica said, interrupting him.

"I'm French on the outside and Southern inside."

She laughed softly. "What if we compromise?"

"What are you proposing?"

"We split the check."

"I'm only agreeing because I want to see you," Kumi admitted softly. "What time is dinner?"

"Be here at around five-thirty."

"I'll see you then."

Kumi ended the call, exhaling a long sigh of contentment. It would be less than twenty-four hours before he saw Veronica again.

A threat of rain persisted throughout the next day with dark clouds and an intermittent roll of thunder. Veronica had made dinner reservations at Gabrielle's. The restaurant, with its beautiful Victorian dining room, offered Southern dishes that were transformed into classic entrées without losing their roots. The highlight of dining at Gabrielle's was a splendid view of Asheville from the restaurant's wraparound porch.

She'd spent the day putting up several loads of laundry, dusting and weeding and pruning her flower garden. Now she looked forward to relaxing and spending time with Kumi. She smiled when she thought of the man who'd put the glow back in her cheeks and her eyes. He'd become her friend and confidant—someone she'd confided her most closely guarded secret. There was so much about him she liked—so much she could love if only he'd been older. She still had to convince herself the ten-year difference in their ages wasn't an issue.

When, she thought, had she become so insular and narrow-minded? Had she become like the very people she'd left Atlanta to avoid? Could she open her mind and her heart to accept whatever life was offering her? A knowing smile softened her delicate features.

Yes, her heart sang.

"Yes, I can," she whispered softly.

The doorbell rang and she left her bedroom, made her way down the winding staircase and crossed the living room to the front door. A bright smile tilted her eyes at the corners when she opened the door to find Kumi staring at her as if she were a stranger. Her penetrating gaze lingered on his impassive expression.

Unlatching the screen door, she pushed it open. "Come in."

Kumi stepped into the living room, his gaze fixed on Veronica's face. She looked beautiful, but fragile and untouchable.

Moving closer, he curved an arm around her waist, pulling her up close. His free hand cradled her chin, raising her face to his. "I missed you like crazy," he whispered seconds before he claimed her mouth with an explosive kiss that sucked the breath from her lungs.

He kissed her with the passion of a predator tearing into its prey, holding her in a strong grip that brooked no resistance. The uneasiness and frustration that had welled up in Kumi overflowed as he staked his claim. He'd confessed to Veronica that he loved her—that was something he'd never told another woman. And his confession made him vulnerable to a pain that was certain to surpass his alienation from his family and country.

Veronica opened her mouth to accept everything Kumi offered. Pleasure, pure and shocking, radiated from her mouth to every nerve in her body as she was transported to a place where she'd never been before. Her senses reeled as if short-circuited. The blood pounding in her head rushed to her heart, and then down to the lower part of her body, pooling in the sensitive area between her thighs. Her trembling knees buckled, and she slumped weakly against Kumi's solid chest. He'd aroused her to heights of desire that threatened to incinerate her with its hottest flame.

Winding her arms around his waist under his jacket,

her fingertips bit into the muscles in his back through the crisp fabric of his laundered shirt. Tasting him, inhaling his distinctive male scent nearly sent her over the edge.

Kumi's ravishing mouth moved from her lips to the side of her neck, his chest rising and falling heavily. "Don't ever do that to me again," he groaned close to her ear.

Veronica went completely still, her heart pumping wildly under her breasts. "Do what?" she gasped.

Kumi's large hands slipped down her spine and cradled her hips. "Go away without telling me."

The scalding blood in her veins suddenly ran ice-cold. His words and coolly disapproving tone slapped at her while her delicate nostrils flared.

"I didn't know I was obligated to apprise you of my every move."

Easing back, he glared at her. "You're not obligated to me, but out of common courtesy you could've at least let me know you weren't going to be home." He'd made a fool of himself calling and leaving three messages on her answering machine.

The tenuous rein she had on her temper snapped and she jerked out of his embrace. "There's one thing you should know about me, Jerome Walker. I'm my own woman and I don't answer to or check in with anyone— especially *a man.*"

He winced when she called him Jerome. He'd grown up with everyone calling him Kumi—everyone except his parents. His father had attended college with a young African student who'd become his roommate and a lifelong friend. The two men had promised each other that if they ever fathered a son they would name him after the other. Years later, Lawrence kept his promise. However, it had been five-year-old Deborah Walker who had begun calling her parents' last-born Kumi, which meant *strong* in Ghana, and the name stuck.

Taking a deep breath, he forced a smile he didn't feel. "I don't want to monitor your whereabouts, Ronnie. I just want more involvement in your life."

She waved a hand. "How much more involved do you want to be? We eat together practically every day."

"I'm not talking about sharing a meal. I want to take you out. I don't like hiding out here."

"We go out," she countered hotly.

"Where, Veronica? We ride my bike," he said, answering his own question. "We've gone to one movie, then ate at a place situated so deep in the woods that even the regulars have a problem finding it in the dark."

His accusing tone stabbed her. Why was he making her the bad guy? "I didn't come to North Carolina to become involved with a man," she countered, "especially not one as young as you."

Reaching out, he caught her shoulders, pulling her to his chest. "You're back to that, aren't you? You're beginning to sound like a broken record. You're not old enough to be my mother, so I suggest you drop what has become a lame, tired-ass excuse about my being too young for you."

Rage rendered her speechless until the silence looming between them became unbearable. Veronica felt her body trembling—not from fear but a rising fury.

"Take your hands off me." Her eyes narrowed. "And I think you'd better leave before I say something I might regret later." She was surprised she sounded so calm when all she wanted to do was scream at him.

Kumi's hands fell away and he moved past her, taking long, determined strides to the door. Veronica did not turn around until she heard the soft click of the screen door closing, and then the sound of a car starting up. After he'd driven away she turned around, her golden eyes shimmering with unshed moisture.

He'd ruined it. She was ready for Kumi, ready to sleep with him, and ready for whatever they would offer each other and he'd sabotaged everything with his display of wanting to control her life. She'd believed he was mature enough to have an affair without becoming obsessive.

Turning on her heel, she headed for the staircase. Ten minutes later, dressed in jeans and a pair of running shoes, she walked out of the house and headed for the narrow path leading into a wooded area several hundred feet away. She had to think and she always thought best when she walked.

Kumi lay across his bed, in the dark, listening to the steady beats of his own heart resounding in his ears. A warning voice had whispered in his head that he was going to lose Veronica even before he claimed her— all of her. He hadn't realized what he'd said to her until after the words slipped past his lips—words he could not retract.

"I can't lose her," he whispered. Not because of a few carelessly uttered words. Sitting up, he turned on a bedside lamp, and then swung his legs over the side of the bed. He hadn't stood up to his father—to demand his respect. He'd taken the easy way out and run away, and he'd been running for fourteen years.

Pulling on a pair of jeans, a pullover cotton sweater and boots, he made his way out of the small bedroom, through the parlor and out into a lightly falling mist. Opening the door to the Camry parked under the carport, he slipped behind the wheel, turned the key in the ignition and switched on the headlights.

His expression was a mask of stone as he concentrated on navigating the dark winding road. He did not intend to give Veronica Johnson up without a fight. A muscle throbbed spasmodically in his jaw as he maneuvered up the hill to Trace Road. The half-dozen structures along the stretch of paved road were ablaze with light.

He hadn't realized how fast his heart was beating until he turned into the driveway behind Veronica's vehicle. Inhaling deeply, he cut off the engine, pushed open the door and placed a booted foot on the wet driveway. Golden light from table lamps illuminated the first floor, beckoning him closer as he made his way to the open door.

He peered through the screen at the same time he rang the bell. The melodious chiming echoed throughout the house. Waiting a full sixty seconds, he rang the bell again before trying the doorknob. It opened to his touch. She hadn't locked it.

"Veronica," he called out, stepping into the living room. He called her again as he walked through the living/dining room, into the kitchen and to the patio.

He searched the downstairs, not finding her, then headed for the staircase. "Ronnie!" His voice bounced off the walls in the hallway as he rushed in and out of bedrooms. A rising panic enveloped him; he couldn't find her. A wave of hysteria paralyzed him until he heard the familiar voice behind him.

"What are you doing here?"

Turning, he breathed out an audible sigh of relief when he saw Veronica standing less than five feet away from him; she was safe. She stood motionless, moisture dotting her velvety skin. Her silk blouse was pasted to her chest, offering him an erotic display of large dark nipples showing through a sheer bra.

Veronica stared at Kumi, light smoldering in her gold-flecked eyes as she battled the dynamic vitality he exuded. She'd fought her emotions and lost miserably. Since meeting Kumi, she had made up so many excuses, spoken and unspoken, as to why she should not permit herself to become involved with him that she was even tired of them herself.

And the reason was always the same: his age.

Why was she so fixated on his being ten years younger when she'd married a man thirty years her senior? She knew the answer as it formed in her mind.

It was because she wanted to shield Kumi from what she'd experienced with Bramwell: the sly looks, whispers, alienation and the blatant references to her husband being her father. All she wanted to do was protect Kumi—she loved him that much.

A small smile of enchantment touched her lips. She loved him; that much she could admit to herself, and it was only a matter of time before she would reveal to Kumi what lay in her heart.

Kumi saw her smile, taking it as a clue that her former hostility had faded. Taking two long strides, he pulled her to his chest, burying his face in her wet hair. She smelled like a clean spring rain shower.

"Kumi?" Veronica's face was pressed against his shoulder, her arms hanging stiffly at her sides.

"Yes, sweetheart."

"Why did you come back?"

He tightened his grip on her waist. "I'm surprised you're asking that question."

The heat from Kumi's body seeped into Veronica's, warming her. She'd walked too far from the house and couldn't get back before the heavens opened, soaking her and the earth with its life-giving moisture.

"I have to ask, because I need to know."

"I came back to apologize for saying what I said." He pressed a kiss along the column of her neck. "I don't want to fight with you. Please, Ronnie, don't send me away again."

"Why shouldn't I send you away?"

"Because I love you, Veronica Johnson. I love you more than life itself."

Wrapping her arms around his slim waist, Veronica moved closer. He loved her and she loved him. Loved him despite his age and his arrogance.

Easing back, she tilted her chin, meeting his tender gaze. She could no longer deny herself his presence or his touch.

The fingers of her right hand traced the outline of his mouth. "I'm not going to send you away—at least not tonight."

Dipping his head, he brushed a kiss over her parted lips. "If that's the case, then I want to spend the night and wake up with you next to me in the morning." He wanted to tell her of the dreams that kept him from a restful night's sleep. Increasing the pressure, he deepened the kiss, his tongue parting her lips. "May I stay the night, Ronnie?"

His kiss left her weak, pulling her into a slow, drugging intimacy. Her tongue met his, testing the texture before she pulled it into her mouth, making him her willing prisoner.

Veronica kissed him back with a series of slow, shivery kisses that left his mouth burning with fire—a blaze that matched the inferno raging out of control in his groin.

Kumi groaned aloud when her fingers searched under his sweater and found his straight spine. She was touching him, but he wanted to touch her.

"Yes, Kumi," she moaned against his searching, plundering mouth. "You can stay the night."

Raising his head, he stared at her. His eyes appeared larger, near black in the diffused light in the hallway lit by wall sconces outside each bedroom. Bending slightly, he swept her up in his arms, her arms curving around his neck.

"Merci, ma chérie."

Veronica rested her cheek on his shoulder, closing her eyes. There was something else she had to tell Kumi before what they shared could be taken to another level.

She opened her eyes, staring up at him. "You're right about my not being old enough to be your mother. You being ten years younger than I is really not an issue."

A slight frown furrowed his forehead as he shifted her weight. "Then what is?"

"My late husband was thirty years my senior, and there were people in Atlanta who reminded us of that in every subtle way imaginable—especially his children.

"They were vicious, Kumi, and if I hadn't been so in love with Bram I would've divorced him to spare him the insults and humiliation. I've been called everything from a hooker to high-price whore.

"I want to invite you to my family reunion in early August, but I shudder to think of the reaction from those—"

"Don't worry so much, Ronnie," he said, interrupting her. "Words are harmless."

Closing her eyes, she shook her head. "Not when

you're on the receiving end," she countered. Pressing her nose to his sweater, she sneezed softly.

"We'll talk later after I get you out of these wet clothes."

She nodded. "You can put me down now."

He ignored her request, asking, "Which one is your bedroom?"

"It's the one on the left."

It took less than half a dozen steps before Kumi found himself standing in the middle of the bedroom with a four-poster mahogany bed covered with a sheer creamy drapery. His gaze swept around the space, cataloging a massive armoire carved with decorative shapes of leaves, vines and pineapples, and a matching triple dresser and rocker boasting the same design. Diaphanous sheers, flanking a double set of French doors, matched the filmy drapery falling sensuously around the bed. Soft light from a table lamp in a sitting room cast soft golden shadows throughout the large space.

He carried Veronica over to the bed, wondering if this was where she'd slept with her husband. Parting the sheer fabric, he placed her in the middle of the bed, his body following. He stared at the serene look on her face. There was no doubt she was as ready for him as he was for her.

Leaning closer, he buried his face against the side of her slender neck. "I'm not going to do anything to you you don't want me to do. If at any time you want me to stop, just say so."

Turning her head, she gave him a bold direct stare. "Will you be able to stop?"

He returned her penetrating look, nodding slowly. "With you I will."

And he could. He loved her too much not to adhere to her wishes. She'd carried pain too long for him to compound it because of his own need to pour out his passions inside her fragrant body.

Raising her arms, Veronica circled his neck, pulling his head down. Then she kissed him, offering all of herself—holding nothing back. She kissed him with a hunger that belied her outward calm. Her tongue slipped between his parted lips, tasting, testing and savoring the flavor and texture of his mouth.

Kumi kissed her, his slow, drugging kisses masking the explosive fire roaring unchecked through his body. There was something about Veronica that wanted him to forgo a lingering foreplay. He hadn't known her long, but it felt as if he'd been waiting for her for years—for all of his life.

His lips continued to explore her soft, lush mouth, as his fingers were busy undoing the buttons on her blouse. The silken garment parted and he pulled back to stare at her heaving chest. A groan escaped him when he feasted on the fullness of a pair of golden breasts tipped with large nut-brown nipples clearly outlined under a sheer white bra.

The image of a child suckling from her ripe breasts—his child—flashed through his mind and he froze. Did he love Veronica enough to offer marriage?

Did he love her enough to hope she would ever bear his child?

Yes, the inner voice whispered to him. He wanted Veronica as his wife and the mother of his children, but he would wait to ask her, wait until she'd come to love him as much as he loved her.

Sliding his palms under her back, he released the hook on her bra, eased the thin straps off her shoulders and then slid it off. He stared at her for a full minute before closing his eyes to conceal the lust in his gaze.

"You are perfect," he murmured in French.

Veronica lay motionless, watching the gamut of emotions cross her soon-to-be-lover's face as he continued to slowly undress her. Desire pulsed her veins like a slow-moving stream of burning lava incinerating everything in its wake.

It was her turn to close her eyes when he removed her blouse, jeans and shoes. Only her panties remained—a thin barrier concealing her femininity from his gaze and his possession. She opened her eyes and stared at him as he left the bed to undress. Watching intently, she admired the muscles in his long, ropy arms as he pulled the cotton sweater over his head.

Her mouth went suddenly dry when he bent over to remove his boots. Turning his back, he unsnapped his jeans, pushing them down over his firm hips. She breathed audibly through parted lips as he removed his briefs. He paused, retrieving the small packet of protection from a pocket of his jeans and slipping it on his redundant erection, and then turned to face her. The shadowy light from the lamp in the sitting area silhouetted his tall muscular body. Her gaze slipped down the broad expanse of chest covered with a fine layer of dark hair, flat, hard belly and then even lower to the rigid flesh jutting majestically between powerful thighs.

Chapter Eight

Veronica gasped as his blood-engorged arousal brushed her inner thigh. Instinctively, her body arched toward him, she caressing the length of his spine, and her fingernails raising goose bumps along his flesh.

Kumi's tongue explored the skin on her neck and shoulders, moving down to stake his claim on her entire body. His mouth covered the peaks of her breasts, teeth tightening on the turgid nipples. He didn't just love her—he worshiped her, ignoring her soft moans, as he tasted the taut flesh over her flat belly. Her moans escalated to gasps when he eased her panties down her hips and legs, tossing them aside.

Sitting back on his heels, Kumi surveyed the exquisite perfection of the woman with whom he'd fallen in love. He was glad he'd waited for her, because he couldn't remember the last time he'd slept with a woman.

Sinking back down to the mattress, he rested his cheek on her belly, brushing tender kisses over the velvety flesh. Moving lower, he left a trail of moisture before he buried his face between her thighs. His hot breath seared the tangled curls concealing the warm moistness of her femininity.

Veronica wasn't given the opportunity to react when she felt Kumi's tongue lathe her dormant flesh. Her body bucked as his teeth found and gently worried the swollen nodule hidden in the folds at the apex of her thighs. She writhed in exquisite ecstasy, her chest heaving from a sensual assault that made it difficult for her to draw a normal breath.

"Kumi, Kumi, Kumi…"

His voice became a litany as she felt herself drowning—drowning in a flood tide of sweetest agony that threatened to shatter her into thousands of particles of sexual bliss.

Passion pounded, whirling the blood through her heart, chest and head until she was mindless with desire for a man she hadn't planned to love.

Shock after shock slapped at her when Kumi's finger replaced his tongue once he moved up her body. His mouth swooped down over hers, permitting her to taste herself on his lips.

His hand worked its magic as he gently eased a second finger into her, moving them in and out of her tender celibate flesh in a quickening motion that matched the movement of her hips, a pulsing growing stronger with each stroke. Waves of ecstasy throbbed through Veronica and she swallowed back cries of release. She did not want it to end—not now—not when she'd waited twenty years to rediscover a passion she thought was beyond her.

Kumi felt the tight walls pulse around his fingers, and without warning he withdrew his hand and positioned his rigid flesh at the entrance to her feminine sex. Guiding his maleness with one hand, he pushed slowly, registering Veronica's gasps against his ear.

"I'll try not to hurt you," he whispered softly, gentling her, while he gritted his teeth against the passion threatening to erupt before he entered her tight body. "Relax, baby, relax," he crooned over and over as each inch of his blood-engorged flesh disappeared into the throbbing folds squeezing him like a hand in a glove a size too small.

Veronica felt Kumi's hardness fill every inch of her body, reviving her passion all over again. He pushed gently, in and out, setting a strong thrusting rhythm she followed easily. She rose to meet his thrusts, her hips moving of their own accord, their bodies in perfect harmony with one another.

Her fingernails bit into the tight flesh over his hips as she once again felt the escalating throbbing searching and seeking a means of escape. She and Kumi had become man and woman, flesh against flesh. He'd become her lover and she his, and together they found the tempo that bound their bodies together.

If possible, Kumi felt his flesh swell and become harder, as he tried to absorb Veronica into himself. Her eager response matched his, while his hunger for her intensified. He wanted to lie in her scented embrace forever; lie between her thighs for a lifetime. He wanted her more than he'd ever wanted any woman he'd ever known.

Heat rippled under his skin, settling at the base of his spine. He knew it wasn't long before it would be over. It would take less than a minute for him to spill his passions into the latex sheath protecting the woman he loved from an unplanned pregnancy.

He withdrew from her, but seconds later he anchored her legs over his shoulders. He reentered her with a strong thrust, his gaze fixed on her glistening face. The memory of her expression would be branded in his mind for an eternity as he memorized the curve of her lush parted lips, fluttering eyelids and trembling breasts, as she was aroused to a peak of desire that swept away the fear that had haunted her for two decades.

Kumi quickened his cadence and within seconds he, too, closed his eyes, lowered his head and groaned deeply in his throat as the hot tide of passion swept through him, leaving an awesome, powerful and pulsing climax that radiated from his core.

He did not know where he found the strength, but he withdrew from her body and collapsed, facedown, beside her. Draping an arm over her belly, he kissed the side of her neck.

Veronica flashed a sated smile, but didn't open her eyes. "Kumi?" He moaned softly in response. "I love you." Her voice was soft, the admission reverent.

Raising his head, he stared at her profile. In a motion too quick to follow, he pulled her over his chest, her legs resting between his. Burying his nose in her hair, he kissed her scalp.

"Thank you, my darling."

They lay together, savoring the aftermath of their lovemaking and a love that filled both with a gentle peace that promised forever.

Veronica eased out of Kumi's loose grip on her body, slipping out of the bed. His soft snoring faltered, and then started up again. Grimacing, she made her way to the bathroom. She ached where she hadn't realized she had muscles.

Turning on a light in the bathroom, she closed the door softly behind her. Walking over to a black marble Jacuzzi, she pressed a dial, then brushed her teeth and rinsed her mouth before stepping into the warm swirling waters.

She lounged in the tub, the water caressing her tender flesh and unused muscles. Closing her eyes, Veronica smiled. Making love with Kumi had been an incredible experience. She thought she was going to faint when he'd put his face between her thighs.

"Would you mind if I come in and share your bath?"

Her eyes opened quickly. Kumi stood several feet away resplendently naked and magnificently male. He had the body of an ancient god sculpted by artisans in centuries past. She flashed a shy smile, sinking lower in the water to conceal her breasts.

"You're going to smell like me."

Moving closer to the oversize Jacuzzi, he stared at her, noticing the evidence of his lovemaking on her throat and along the tops of her breasts. "I already smell like you. The scent of your perfume is on my skin and the taste of you is in my mouth."

Veronica couldn't stop the wave of heat in her face as she glanced away demurely. "There're toothbrushes in the top right drawer of the dressing table."

Kumi smiled at her display of modesty. He had to remember Veronica hadn't shared her body with a man for twenty years despite the fact that she'd been married—a marriage that had been in name only.

Turning, he made his way to the dressing table and opened a drawer filled with an ample supply of toothbrushes and disposable razors. He brushed his teeth before joining Veronica in the warm water.

The black marble tub was large enough to accommodate four adults. The bathroom's ebony-and-platinum color scheme was modern and sophisticated.

Resting his arms along a ledge surrounding the Jacuzzi, he gave Veronica a penetrating stare. "Did I hurt you?"

She shook her head, limp strands of hair moving with the slight motion. "No."

The recessed ceiling lights slanted over her face, highlighting the gold in her skin and eyes. Kumi floated over to her, stood up and watched her face for a change in expression. He wanted to make love to her again; now that he'd had her he didn't think there would ever be a time when he wouldn't want to make love to her; he was certain he would want her even when he was old and gray.

Cradling her face between his palms, he eased her to her feet and pressed a kiss over each eye. "You are so incredibly beautiful, Ronnie. Beautiful and sexy."

Rising on tiptoe, she wound her smooth legs through his hair-roughened ones, making him her willing prisoner. Holding tightly to his neck, she kissed him tentatively as if sipping a cool drink.

"You make me feel sexy," she murmured, inhaling his mint-scented breath.

"No, baby, I have nothing to do with that. You *are* sexy."

His right hand moved down and cradled a breast, his head following. She gasped loudly when he took the nipple into his mouth and suckled her until she felt the pull in her womb.

She managed to free herself from his rapacious mouth, her body splayed over his. Both were breathing heavily. Waiting until her pulse slowed, she moved sinuously down his chest, her tongue sweeping over his breasts and suckling him as he had her. She moved even lower, her nose pressed against his thigh; then she registered his labored breathing as she took him into her mouth, his flaccid flesh hardening quickly.

"No, Ronnie!" His voice bounced off the walls, but

it was too late. Her magical tongue caressed the length, tip and the root of him like someone savoring an exquisite dessert.

His hands curled into tight fists as he resisted the urge to explode in her mouth. The muscles bulged in his neck, shoulders and biceps. He embarrassed himself with the moans of ecstasy escaping his compressed lips. Electric shocks shook him until he convulsed uncontrollably.

His right hand moved down, his fingers entwined in her hair, easing her head up as he spilled his seed into the swirling waters. His fingers loosened and she stood up, curled against his body, smiling.

"Now we're even," she whispered, "because the taste of you is in my mouth."

Curving a hand under her chin, he lowered his head and kissed her tenderly, his tongue meeting hers. He tasted himself on her lips, loving her even more for her selflessness.

Lifting her from the Jacuzzi, he carried her to the shower stall and together they frolicked under the flowing water like little children until it cooled and their fingers and toes wrinkled like raisins.

Half an hour later, Veronica, wrapped in a silky red robe, sat on a stool in the kitchen, watching Kumi prepare baked chicken breasts with mustard, tarragon, carrots and leeks over a serving of boiled egg noodles with an accompanying salad made with field greens.

They ate on the patio, listening to the latest Enya CD

with the flowing waters of the indoor waterfall providing the perfect backdrop to the soothing selections.

Both were content to listen to the music and enjoy the comfortable solitude. What had occurred between them earlier was still too new and shockingly sensual to absorb in only a few hours.

They cleared the table, cleaned up the kitchen, then hand in hand mounted the staircase to the bedroom. Veronica straightened the twisted sheets, while Kumi stood on the veranda staring out at the night. She was in bed when he returned to the bedroom, closing the French doors behind him.

She turned in to his embrace as if she'd been doing it for years instead of a few hours. He held her protectively until she fell asleep. Sleep did not come as easily for Kumi. Thoughts of when he would leave the States to return to Europe tortured him. For the past ten years he'd made Paris his home when he could've returned to Asheville, North Carolina. Before meeting Veronica Johnson he'd thought he would live out his life on European soil, but now he wasn't so certain.

Could he leave her? Would he return to France without her?

The questions attacked him until fatigue overtook him as he succumbed to a sleep filled with mental images of their erotic lovemaking.

Veronica came to know a different Kumi a week after they'd begun sleeping together. She'd heard the excitement in his voice when he spoke of owning and operating his own restaurant, his anxiety when he talked about returning to Paris and she also registered his pain when he revealed his strained relationship with his father.

Reaching for her hand, he threaded his fingers through hers. "How can a man reject his own flesh and blood because he refuses to follow his wishes?" he questioned.

Veronica stared up at the netting floating around the bed. Cool air filtered into the bedroom through the open French doors, and she snuggled closer to Kumi for warmth. "Because he's a control freak," she said softly, "and because he believes he knows what's best for you."

"That may have been okay when I was a child."

"Some parents never see their children as adults." Turning on her side, she smiled at him. "My mother still tries to tell me how to live my life. She doesn't like the fact that I live here alone, and she took to her bed for a month when I told her that I was marrying a man old enough to be my father."

"How do you deal with her?"

"I used to argue with her, but that got me nowhere, so now I just 'yes' her into silence. I've always been the renegade, while my younger sister has always conformed. She married a wonderful man and gave birth to two perfect children."

Releasing her hand, Kumi cradled his arm under his head. He gave Veronica a steady look. "What about you, Ronnie? Would you marry again?"

Running a finger down the middle of his furred chest, she shrugged a shoulder. "I doubt it."

His gaze widened, searching her face and reaching into her thoughts. "Would you consider marrying me?"

She wavered, trying to comprehend what she was hearing. "I don't know," she said honestly. And she didn't know. She loved Kumi, enjoyed sleeping with him, but hadn't given any thought to a permanent relationship because she knew he planned to return to France at the end of the summer.

Moving closer, he kissed her forehead. "At least you didn't say no."

"Are you proposing marriage?" she asked with a wide grin.

He hesitated, measuring her for a moment. He'd done it again—opened his mouth to say something before he'd thought it through. He did want to marry Veronica, even if she smiled at him as if he'd told her a joke.

"No," he said glibly. The tense moment passed when he reached for her and flipped her over on her back. "I want you to come with me to see my sister's place."

She lifted her eyebrows. "When?"

"Today."

Veronica shook her head. She wasn't ready to meet Kumi's family. "I don't think so."

"Please," he whispered, lowering his body over hers. "Don't make me beg, Ronnie."

She felt the crush of his muscular body bearing down on her slender frame. Bracing her hands against the solid wall of his chest, she closed her eyes. "You're going to have to do more than beg, sweetheart."

Burying his face against the side of her neck, he nipped at a spot under her ear. "What do you want?" Curving her arms around his neck, she whispered what she wanted him to do for her. Kumi threw back his head and laughed loudly. "Of course. You're so easy to please," he crooned sensuously.

Rolling off her body, he parted the netting, scooped her off the bed and carried her into the bathroom. She'd asked that he accompany her to her family reunion in August.

He would go to Atlanta with her, while she would finally get to meet Debbie. When his sister had questioned Kumi about not being able to reach him at his cottage one night, he'd smiled at her, saying he had been occupied elsewhere.

Debbie had followed him around, taunting him until he finally blurted out that he had a friend. Flashing a smug smile, she sweetly invited him and his *friend* to come to the B and B.

Deborah had let go of some of her anxiety that Maxwell's B and B wouldn't open on its projected date, after Kumi hired the third assistant chef. Only one of the three had more than six years' experience working in a full-service kitchen. The other two were recent culinary school graduates. Kumi had offered to act as executive chef if he hadn't hired one with more than ten years' experience by opening date. He was scheduled to meet with the new hires to plan dinner menus.

* * *

Veronica waited for Kumi to come around the Lexus and open the passenger-side door for her. She hadn't realized her pulse was racing until she saw a woman standing on the wraparound porch of a magnificent Victorian house, waving at Kumi.

Veronica had given special attention to her appearance. She blew out her hair, and then pinned it up off her neck in a chic chignon. Her dress was a simple sleeveless black silk sheath that barely skimmed the curves of her body, while Kumi had elected to wear a pair of black tailored linen gabardine slacks, jacket, and a banded collar white silk shirt. He looked incredibly handsome with his freshly shaven face and neatly brushed hair.

Veronica liked Kumi's sister on sight. She was tiny—barely five-two—and very pretty. Her delicate features, large dark eyes, and quick smile made her appear almost doll-like.

Arching eyebrows lifted in a face the color of rich cinnamon, she peered closely at Veronica. "Now I see why my brother needs a pager to monitor his whereabouts. You're absolutely gorgeous."

Veronica couldn't stop the flush darkening her cheeks. Pulling her hand from Kumi's loose grip, she extended it. "Thank you, Deborah. I'm Veronica Johnson."

Deborah shook her hand, smiling up at the taller woman. "My pleasure, Veronica. Please, come in." Still holding Veronica's hand, she pulled her into the large house.

Pushing his hands into the pockets of his slacks, Kumi followed the two women, a hint of a smile playing at the corners of his mouth. Bubbly, spontaneous Debbie could get the most uptight person to relax. She would be the perfect hostess for Maxwell's. His smile was still in place as he headed for the kitchen.

Veronica was awed by the interiors of the proposed bed-and-breakfast as Deborah led her in and out of every room on the first and second levels. Highly waxed bleached oak floors gleamed under the brilliance of chandeliers, windows framed in stained glass sparkled from bright sunlight and walls were graced with patterns of wallpaper made popular at the beginning of the last century.

Veronica ran her fingers over the smooth surface of a desk in the sitting room of one of the larger bedroom suites. "This piece is exquisite." There was no doubt it was an original.

Crossing her arms under her small breasts, Deborah gave Veronica a curious look. "You have a good eye for antiques." Veronica nodded, her fingers tracing the outline of one of the five leaf-and-scroll-carved cabriole legs ending in hairy paw feet.

Turning, she stared at Deborah. "And you have exquisite taste in decorating."

It was Deborah's turn to nod. "And you have wonderful taste in men."

Veronica lifted an eyebrow. "I assume you're talking about Kumi?"

"But of course."

"It doesn't bother you that I'm older than he is?"

"Does it bother my brother?"

"Not in the least."

"Then it's fine with me. I'm five years older than Kumi, and I had always assumed the responsibility of protecting him from my father. But then Kumi went away, and when he didn't come back after his tour with the Marine Corps I blamed myself.

"Dad was consumed with Kumi becoming a doctor because my two older brothers were better suited for careers in business. Larry is an actuary and Marvin is branch manager of a local bank. We all knew Kumi was gifted when he was able to read at three. Dad used to brag to his colleagues that his youngest son was able to solve mathematical and chemical equations in his head even before he entered high school.

"There's been a Dr. Walker in our family for three generations, so the responsibility fell on Kumi to continue the tradition. I'm certain he would've gone to medical school if Dad hadn't been so controlling.

"I kept saying I should've done more, said more." She shrugged a shoulder, exhaling audibly. "I beat myself up for years until Kumi made me realize that we can't change people, and if they don't change, then you accept them for who they are.

"Dad's not too old to change, it's just that he doesn't want to change." Dropping her gaze, Deborah bit down on her lower lip. "I know that I've been running off at the mouth. I said all that to say that if Kumi wants you in his life, then who am I to question his decision? He's never spoken or written to me about a woman before, therefore, you must be very special for him to introduce you to us."

Veronica flashed a warm smile. "I'm very fond of Kumi."

Deborah gave her a skeptical look. "Fond?"

"Yes, fond." She didn't know Deborah well enough to bare her soul to her. She had to know that she and Kumi were sleeping together, therefore, Veronica decided to let Deborah draw her own conclusions.

Deborah glanced at the watch on her wrist. They'd been gone for almost three quarters of an hour. She grinned mischievously. "Mom should be here now."

Veronica recoiled as if she'd been punched in the stomach. "Kumi didn't tell me he wanted me to meet his mother."

"He doesn't know I invited her. I wanted it to be a surprise."

"What about your father?"

"He went fishing with a few of his retired friends. He'll be away for at least three days."

Deborah clasped her hands together. "We'd better get back downstairs." She winked at Veronica. "Your *boyfriend* has offered to do the cooking."

She followed Deborah across a carpeted hallway and down a staircase with a solid oak banister and massive newel posts. She was certain Kumi would be surprised to see his mother, but Veronica wondered how Mrs. Walker would react when he introduced her to his *friend*.

Chapter Nine

Veronica walked into the dining room, her footsteps muffled in a thick forest-green carpet as she met Kumi's gaze over his mother's shoulder. His near-black eyes burned her face with their intensity. She stopped less than three feet away, her arching eyebrows lifting in a questioning expression. He had changed from his jacket and shirt into the white tunic favored by chefs. All he was missing was the *toque blanche* for his head.

Smiling, Kumi placed both hands on his mother's shoulders, turning her around. "Mother, I'd like you to meet a good friend of mine, Veronica Johnson. Ronnie, this is my mother, Mrs. Jeanette Walker."

Veronica successfully bit back a knowing smile when she registered the older woman's stunned expres-

sion. Walking forward, she offered her hand. "I'm honored, Mrs. Walker."

Jeanette placed a tiny manicured hand over her throat. Recovering quickly, she shook the proffered hand. "It's nice meeting you, Veronica. How long have you known my son?"

This time she did smile. Now she knew from whom Kumi had gotten his direct in-your-face attitude. "A month."

Jeanette glanced over her shoulder at her son, who stared down at her with a pair of large dark eyes that mirrored her own. "Oh, really...that long?" Her tone was soft *and* accusatory.

Curving an arm around Jeanette's narrow waist, he kissed the top of her head. "Come along, Mother." He winked at Deborah. "We can sit down to eat now."

Kumi extended his free hand to Veronica, leading her and Jeanette to the only table covered with a snowy-white linen cloth. Place settings for four were set with fine-bone china, monogrammed silver bearing a bold M, and crystal, along with bottles of white and red wine, as well as sparkling water. He seated his mother, Veronica and finally Deborah.

"Where's Orrin?" Jeanette asked Deborah after Kumi retreated to the kitchen. Deborah's husband was missing.

"He went to Waynesville to pick up several quilts I want to use as wall hangings." She glanced at her watch. "He called me from his truck about an hour ago,

saying he was going to stop and look at some vintage doorknobs at Hargan's Hardware."

Veronica studied Kumi's mother. She estimated Jeanette to be in her late sixties, but her natural beauty hadn't faded with age. And despite bearing four children, her body was still slender. Her naturally wavy stylishly coiffed short silver hair was elegant and sophisticated, her face a smooth red-brown, while her large dark eyes were bright, alert. It was only when she smiled that attractive lines were visible around those penetrating eyes.

Jeanette cocked her head and smiled at Veronica, who returned it with a warm one of her own. She was more than curious about the woman whom Jerome had invited to meet his family. It was apparent she was older than her son, but what she had to reluctantly admit to herself was that Veronica Johnson was perfectly turned out: from her sleek hairstyle, subtly applied makeup to her choice of attire. Her musings were interrupted when her son returned, balancing a large tray on his left shoulder.

"I've sampled everything Kumi's prepared thus far," Deborah announced proudly.

"What are we eating, Jerome?" Jeanette asked.

He placed several serving dishes on the table. "You have a choice between *noisettes d'Agneau, coquilles St. Jacques* or *entrecôte Bercy.* The salad is *salade frisée aux lardons.*"

"Everything looks delicious, but will you kindly translate what you just said, Jerome?"

Placing the tray on a nearby table, Kumi sat down opposite Veronica. "Ronnie, will you please translate for my mother and sister what I just said."

She smiled and said, "We have lamb cutlets sautéed in butter and served with mushrooms and an herb-and-garlic butter." She pointed to another dish. "These are sea scallops cooked in a little butter. Their orange tails, containing edible roe, are delicious. Over here is rib steak cooked in a white wine sauce. And of course the salad, which is made up of endive with diced fried bacon."

There was a stunned silence until Deborah asked, "You speak French?"

Veronica smiled across the table at her lover. "Not as well as your brother, but I manage to get by."

"Don't be so modest, sweetheart," Kumi crooned. "You speak it beautifully." The endearment had slipped out so smoothly that he hadn't realized its import until he saw Jeanette's startled look.

Picking up her napkin, Jeanette placed it on her lap, while staring at her son under her lashes. Seconds later she redirected her penetrating gaze on Veronica. She hadn't missed the sensual exchange when they shared a secret smile. It was a look she was familiar with—one she'd shared with Lawrence Walker more than forty years ago.

She didn't know who this Veronica Johnson was and where she'd come from. But it was apparent she made Jerome happy. And that's all she'd ever wanted for her brilliant son since he was a child—peace and happiness.

* * *

The soft sound of music from a mini stereo system in the sitting room and flickering votives on a table created a magical backdrop for the two lovers sharing the king-size bed.

Veronica lay in Kumi's protective embrace, her back pressed to his chest. She placed her hands over the larger pair resting over her belly.

"Your mother is very charming," she said in a quiet voice.

Kumi chuckled, the sound rumbling deep in his wide chest. "My mother is a snob."

Tilting her chin, she glanced up at him over her shoulder. "How can you say that? I thought you loved your mother."

"I do love her, but I can say that because I know Jeanette Walker née Tillman. It was you who charmed her. You said all of the right things, but more than that you exemplify what she considers a proper young woman. The way you styled your hair, your dress and jewelry were perfect in her eyes. You're educated, well traveled and speak more than one language. All that aside, you're stunningly beautiful, so what is there not to like?"

Turning over, Veronica pressed her naked breasts to his chest. She couldn't quite make out his expression in the darkened bedroom. The afternoon she'd spent with Kumi's mother and sister was perfect. They'd sampled the dishes Kumi had prepared, finding each one more delicious than the other. Orrin Maxwell arrived a quar-

ter of an hour after they'd sat down to dine. He quickly showered, changed his clothes and joined them in the dining room.

Veronica had liked Orrin immediately. He was friendly and unpretentious. He was a tall, light-skinned slender man who was eight years older than his wife. She'd noticed he was still quite formal with his mother-in-law even though he and Deborah had recently celebrated their twelfth wedding anniversary.

"Are you saying I passed inspection?"

Kumi's fingers tightened slightly on her shoulders, pulling her up until her face was level with his. "It wouldn't have mattered what my mother thought of you, because you're the one I love. The day I left home for the Marine Corps I stopped seeking my parents' approval. All that matters is what—"

Veronica's explosive kiss stopped his words as her tongue plundered the moist recesses of his mouth. Everything that was Jerome Kumi Walker seeped into her, and she writhed against him like a cat in heat.

Her hands were as busy as her mouth, sweeping over his chest, down his arms and to his muscled thighs. Raising her hips slightly, she searched for and cradled him in her hand. He hardened quickly with the stroking motion. Flipping her quickly onto her back, he entered her without his usually prolonged session of foreplay.

The outside world ceased to exist as they used every inch of the bed, each drawing from the other what they'd never given another living, breathing person. Kumi withdrew from her moist heat long enough to

kiss every inch of her velvety body from her head to her feet.

Veronica reciprocated, her rapacious tongue wringing deep moans from Kumi as she took all of him into her mouth. His head thrashed from side to side while he gripped the sheets, pulling them from their fastenings. It all ended as she slid up the length of his moist body, rubbing her distended nipples against his chest while kissing him fully on the mouth. Then she straddled him, his hands cupping the fullness of her buttocks, and established a rhythm that he matched stroke for stroke. He rose to meet her, she taking every inch of him into her body as she rode out the storm sweeping over them.

"Yes, Kumi. Oh, yes," she chanted over and over, her husky approval drowning out the soft strains of music. Their breathing quickened, and Veronica did not know where she began or where he ended. She was transported to another time and place as she surrendered to the hard pulsing flesh sliding in and out between her thighs.

Kumi was offering her what Bram had given her— love and protection. But then he'd given her something her much older husband wasn't able to elicit—sexual fulfillment.

Burying her face against the column of his strong neck, she closed her eyes and melted all over him as he climaxed, his body convulsing violently as he left his hot seed buried deep in her womb.

Kumi stroked Veronica's damp hair as he lay, eyes

closed, completely awed by the display of raw, uninhibited sensuality he'd just shared with the woman in his embrace.

He loved her, more than his own life. He felt hot tears burn the backs of his eyelids. He couldn't leave her. Not now, because he knew he could not return to Paris without her.

Before meeting Veronica Johnson he knew exactly what he wanted and where he wanted to be, but all of that had changed the moment he shared her bed.

He opened his eyes, determination shining from their obsidian depths. A confident smile tilted the corners of his strong male mouth as he made a silent vow that Veronica would become a part of his life, whether in the States or in Europe.

The weeks sped by quickly with Kumi caught up in a surreal world of complete enchantment and fulfillment. He spent every night at Veronica's house, leaving by eight the following morning, but only after they'd shared breakfast.

He had finally hired an experienced chef for Maxwell's. He conducted six-hour, four-day-a-week cooking classes for the three men and one woman, checking and rechecking their efforts when they prepared the classic French dishes he had decided to serve the inn's guests. He'd also set up accounts with green grocers, butchers and vendors who sold the finest wines, cordials, imported cheeses and olive oil.

Veronica had accompanied him when he drove to

New Orleans to confer with a fishing establishment who had built their impeccable reputation on shipping freshly caught seafood overnight to restaurants along the East Coast.

They spent two nights in New Orleans, taking in the sights and sampling the dishes that had made the city famous for its gastronomical opulence. The sweltering heat and oppressive humidity did not dampen Veronica's enthusiasm as they stayed up well into the night, visiting several of the popular jazz clubs. They'd returned to North Carolina exhausted and a few pounds heavier.

Maxwell's opened for business mid-July. The event was announced in the local newspapers, and Asheville's mayor and several high-ranking members of his inner circle attended the celebration along with the ubiquitous reporters and photographers. Deborah had managed to get several photographs and a brief article about Maxwell's unique decorating style featured in the latest issue of *Country Inns*.

A restaurant critic had declared the food, service and ambience exquisite, recommending dining at Maxwell's B and B as an experience "not to be missed during one's lifetime."

During the day Kumi smiled when he didn't want to because Veronica, pleading a headache, had stayed home. At first he believed her, but as the night wore on, a nagging voice in the back of his head whispered that she'd elected to stay away because the event had

become a family affair. Lawrence and Jeanette Walker, their sons, daughters-in-law and grandchildren had all turned out to support and celebrate Orrin and Deborah Maxwell's new business venture.

Kumi was reunited with two nieces and three nephews who had been toddlers and preschoolers when he'd entered the marines. His youngest nephew, a handsome thirteen-year-old, hadn't been born at the time.

He gave them a tour of the kitchen, making certain they stayed out of the way of the chefs, who were chopping, sautéeing, stirring and expertly preparing dishes that were not only pleasing to the palate but also to the eye.

Marvin Walker's sixteen-year-old daughter, transfixed by the activity in the large kitchen, caught the sleeve of Kumi's tunic. "Uncle Kumi," she said tentatively, "can you teach me to cook like they do?"

Curving an arm around her shoulders, he smiled down at the expectant expression on her youthful face. She was a very attractive young woman who had inherited her mother's delicate beauty.

"You're going to have to ask your parents if they'll let you come visit me in Paris."

Biting down on her lower lip, she shook her head. "They won't let me drive to the mall by myself, so I know going abroad is out."

"Maybe in two years when you've graduated high school, you can come visit me for the summer before you go to college."

"Really?"

He nodded, smiling broadly. "Really."

She hugged him, surprising Kumi with her impulsiveness. Marlena hadn't celebrated her second birthday the last time he saw her, but she had always been special to him. It was with her birth that he'd become an uncle for the first time.

Turning on his heel, he made his way to a room off the kitchen the staff used as their dressing room. He changed out of the white tunic and checkered pants and into a black silk V-neck pullover and a pair of black slacks. The color emphasized the slimness of his waist and hips, but could not disguise the depth of his solid chest or broad shoulders. At thirty-two he was physically in the best shape he'd ever been in his life. He was stronger and more mentally balanced than he'd been even after he'd completed the Marine Corps' rigorous basic training at Parris Island, South Carolina.

He walked through the spacious lobby of the bed-and-breakfast, coming face-to-face with his father. When he attempted to step around the tall man with slightly stooping shoulders, he felt his egress thwarted.

"Excuse me, please." He was surprised that his voice was so calm when all he wanted to do was brush past the older man as if he were a stranger.

Lawrence Walker placed a heavily veined hand on his son's arm. "I'd like a word with you, Jerome."

Kumi froze, staring at the hand resting on his arm—a hand that had comforted sick patients for forty years until Lawrence's retirement earlier that year, a hand that had caressed his forehead whenever he was

sick and a hand that had patted his head in approval whenever he brought home an exam with a perfect score.

"You want to talk *now?*" A frown creased his high, smooth forehead at the same time he shook his head. "Sorry, I'm on my way out."

Lawrence's grip tightened. "Please, Jerome, hear me out."

There was a pleading in his father's voice Kumi had never heard before. Proud, arrogant Dr. Lawrence Walker asking permission to be heard was something he never thought he would witness in his lifetime.

Giving his father a long, penetrating stare, he motioned with his head. "We can sit over there."

Lawrence dropped his hand and walked slowly over to a pair of facing club chairs covered in a soft beige watered silk fabric, Kumi following. He sat down, his shoulders appearing more stooped than usual.

Kumi sat, staring intently at his father, and for the first time in fourteen years he realized that the man before him wasn't aging well. An even six feet in height, his taupe-colored skin was dotted with age spots that resembled flecks of dark brown paint. His once-coarse dark hair was now sparse, completely white, and his green-gray eyes were no longer bright and penetrating. Lawrence was only sixty-nine, the same age as his wife, but looked years older.

Crossing one leg over the other knee, Kumi folded his arms over his chest, waiting for his father to speak.

Tense seconds turned into a full minute. "What do you want to talk about?" he asked through clenched teeth.

Closing his eyes, Lawrence pressed his head to the chair's back. "I want to thank you for helping Deborah."

"I don't need you to thank me. Debbie did that already."

Lawrence opened his eyes, fire gleaming from their depths. "Dammit, Jerome, don't make this harder for me than it needs to be."

Dropping his arms, Kumi splayed long fingers over the chair's armrests. "You? Why is it always about you, Dad?"

"It's not about me—not this time." Lawrence flashed a tired smile. "It's about you, son. You and me."

A muscle twitched in Kumi's jaw. "What about us?"

He wasn't going to make it easy for his father because it had never been easy for him. The alienation had nearly destroyed him—an alienation that had spread to his older brothers who had always sought their father's approval. Only his mother and sister challenged Lawrence Walker, and had successfully escaped his wrath.

"I can't turn back the clock," Lawrence began slowly, "but I'm willing to begin anew—tonight." He extended his right hand. "I'm sorry."

Kumi stared at the hand as if it were a venomous reptile. He stared at it so long, he expected the older man to withdraw his peace offer. But he didn't.

Reluctantly, Kumi placed his hand in his father's, pulling him gently to his feet. He wrapped his arms

around his body, registering the frailty in the slender frame.

"It's okay, Dad," he said close to his ear. Then he kissed his cheek, unaware of the tears filling Lawrence's eyes.

Taking a deep breath, Lawrence smiled, easing out of his son's comforting embrace. He reached into a pocket of his trousers and pulled out a handkerchief, wiping away the tears before they stained his face.

"Your mother said you've met someone who's very special to you."

Kumi nodded, smiling. "Yes, I have."

Lawrence's smile matched Kumi's. "Why don't you bring her with you when you come for Sunday dinner? We're having a cookout."

"I didn't know I was invited for Sunday dinner," he countered.

"Well, you are. And so is your lady."

"Are you asking or ordering me to come?"

A sheepish expression softened the harsh lines in Lawrence's face. "I'm asking, Jerome."

Kumi inclined his head. "I'll have to ask Veronica if she's free on Sunday."

Standing up straighter, Lawrence pulled back his shoulders and stared at his youngest child. "I know you haven't heard me say this in a very long time, but I'm very proud of you, son."

The beginnings of a smile touched Kumi's mouth before becoming a wide grin. "Thank you, Dad."

Lawrence nodded. "You're welcome, Jerome."

* * *

Kumi drove up Trace Road, feeling as if he'd been reborn. The single headlight from the bike lit up the darkened countryside, matching the brilliance of the full moon overhead. Tonight there were no shadows across the clear summer nighttime sky, or in his heart.

He parked the Harley alongside the house and removed his helmet. Tucking it under his arm, he walked to the front door and rang the bell.

Veronica was slow in answering the bell, but when he saw her face he knew she hadn't lied to him. Her eyes were red and puffy as if she'd been crying.

He stepped into the entry, placed his helmet on the floor and then swept her up in his arms. Shifting her in his embrace, he closed and locked the door before heading for the staircase.

"How are you feeling?"

She moaned softly. "A little better."

He dropped a kiss on the top of her silver hair. "Your head still hurts?"

"Not anymore. It's now my back and legs."

"Do you want me to call a doctor?"

"No. It'll pass in a couple of days."

Walking into her bedroom, he stared at her as she closed her eyes. "You've gone through this before?"

"It usually hits me several times a year. It's PMS."

"What is it?"

"Premenstrual syndrome. Headache, bloating, backache, sore breasts and on occasion temporary insanity."

He placed her on the bed, sinking down to the mat-

tress beside her. "Do you want me to fix you something to eat or drink?"

"I've been drinking mint tea."

He kissed her gently on her lips. "Have you eaten?"

She started to shake her head, but thought better of it. "I'm not hungry. How was Maxwell's grand opening?" She'd smoothly changed the subject.

"Wonderful. Everything went off without a hitch. By the way, my father invited us to Sunday dinner."

Veronica opened her eyes. "You spoke to your father?"

"He spoke to me."

"Does this mean you've declared a truce?"

He ran his finger down the length of her nose. "It only means we're talking to each other."

"That's a start."

"That it is," he confirmed, kissing her again. "Do you want me to stay with you tonight?"

"Yes."

"Do you want more tea?"

"Yes, please."

Pushing off the bed, he smiled at the dreamy expression on her face. "Don't run away. I'll bring you your tea."

Kumi didn't want her to run away, and she didn't want him to go away. But he was going to go away in another eight weeks. He was scheduled to return to Paris September 19—exactly ten days before she celebrated her forty-third birthday.

Closing her eyes, she did what she hadn't done in

months—she prayed. Prayed for an answer because she loved Kumi Walker. She began and ended her day in his arms. He'd given her everything she needed as a woman and even more that she hadn't known she needed.

She was astonished at the sense of fulfillment she felt whenever they were together, and the harder she tried to ignore the truth, the more it persisted: she wanted Kumi in her life beyond the summer. She wanted him for all the summers, springs and seasons in between until she drew her last breath.

Chapter Ten

Kumi's right arm curved around Veronica's waist, leading her around to the back of the imposing Regency-style pale pink limestone structure where he'd spent the first eighteen years of his life. The fingers of his left hand tightened on the handle of a large container of chocolate cream-filled petits fours, coated with dark and light couverture and an exquisite truffle torte filled with a light chocolate cream.

All or most of the Walkers were extreme chocoholics, and he'd decided to fulfill their dessert fantasies with his contributions to what had become the traditional Sunday afternoon cookout.

His parents had been cooking outdoors on Sunday afternoons whenever the weather permitted for as long as he could remember. Unlike many Southern black

families who sat down together for dinner after church services ended, Jeanette and her husband preferred the more informal approach. The only exception had been inclement weather or if his parents had invited guests to share their roof and table with their four children.

He'd gotten up an hour before sunrise, kissing a still-sleeping Veronica, and had returned to his cottage where he'd showered, changed his clothes and then had headed for Maxwell's. By the time the daytime chef had arrived to begin the task of preparing breakfast for the guests at the bed-and-breakfast, he'd finished the petits fours and had been pressing the chocolate flakes to the sides of the cream-filled torte.

Assisting the chef, Kumi had chopped the ingredients needed for omelets, and had rolled out several trays of what would become fluffy biscuits. The chef, one of two recent culinary school graduates, was talented and creative.

They'd spent more than an hour discussing cooking techniques, and before leaving to return to check on Veronica, Kumi had left a note for the pastry chef to include an assortment of chocolate candies for the dessert menu. The suggestions had included cognac balls, kirsch rolls, croquant peaks and the ever-popular chocolate truffles. Preparing the chocolate and inhaling its aroma of chocolate had triggered his craving for what had been referred to as "food of the gods."

Veronica now heard the sounds of laughter and raised voices before she saw Kumi's immediate family. The PMS had eased with the onset of her menses. She

hadn't thought she would be so thrilled by the obvious sign when she'd left her bed earlier that morning; a lingering fear had gripped her after she and Kumi had made love without protection the day she'd shared lunch with Jeanette and Deborah at Maxwell's.

At forty-two I'm much too old to think about having a baby. Her declaration to her sister had haunted her once she'd realized the recklessness of her actions. She loved Kumi, but she wasn't certain she loved him enough to bear his child.

Sixteen-year-old Marlena Walker spied her uncle first. "Uncle Kumi's here," she announced in a loud voice.

A petite slender woman, an older version of the teenage girl, shifted on her webbed lounger, frowning. "Marlena Denise Walker, please. It's not becoming for a young lady to scream like that."

Marlena's smile faded quickly and she rolled her eyes upward. "Give it a rest, Mom," she said under her breath.

Bending slightly, Kumi kissed his niece's cheek. "Chill," he warned softly. Glancing at Veronica's composed expression, he silently admired her flawless skin. She had forgone makeup with the exception of lipstick. She'd brushed her hair back, securing it in a ponytail. She was appropriately dressed for the occasion: a pair of black linen slacks, matching ballet-slipper shoes and a sleeveless white cotton blouse that revealed her toned upper arms.

"Veronica, this little minx is my niece Marlena. Marlena, I'd like for you to meet Miss Veronica Johnson."

Marlena smiled. "Nice meeting you. You're very pretty. I like your hair color." The words rushed out like a run-on sentence.

Veronica returned the friendly open smile. "It's a pleasure to meet you, Marlena. And thank you for your compliment."

"Well, it's true," the teenager insisted.

Kumi handed her the large container. "Please take this into the house and refrigerate it for me, princess. Don't tilt it," he warned softly.

"I bet it's chocolate."

"And don't open it," Kumi called after her as she turned and retreated to the house.

Over the next quarter of an hour Veronica was introduced to Dr. Lawrence and Jeanette Walker's children and grandchildren. Kumi's older brothers—Lawrence, Jr., whom everyone called Larry, and Marvin, were exact physical replicas of their father. Both were tall, slender and had inherited the older man's complexion, eye coloring and slightly stooped shoulders. Their collective offspring of four boys and two girls had compromised—the boys resembling their fathers and the girls their mothers. Both of Kumi's sisters-in-law were petite women with delicate features. She found everyone friendly, but curious, judging by surreptitious glances whenever her gaze was elsewhere.

Veronica sat on a webbed lounge chair, staring at

Kumi through the lenses of the dark glasses she'd placed on her nose to shield her eyes from the harmful rays of the hot summer sun, while taking furtive sips of an icy lemon-lime concoction through a straw. Kumi wore a pair of khaki walking shorts with a navy blue tank top. His youngest nephew had stopped him, pointing to the small tattoo on his left bicep. She smiled when he translated the two words that made up the Latin motto of the United States Marine Corps: *Semper Fidelis—Always Faithful.*

His eyes widened as his gaze went from the tattoo to his uncle's smiling face. "Mama," he said loudly. "I want a tattoo like Uncle Kumi."

Marvin's wife glared at her son, then turned to her husband. "I think you'd better talk to that child or he won't be around for his fourteenth birthday."

Marvin, who had assumed the responsibility for grilling meats, waved to his youngest child. "Come here, Sean. Kumi, please take over while I have a heart-to-heart with my son."

Larry patted Kumi's back. "Go to it, brother. I don't know why Marvin thinks he can cook, but every once in a while we humor him and let him think he's doing something."

"I heard that," Marvin called out.

"Good," Larry countered. "Now that Kumi's here, we really don't need your *expertise.*"

The eating and drinking continued well into the afternoon and early evening. Veronica sat at a long wooden table with all the Walkers, enjoying their camaraderie. There was an underlying formality about them, as if they feared letting go of their inhibitions. It was if they had to be careful of how others viewed them. Then, she remembered Kumi telling her that his mother was a snob. Having the right family pedigree was very important to Jeanette; however, it appeared as if some of her grandchildren exhibited streaks of rebellion—a trait that was so apparent in Jerome Kumi Walker.

There was a lull in conversation as everyone concentrated on eating mounds of meats, vegetables and salads set out in serving platters. Veronica had sampled Jeanette's delicious potato salad, declaring it one of the best she'd ever eaten. Kumi, assuming the grilling duties from Marvin, grilled rock lobster tail with a red chili butter dipping sauce, swordfish, chicken, butterflied lamb and filet mignon with a brandy-peppercorn sauce.

Marlena wiped her hands and mouth, then said, "I think I want to become a chef."

Her mother's jaw dropped. "I thought you wanted to become a lawyer."

"I've changed my mind. You know I love to cook."

"We'll talk about it later," Marvin said, smiling.

"Really, Daddy?"

"Really, princess," he confirmed, ignoring his wife's scowl.

Leaning closer to Kumi, her bare shoulder touching his, Veronica whispered for his ears only, "I think you're responsible for spawning the next generation of insurgents."

Turning his head, he smiled down at her. "I believe you're right," he said softly. "Tattoos and cooking instead of medicine and law. What are the Walkers coming to?"

She smiled and wrinkled her nose. "What would you do if your son decided he wanted to become a ballet dancer?"

Lowering his head, his mouth grazed her earlobe. "Have my son and you'll find out."

Veronica stared at Kumi as if he'd touched her bare flesh with an electrified rod. He wanted her to have a baby—his child. He wanted a child, but it was he who had always assumed the responsibility of protecting her whenever they made love—all except the one time she had initiated the act. The one time she hadn't been able to hold back—the one time she'd risked becoming pregnant because it had been her most fertile time during her menstrual cycle. But her menses had come on schedule, belaying her anxiety that she might be carrying his child.

"That's not going to become a reality."

Kumi recoiled as if she'd slapped him. He stood up, stepping over the wooden bench, while at the same time anchoring a hand under Veronica's shoulder and gently pulling her up.

"Please excuse us," he said to the assembled group staring mutely at them. "I have to talk to Veronica."

If there was ever a time she wanted to scream at him,

it was now. Whatever he wanted to talk to her about could have waited until they returned home.

Kumi led Veronica across the spacious backyard and into the flower garden. Sitting down on a stone bench, he eased her down beside him, his arm circling her waist.

Unconsciously, she rested her head against his shoulder. "What do you want to talk about that couldn't be discussed at another time?"

"Us."

"What about us?"

There was slight pause before Kumi spoke again. "I love you, Ronnie, and you love me. But where are we going with this? Our feelings for each other?"

Raising her head, she stared at his composed expression. "What is it you want from me?"

"I want you to marry me, Veronica Johnson. I want you to become my wife and the mother of my children," he said smoothly, with no expression on his face.

"I'm too old to have children—"

"Then *one* child!" he snapped angrily, interrupting her.

A slight frown marred her smooth forehead. "There's no need to take that tone with me, Kumi." Her father had never raised his voice to her, and she would not tolerate the same from any man.

His shoulders slumped. "I'm sorry, Ronnie." His voice was softer, apologetic. "Wanting you in my life permanently is eating me up inside. I think I'm losing my mind."

Closing her eyes, she bit down hard on her lower lip. Kumi was offering her what every normal woman wanted—a man who loved her enough to offer marriage and children. He wanted to marry her when too many men were willing to sleep with or live with a woman without committing to a future with them.

She opened her eyes, forcing a smile she did not feel. "Will you give me time to consider your proposal?"

An irresistibly devastating grin softened his stoic expression. Shifting, he picked her up, settling her across his lap. "Of course, sweetheart." He curbed the urge to pull her down to the grass and make love to her.

When he'd returned to her house earlier that morning she'd given him the news that she wasn't pregnant, and it wasn't until after he'd recalled the time they'd made love and he hadn't protected her that he understood her revelation. He wanted Veronica to have his child, but only after she committed to sharing her life with him.

Cradling her face between his palms, his lips brushed against hers as he spoke. "Thank you for even considering me."

Veronica felt his lips touch hers like a whisper. "You honor me with your proposal."

"No," he argued softly. "I'm honored that you've permitted me to become a part of your existence." *Even if it is only temporary,* he added silently. There was still the remotest possibility that she would reject him. And what he had to do was prepare himself for that time, because it was just six weeks before he was to return to Paris either with or without Veronica Johnson.

* * *

"Make a left at the next corner."

Kumi followed Veronica's directions, after they'd left a security gatehouse in a private community, overwhelmed by the magnificence of the structures situated five miles north of downtown Atlanta, spreading outward from the nexus of Peachtree Street, Roswell and West Paces Ferry Roads. He'd visited Atlanta the year before he'd applied to Morehouse College, but he hadn't been to Georgia's capital city's wealthiest neighborhood.

He'd agreed to accompany Veronica to her family reunion, committing to spend a week with her before returning to North Carolina. He'd also agreed to drive her Lexus back to North Carolina, because she had planned to fly back a week later. He maneuvered around the corner she indicated, his gaze widening as he encountered a cul-de-sac. Four large, imposing Colonial-style structures were set on the dead-end street, each a gleaming white in the brilliant Atlanta summer sun.

"I'm the first one on the right."

Kumi stared numbly through the windshield. A sloping sculpted lawn, precisely cut hedges, a quartet of towering trees and thick flowering shrubs provided the perfect reception for the place Veronica and Bram had called home.

Veronica reached under the visor and pushed a button on an automatic garage opener. The door to a three-car garage slid open silently. Kumi drove into the garage next to a Volkswagen Passat and turned off the engine, while she removed another small device from her purse and pressed several buttons, deactivating a sophisticated alarm system.

Kumi got out of the truck, coming around to open the passenger-side door for Veronica. She smiled at him when he curved an arm around her waist and helped her down.

"It's going to take at least an hour to cool the place to where it's comfortable."

He nodded. It was as if the words were stuck in his throat. It was as if he were seeing Veronica for the first time. He hadn't even seen the interior of this house, but he knew instinctively that it would be nothing like the one on Trace Road. That one was modest while this one quietly shouted opulence. He did not have to read a real estate listing to know that the homes in the cul-de-sac were probably appraised for a million or more.

Veronica opened a side door, leading into the house, while he lingered to retrieve his luggage from the cargo area. He followed her into the house, mounting three steps and walking into a spacious kitchen. He didn't know what to expect, but he went completely still, staring at a kitchen that could've been in any French farmhouse. A massive cast-iron stove from another era took up half a wall.

He walked numbly through the kitchen and into a hallway that led in four directions. Antique tables, chairs and priceless lamps were displayed for the admiring eye. Shifting his luggage, Kumi ambled around the downstairs, peering into a living and dining room decorated in the recurring country French design. A smile crinkled his eyes. It was apparent Veronica hadn't let go her love for France as evidenced by her home's furnishings. He made his way up a flight of stairs, feeling the cool air flowing from baseboard and ceiling vents.

"I'm in here," Veronica called out from a room near the top of the carpeted staircase.

He entered a large bedroom boasting a queen-size mahogany sleigh bed. All of the furnishings in the room were white: a counterpane with feathery lace, a nest of piled high gossamer pillows, embroidered sheers at the tall windows and the cutwork cloths covering the two bedside tables.

Staring at her smiling face, Kumi felt a fist of fear knot up his chest. Veronica's home and its furnishings were priceless. And if she married him, would she be willing to leave it all behind?

Veronica smiled up a Kumi as they made their way up the path to Bette Hall's house. They had to park on a side street because of the number of cars and trucks lining the Halls' circular driveway. Veronica's and Kumi's arms were filled with desserts they'd made earlier that morning. She'd baked two sour-cream pound cakes and a sweet potato pie. Kumi had put his professional touches on a *gâteau des rois,* a marzipan-filled puff French pastry that was served on the final feast of Christmas—Twelfth Night—to mark the arrival of the

Three Kings to Bethlehem, and a traditional American chocolate pecan pie.

The screen door opened with their approach and Veronica came face-to-face with her sister and brother-in-law, who had just arrived. The spacious entryway and living room were filled with people of varying ages. Infants in their parents' arms cried and squirmed; toddlers were scampering about, seeing what mischief they could get into; teenagers with earphones from disc players and portable tape players gyrated to the music blasting in their ears.

Candace's gaze lingered briefly on Kumi before she turned her attention to Veronica. Curving an arm around her neck, she kissed her cheek. "Hey, big sis. Who is *he?*" she whispered sotto voce.

A mysterious smile touched Kumi's mouth. There was no doubt Veronica would be asked the same question over and over before the day ended.

"Kumi, this is my sister, Candace, and brother-in-law Ivan Yarborough. Candace, Ivan, Kumi Walker."

Kumi flashed his hundred-watt smile, charming Candace immediately. "My pleasure."

"Oh, no," Candace crooned, "It's *my* pleasure."

Ivan and Kumi nodded to each other, exchanging polite greetings as Candace and Veronica carried the desserts into the kitchen where every inch of counter space and tables were with filled platters and pots emanating mouthwatering aromas.

Half a dozen fried turkeys, hundreds of pounds of fried chicken and countless slabs of spareribs were transported from the kitchen to the backyard by relatives Veronica hadn't seen in a year. Candace clutched her arm, pulling her out of the path of people coming and going in the large kitchen.

"He's gorgeous. Where on earth did you find him?"

Veronica stared at Candace, baffled. "What are you talking about?"

"Kumi. That is his name, isn't it?"

"Yes. Why?"

Candace shook her head. "What am I going to do with you? I can't believe you brought your man to a family reunion where every woman from eight to eighty will be drooling, analyzing and dissecting him within the first five minutes of his arrival. And you know how Aunt Bette likes young men."

"Kumi will be able to take care of himself."

"It looks as if he's been taking good care of you, Veronica."

Heat stole into her face, burning her cheeks and for once she did not have a comeback. "Let's go outside," she said instead.

Bette Hall's house was built on five acres of land, most of which had remained undeveloped. She'd had a landscaping company cut the grass, and she'd set up eight tents to accommodate the eighty-three family members who were confirmed to attend the annual gathering.

The weather had cooperated. The early afternoon temperature was in the low eighties, and a light breeze offset the intense heat from the sun in a near cloud-less sky.

Veronica was handed an oversize T-shirt with Ward-law Family Reunion inscribed on the back, along with the date. She slipped it on over her shorts and tank top, the hem coming to her knees.

Reaching for a pair of sunglasses from the small cro-cheted purse slung over her chest, she put them on the bridge of her nose. She waved to a cousin who'd trav-eled from Ohio, before moving around the grounds to find her parents. She found them in a tent with several other older couples.

She kissed her mother, then her father. "I have some-one I'd like you to meet," she said mysteriously.

"Who?" Irma asked, smiling.

"Don't move."

Veronica left the tent, searching for Kumi. She spied him with Aunt Bette's teenage granddaughter. It was obvious the scantily dressed young woman was openly flirting with him, despite his impassive expression.

"Excuse me, Chantel, but I'd like to borrow Kumi for a few minutes."

Chantel Hall's jaw dropped when Veronica curved her arm through Kumi's and led him away. She was still standing with her mouth open when an older cousin came over to her.

Chantel sucked her teeth while rolling her head on her neck. "Isn't he too young for her?"

"Don't be catty, cuz. If he can drive, vote, buy cigarettes, liquor, serve in the military and not be drinking Similac or wearing Pampers, then he's not too young."

Chantel sucked her teeth again, rolled her eyes and walked away with an exaggerated sway of her generous hips.

Veronica led Kumi into the tent where her parents sat on folding chairs, drinking iced tea. All conversations ended abruptly at the same time all gazes were trained on the tall man with Veronica Johnson-Hamlin.

"Mother, Daddy—" her voice was low and composed "—I'd like you to meet a very good friend, Kumi Walker. Kumi, my parents, Harold and Irma Johnson."

Leaning over, Kumi smiled at Irma, who stared up at him as if he had a horn growing out the center of his forehead. The spell was broken when she returned his sensual smile.

"I'm so glad you came with Veronica."

His smile widened appreciably. "So am I, Mrs. Johnson." He extended his hand to Veronica's father, who rose to his feet and grasped his fingers in a strong grip.

"Nice meeting you, Kumi."

Everyone stared at Veronica in suspended anticipation. She ended the suspense, saying, "This is Kumi Walker. Kumi, these wonderful people are my aunts and uncles."

There was a chorus of mixed greetings before several put their heads together and whispered about their niece's choice in male companionship.

It was something Veronica overhead many more times before night descended on the assembled. Most of the younger women whispered about how "hot" and "fine" he was, but the older ones shook their heads claiming Veronica had gone from one extreme to the other. First she'd taken up with an old man, and now a young boy. Poor Irma must be so embarrassed.

Dusk came, taking with it the heat, while the volume of music escalated. The hired deejay played the latest number-one hip-hop tune and couples jumped up to dance.

Veronica sat on the grass, supporting her back against a tree, watching her extended family enjoying themselves while Kumi lay on the grass beside her, eyes closed.

She stared at him. "Don't go to sleep on me, darling. I'll never be able to move you."

He smiled, not opening his eyes. "I'm just resting. I think I ate too much."

"You're not the only one."

"I like your family, Ronnie. They're a lot less uptight than mine."

"That's because we have a few scalawags and riff-raff who managed to sneak in under the guise that they were respectable ladies and gentlemen. Personally, I think it's good because they add a lot of flavor to the mix."

"Who made the punch?"

Veronica laughed, the sound low and seductive in the encroaching darkness. "That had to be cousin Emerson. His grandfather used to make moonshine during *and* after Prohibition. The recipe was passed down from grandfather to son, and finally to grandson."

Kumi blew out his breath. "That stuff is potent."

"How much did you drink?"

"At least two, maybe even three glasses."

"It's no wonder you can't move. Didn't somebody warn you?"

"Nope. At least I wasn't doing shots like some of the others."

"Kumi! Were you trying to kill yourself?"

He opened his eyes, a sensuous smile curving his strong mouth. "No. I'm not ready to die—at least not for a long, long time."

Chapter Eleven

Kumi lay quietly, watching Veronica stretch like a graceful feline. She turned to her left, throwing her right leg over his and snuggled against his shoulder. A soft sigh escaped her parted lips at the same time her eyes opened.

Cradling the back of her head in one hand, he pressed his mouth to her vanilla-scented hair. "Good morning, sweetheart."

Inching closer to Kumi's hard body, Veronica smiled. "Good morning." She noticed the abundance of sunlight pouring into the bedroom through the lace sheers. It was apparent she'd overslept. "What time is it?" Her voice was heavy with sleep.

Kumi turned, peering at the clock on his side of the bed. "Eight-ten."

"It's not that late," she moaned.

"What time are you scheduled to get your hair done?"

"Eleven."

She and Kumi had been in Georgia for three days and they were invited to attend a fund-raising dinner dance to benefit AIDS victims in the Atlanta area. It was one of many organizations she'd joined after she'd married Bramwell.

Kumi pulled Veronica closer and settled her over his chest. Attending the formal affair would give him a glimpse of what his life would be like if he married Veronica and relocated to Georgia. She'd been forthcoming when she revealed what her marriage to Dr. Bramwell Hamlin had been like.

Even though Kumi hadn't lived in the States for a decade, he had been familiar with her late husband's name. And after spending time with Veronica in her hometown he'd come to understand who she was.

They'd shared dinner with her parents and with her sister's family, and the contents of their respective homes were comparable to the furnishings in Veronica's. It didn't take him long to conclude that the Wardlaws and Johnsons were a product of old-black Southern aristocracy, much like his own family lineage, concluding their backgrounds were more similar than dissimilar.

His right hand moved up and down her spine, lingering over her hips. A slight smile curved his mouth. She was putting on weight. He'd noticed the night before when she'd undressed in front of him that her breasts were fuller, the nipples darker and more prominent.

The muscles in his stomach contracted when he recalled the vision of her lush body in the warm golden glow of a table lamp. The flesh between his thighs stirred as it hardened with his erotic musings. He wanted her, and since they'd begun sleeping together there was never a time when he did not want her.

Veronica felt Kumi's arousal and as his passion swelled, so did hers.

Writhing sensuously atop him, she pressed a kiss under his ear. "Don't start what you can't finish," she murmured.

The words had just left her lips when she found herself on her back, staring up at Kumi. His large eyes captured her gaze, holding her prisoner. He smiled as he lowered his body and brushed a kiss over her parted lips. She closed her eyes, letting her senses take over as he kissed her chin, throat before moving slowly down her chest.

He eased down her body, leaving light whispery kisses over her belly. Her respiration quickened, fingers curling into tight fists as she struggled not to touch him. His moist breath swept over her thighs and she swallowed back a moan. This was a different kind of lovemaking—one in which the only part of his body that touched her was his mouth.

He kissed her inner thighs, she rising slightly off the mattress. This time she did moan audibly. Turning her over, he explored the backs of her knees, leaving her shaking uncontrollably. He was torturing her, and at that moment if Kumi had asked her for anything she would've given it to him.

It all ended when he moved up and staked his claim on her breasts, she keening like someone in excruciating pain. She felt the sensations in her womb.

"Kumi?"

"Yes, baby?" A turgid nipple was caught between his teeth.

"Please."

He released her breast and stared at her. "What is it?"

She opened her eyes. They were shimmering with moisture. "Don't torture me."

Holding her close, he glared at her. "Why shouldn't I? You torture me, Veronica. You've tortured me every day since I first saw you."

Closing her eyes against his intense stare, she shook her head. "What do you want?"

Burying his face between her scented neck and shoulder, he said, "You know what I want."

She knew exactly what he wanted. He wanted a wife and a child. He wanted her.

And she wanted to be his wife and the mother of his children.

"Yes, Kumi," she whispered.

"Yes, what, Ronnie?"

She took a deep breath, held it and then let it out slowly. "I will marry you."

First he kissed the tip of her nose, then her eyes and

finally he kissed her soft mouth. "I love you so much," he whispered as his hands moved slowly over her body. "Thank you, thank you, thank you." His voice was thick with emotion.

Lifting his hips, he eased his thick long length into her awaiting body, both sighing as her flesh closed possessively around his. Knowing they'd committed to sharing their lives and futures made their coming together all the more sweet.

A deep feeling of peace entered Veronica. Her whole being was flooded with a desire that filled her heart with a love she'd never known. Passion radiated from the soft core of her body, igniting a fire in Kumi's loins. He moved sensuously against her, his hips keeping perfect rhythm with hers.

They were no longer man and woman, but soon-to-be husband and wife—one.

Her body vibrated liquid fire and she wanted to yield to the burning passion that seemed to incinerate her with the hottest fire. Kumi quickened his movements, taking her with him as they were swept up in the hysteria of ecstasy holding them captive.

Great gusts of desire shook her from head to toe, and her lips quivered with silent words of unspoken passion.

Tears streaked her cheeks and she moaned over and over when she surrendered to the hot tides of love carrying her out to a weightless sea where she welcomed drowning in the delight of a never-ending love.

Kumi's passions overlapped Veronica's and seconds later he groaned out his own awesome climax. It was the second time in his life that he'd made love to a woman without using protection. Both times it had been with Veronica Johnson. But that was inconsequential because he would willingly repeat the act over and over until her belly swelled with his child.

Veronica entered the brightly lit ballroom, her hand resting lightly on the sleeve of Kumi's white dinner jacket. A brilliant diamond butterfly pin on the strap of her one-shoulder black crepe de chine dress glittered under the prisms of light from two massive chandeliers. The pin was a preengagement gift from Kumi. He sheepishly admitted he had selected the delicate piece of jewelry while waiting for the slacks to a rented tuxedo to be altered.

She'd wanted to admonish him for spending his money, but quickly changed her mind. She hadn't wanted to appear ungrateful nor bruise his pride. She'd thanked him instead, kissing him passionately. They'd stopped just in time or they never would've made it to the fund-raiser on time.

She took a surreptitious glance at his distinctive profile, her breath catching in her chest. His good looks were complemented by a self-confident presence that elicited an inquisitive glance or smile from several formally dressed women standing around in the ballroom talking quietly or sipping from champagne flutes.

While Veronica had spent four hours at a full-service salon wherein she'd had the roots of her hair touched up with a relaxer, her face hydrated by a European facial, followed by a manicure and pedicure, Kumi had visited the adjacent barbershop to have his curly hair cut and the stubble of an emerging beard removed from his face with a professional shave. He then went to select formal wear for the fund-raiser before he returned to pick her up from the salon.

When he'd walked in, all conversation had come to a complete halt, and gazes were fixed on his smooth face and tall, muscular body. Veronica had risen from her sitting position in the reception area, curved her arm through his amid whispered choruses of "Damn!" and "Oh, no, she didn't!"

She hadn't expected the rush of pride filling her as she clung to his arm, and it was not for the first time she'd found it difficult to believe that she had fallen in love with Kumi—that she had pledged her future to his.

Kumi's right hand covered the small one resting on his sleeve, his admiring gaze lingering on Veronica's swept-up hairdo. Wearing her hair off her neck gave him an unobstructed view of her long, slender, silken neck. She hadn't worn any jewelry except for a pair of brilliant diamond studs and his gift.

Filled with masculine pride, he noticed men turning and staring at the woman on his arm. The soft fabric of her dress draped her body as if it had been made expressly for her. The garment bared a shoulder and the expanse of her back. The single strap crossed her velvety back, ending at her narrow waist; a generous display of long shapely legs were exposed by a back slit each time she took a step. Dropping her hand, he splayed the fingers of his left one across her bare back. The possessive gesture was not lost on those who were shocked to see Veronica Johnson-Hamlin in attendance with a man. Since her husband's death she had continued to attend the annual fund-raiser, but had elected to come unescorted.

Lowering his head, Kumi asked, "Would you like something to eat or drink?"

Waiters, balancing trays on their fingertips, weaved their way through the burgeoning crowd, offering a plethora of hors d'oeuvres and glasses of sparkling champagne. The annual fund-raiser was a sellout.

"I'd like a seltzer, thank you."

Leaning closer, he pressed his lips to her forehead. "Wait here for me. I don't want to lose you."

Nodding, she positioned herself with her back against a massive column, watching Kumi as he made his way toward one of the bars set up at either end of the expansive ballroom of a former antebellum plantation house.

She exchanged polite smiles and greetings with people she'd known for years and others she'd met once she married Bram. Her late husband had been medical adviser for the foundation for several years after documented cases of the disease increased with rising fears and ignorance of the epidemic affecting the African-American population.

"I'm surprised to see you here, Veronica," drawled a familiar male voice. "I was told you had gone to the mountains for the summer."

Turning to her right, Veronica looked at the man who had prompted her to leave Atlanta. Regarding her with impassive coldness was Clinton Hamlin, Bramwell Hamlin's eldest son.

Older than Veronica by only three years, she'd been initially attracted to his lean face with its perfectly balanced features. His smooth mocha-colored face was tanned from the hot summer sun, which brought out the shimmering lights in his dark gray eyes. Tall, slender and impeccably attired, Clinton was a masculine version of his once-beautiful mother before she embarked on a slow descent into a world of substance abuse.

She affected a polite smile. "You should know that this event is very important to me—to all of our people."

Vertical lines appeared between his eyes. "What I do know is that you're a *slut*." He spat out the last word. "You seduced my father, got him to marry you and now you come here and flaunt your pimp in front of everyone. Thank God my mother isn't here to witness this."

Veronica recoiled as if Clinton had slapped her. She wanted to scream at him that his mother couldn't witness anything because she probably was too drunk to even get out of bed.

Of Bram's three children, Clinton had been the only one to befriend her once his father announced his decision to marry a much-younger woman. But his conciliatory attitude changed abruptly with the disclosure of his father's last will and testament. He'd had to share three million dollars with his brother and sister—the amount a pittance compared to what Veronica had received, and he was convinced she'd talked his father into leaving half his estate to whom he referred to as "hood rats."

Only pride kept her from arguing with Clinton. "Thank you for the compliment," she drawled facetiously. She glanced over his shoulder to see Kumi coming toward them. "Now I suggest you leave before my *pimp* gets here. He has a rather nasty temper."

Clinton turned in the direction of her gaze. The man who'd come with his stepmother was formidable-looking, even in formal attire. "We'll talk again," he warned softly.

"No, Clinton, we *won't* talk again," she countered. "The last thing I'm going to say to you is get some help for your problem."

Leaning closer, he said between clenched teeth, "I don't have a problem."

"Right now the only Hamlin who doesn't have a *problem* is your sister."

Rage darkened his face under his deep tan. "You'll pay for that remark." Turning on his heels, he stalked away, his fingers curling into tight fists.

She was still staring at Clinton's stiff back when Kumi handed her a glass filled with her beverage. She missed her lover's narrowed gaze as he studied her impassive expression.

Kumi didn't know why, but he felt a sudden uneasiness that hadn't been there when he first walked into the ballroom with Veronica. There was something about her expression, the stiffness in her body that boded trouble. Had the man who'd walked away with his approach said something to upset her? Was he one of the ones whom she'd spoken about who had sought to defame her character?

Shifting his own glass of sparkling water to his left hand, he curved his right arm around her waist, pulling her closer to his side. He would not leave her alone again for the rest of the night. If anyone had anything disparaging to say to Veronica Johnson, then they would have to deal with him.

Veronica scrawled her signature across several documents that gave her lawyer power of attorney to negotiate and finalize the sale of her properties. It had taken almost a week to list her Atlanta and North Carolina holdings with a Realtor before she set up an appointment with an appraiser to catalog the contents of her Buckhead home. All that remained was the transfer of the titles of her cars to her sister and brother-in-law.

The night before Kumi left Atlanta to return to Asheville, they'd lain in bed, holding hands, planning their future. Her disclosure that she would live with him in France had rendered him mute. Once he'd recovered from her startling revelation, he told her he would make certain she would never regret her decision to leave her home and family.

Replacing the top on the pen, she dropped it into her purse, a knowing smile softening her mouth. In two days she was scheduled to return to her mountaintop retreat and the man she loved.

She and Kumi had planned to marry in North Carolina on September 18—a day before they were scheduled to leave for France, a day before she would board a flight with her husband to begin a new life in another country and eleven days before she would celebrate her forty-third birthday.

Kumi had called his sister with the news of their upcoming nuptials, and Deborah had offered Maxwell's for the reception and lodging for family members and out-of-town guests. Veronica was adamant that she wanted a small gathering, with only immediate family members in attendance.

Leaving the documents with the lawyer's administrative assistant, Veronica walked out of his office, making her way to the parking lot to pick up her car. She'd just opened the door and slipped behind the wheel when it swept over her. A wave of nausea threatened to make her lose her breakfast. A light film of perspiration covered her face as she struggled not to regurgitate. Turning the key in the ignition, Veronica switched the fan to the highest speed, and waited for the cold air to cool down her face and body. What had made her sick? Was it something she'd eaten?

She sat in the car for ten minutes before she felt herself back in control. Reaching for her cell phone, she dialed Candace's number, canceling their luncheon date. Half an hour later she lay in her own bed, swallowing back the waves of nausea that attacked when she least expected.

It was late afternoon before she finally called her doctor's office, explaining her symptoms to the nurse, who told her that the doctor had had a cancellation and could see her at five-thirty.

Veronica sat in the darkened kitchen not bothering to turn on a light, staring across the large space with unseeing eyes. A single tear rolled down a silken cheek, followed by another until they flowed unchecked.

She was pregnant!

She'd argued with the doctor that she'd had her period in July—although scant—but that she couldn't be pregnant. The young internist reassured her that the test was ninety-five percent accurate before he cautioned her because she was high-risk, she should see her gynecologist as soon as possible if she planned to carry her baby to term.

The shock that she was going to be a mother eased, replaced by a quiet, healing sense of joy. Kumi would get his wish: a wife and a child.

Kumi waited at the Asheville Airport for Veronica's flight to touch down. A bright smile lit up his face when he spied her. Waving to her, he gently pushed his way through the crowd. Curving an arm around her waist, he swept her off her feet and kissed her.

Veronica tightened her hold around his strong neck,

melting into him. "Please, don't squeeze me too tight," she murmured against his searching parted lips.

Easing his hold on her body, he noted the liquid gold glints in her clear brown eyes. "Did you hurt yourself?" He knew he hadn't held her that tightly.

She shook her head, saying, "I'll tell you once we get back to the house."

He gave her a questioning look. "Are you okay?"

A smile fired her sun-lit eyes. "I'm wonderful." And she was. After she'd gotten over the initial shock that a tiny life was growing under her heart, she found it difficult to conceal her joy from her sister and parents. However, she'd decided to tell Kumi first before announcing her condition to others.

Kumi swung Veronica effortlessly up into his arms, spinning her around in the middle of her living room. He'd missed her—more than he thought he ever would.

"What is it you want to tell me?"

Holding on to his neck and resting her head against his shoulder, Veronica smiled. "We're going to have a baby."

Kumi went completely still at the same time his heart pumped painfully in his chest. He registered a roaring in his head and suddenly felt as if he was going to faint. His knees buckled slightly as he eased down to the floor holding Veronica.

He sat on the floor, her cradled on his lap and held her to his heart. "I don't believe it," he said over and over. "Thank you, darling. Thank you," he whispered hoarsely.

Her hands cupped his face as she kissed his lips. Seconds later, she began to cry as they shared a joy that neither had ever experienced in their lives.

Chapter Twelve

Veronica stared at her ripening figure in the full-length mirror, praying she would be able to fit into the dress she'd selected for her wedding. She was nine weeks into her term, and gaining weight at a rate of a pound a week. Her Atlanta gynecologist had referred her to a colleague in Asheville, who had put her through a series of tests. At eight weeks she'd undergone a transvaginal ultrasound for a better view of her baby and placenta, and the results revealed not one fetus but two. She and Kumi were expecting twins.

Her moods vacillated with the changes in her body—she'd be screaming at her fiancé, and then sobbing in his arms seconds later. The realization that she was going to permanently leave her home, her family and the country of her birth had washed over her like a cold ocean wave, adding to the stress of planning a wedding. The night before, she'd threatened to cancel the ceremony, eliciting an outburst of anger from Kumi that left her with her mouth gaping after he'd stormed out of her house, slamming the door violently behind him. Forty minutes after his departure he'd called her, apologizing. She'd accepted his apology, and then offered her own, pleading for patience. They'd ended the call declaring their undying love for each other.

All of the arrangements for the wedding were finalized: the license, rings, flowers, menu and lodging arrangements for out-of-town guests. She'd decided to exchange vows in North Carolina rather than Atlanta, because she wanted to begin her life as Mrs. Jerome Walker without whispers and innuendos. Jeanette Walker had contacted the minister at the church where the Walkers had worshiped for generations, asking him to perform the ceremony. Deborah and Orrin had offered Maxwell's for the ceremony and the reception dinner. Veronica had chosen Candace as her matron of honor and Kumi had asked his father to be his best man.

Her dress was a Victorian-inspired tunic over a full-length slip in shimmering platinum. The Chantilly lace overblouse, sprinkled with pearl and crystal embroidery, added romantic elegance to a garment reminiscent of a treasured heirloom.

Glancing at the clock on a bedside table, she noted the time. Her parents, sister, brother-in-law and nephews were expected to arrive from Atlanta within the hour. Deborah had made arrangements for them to stay over at Maxwell's instead of at a nearby hotel.

Veronica buttoned the shirt that had belonged to Kumi. She'd begun wearing his shirts because they were more comfortable than her own. After they arrived in Paris she planned to purchase enough clothes to accommodate her rapidly changing figure.

The chiming of the doorbell echoed melodiously throughout the house. Turning on her heel she headed for the staircase. Kumi had promised to pick her up and take her to his parents' house to meet several of his cousins who had come in early for the wedding. Then everyone would retreat to Maxwell's for dinner.

She opened the door, her eyes widening in surprise when she stared through the screen door at Clinton Hamlin. "What are you doing here?"

He affected a polite smile. "May I come in? I'd like to talk to you."

Her gaze shifted to a racy sports car parked alongside her SUV. "You drove all the way from Atlanta just to talk to me? You know my telephone number. Why didn't you call me?"

Clinton shrugged his shoulders and ducked his head. "What I'd like to talk to you about is better discussed in person."

She pushed it open, permitting him to come in. He took several steps, then turned and stared at her. There was something about the way he looked at her that made Veronica feel uncomfortable. It was as if he could see through her oversize shirt to see her expanding waistline and ripening breasts. But she was being ridiculous. Only her family and Kumi's knew she was pregnant.

"What do you want to talk to me about?"

He lifted an eyebrow. "Where are your manners, *Mrs. Hamlin?* Aren't you going to invite me to sit down?"

"No, I'm not, because you should know better than to come to a person's home without an invitation."

His gray eyes glittered like sparks of lightning. "Your *home?* You keep forgetting that this was my father's home. Just like the place in Buckhead. My father purchased that place before you seduced him and turned him against his own children."

Veronica pushed open the door. "You can leave now." She wasn't going to permit Clinton to insult her—not in *her* home.

Clinton shook his head. "I'm not going anywhere until you give me what's due me, my brother and my sister."

"Get out!" The two words were forced out between clenched teeth.

A rush of blood suffused his face. A feral grin distorted his handsome features as he moved closer. Without warning, his right hand came up, holding her upper arm in a savage grip. "Not until I get what I want. What you're going to do is get your checkbook and write me a check for my share of my father's estate."

Veronica struggled to control her temper. "You got your share."

"I got nothing!"

"Your father left you almost a million dollars," she argued.

"And you got almost three," he countered. "And because of you he left those worthless hood rats five million."

She tried extracting herself from his punishing grip. "This discussion is over. Now, get out before I call the police and have you arrested for trespassing."

Clinton's fingers tightened savagely. "I have nothing to lose. Either it's the police or my bookie."

Veronica went completely still, and then swung at Clinton, her fist grazing a cheekbone. Howling, he let go of her arm, but came after her as she raced to a table in the living room to pick up a cordless telephone resting on its console. The phone was ripped from her hand and flung across the room. It hit a wall and bounced to the floor.

Veronica turned to face Clinton, seeing rage and fear in the dark gray eyes. In that instant she felt a shiver of fear shake her. She feared for herself and that of her unborn children. She took a step backward as he moved toward her. Where could she run? There was no way to escape him.

"Think about what you're about to do." Her voice was low, soothing.

He shook his head. "I've thought about it, Veronica. I've thought about it a long time, and it has to end this way. If I don't come up with a hundred thousand dollars by tomorrow, then I'm not going to be around to face another sunrise."

Her heart pounded painfully in her chest. She had to reason with him—had to get him to see that hurting her would not solve anything. "I can't write you a check."

Clinton's hands curled into tight fists. "And why the hell not?" he shouted as veins bulged in his neck.

"I've invested it." And she had, along with the proceeds from the sale of her art gallery.

He stopped his stalking, glaring at her. "You don't have a checking account?"

She nodded. "Yes. But I don't have a hundred thousand in it."

"How much do you have?"

"I have about eleven thousand in one and about eight in another."

"I'll take it," he snapped.

Closing her eyes, she nodded. She would agree to anything to get him to leave. "Wait here while I get my purse."

"How stupid do you think I am, Veronica? Do you actually think I'm going to let you out of my sight?"

You are stupid, she thought. Didn't he know that she could place a stop on the checks with one telephone call? "My purse is upstairs."

He followed her as she mounted the staircase. He was close enough for her to feel his breath on her neck. She retrieved her purse, extracted a check and filled out an approximate amount for the balance. Walking over to the armoire, she withdrew another checkbook from a drawer and filled it in, making it payable to Clinton Hamlin.

Snatching the checks from her outstretched fingers, he inclined his head. "I'll be back for the rest. You'd better contact your investment banker and tell him you need to make an early withdrawal."

She forced a smile she did not feel. "Don't push your luck, Clinton."

"You're the one whose luck has just run out."

"I beg to differ with you," came a strong male voice several feet away.

"Kumi!" The relief in Veronica's voice was evident. He had arrived just in time.

"It's all right, Ronnie." He'd spoken to Veronica, but his gaze was fixed on the back of Clinton Hamlin's head.

Clinton spun around, but before he could blink he found himself sprawled on the floor with a knee pressed to his throat. It had taken less than three seconds for Kumi to toss him over his hip and pin him to the floor.

The fingers of Kumi's right hand replaced his knee as he forcibly pulled Clinton to his feet. "You better call the police, Ronnie, or I'll forget that I'm getting married in two days and snap this piece of vermin's scrawny neck."

"Don't hurt me," Clinton pleaded, gasping. "Please don't hurt me."

Kumi released his throat and slapped him savagely

across the face. "Shut up before I make you sorry you ever drew breath."

Veronica walked over to a bedside table and picked up the telephone. She made the call, one hand resting over her slightly rounded belly. The call completed, she made her way over to her sitting room and sank down in the cushioned rocker. Her gaze met Kumi's before he caught the front of Clinton's shirt and led him out of the bedroom. It wasn't until the police arrived that she went downstairs and gave them a report of what had happened. Clinton was read his rights and led away in handcuffs. What she did not tell the senior officer was that she would come in and drop the charges of trespassing and extortion before she and Kumi left for Europe.

Kumi closed the door behind the departing police officers. Turning he smiled, holding out his arms and he wasn't disappointed when Veronica came into his protective embrace.

Lowering his head, he kissed the end of her nose. "Are you all right, sweetheart?"

She smiled up at him. "I don't think I'll be all right until I'm Mrs. Jerome Walker."

He lifted his eyebrows. "We only have another forty-eight hours before that will become a reality."

Resting her head over his heart, she closed her eyes. "I can't wait."

Kumi chuckled softly. "Neither can I."

"I can't wait to see who our babies are going to look like," she said in a soft voice.

"I bet they'll look like you."

She gave him a saucy grin. "How much do you want to bet?"

He ran a finger down the length of nose. "I'm not even going there," he said laughing. "We'll just have to wait and see, won't we?"

"Yes." She sighed.

Kumi released Veronica long enough to pull the checks she'd given Clinton out of a pocket of his slacks. Tearing them into minute pieces, he let them float to the floor like confetti.

"Let's go, sweetheart. Our families are waiting for us."

She followed him out of the house and into the cool night. It was only mid-September, but fall came early in the mountains. She inhaled a lungful of air, savoring it. In another two days she would marry, and the next day she would leave for her new home with her new husband.

She had come to the mountains to heal but found love instead.

Kumi was right: God does set the time for sorrow and the time for joy.

This was her time for joy.

Epilogue

A year later

Kumi cradled his son in the crook of his arm while he extended a free hand to his wife. She smiled up at him while she held an identical little boy against her breasts.

The babies had arrived early to the much-anticipated grand opening of Café Veronique. Veronica had planned to stay for an hour before she returned home to put her five-month-old sons to bed.

Her pregnancy had been difficult—she'd spent the last month in bed. The strain of carrying two babies who'd weighed six and a half pounds each at birth had taken its toll on her back and legs. The infants were delivered naturally after the doctor induced her labor, and when she saw her babies for the first time she couldn't stop crying. They looked enough like Kumi to have been his clones.

Curving an arm around Veronica's waist, Kumi pressed a kiss to her short silver hair. She'd cut her hair after the twins' birth because she claimed it was easier to maintain. The new style was very chic. She'd lost most of the weight she'd gained during her confinement, but her body had changed. It was fuller and more lush. And there was never a time when he didn't want to make love to her.

Jerome Kumi Walker still found it hard to believe his life was so perfect. He'd married a woman he loved, who'd given him two healthy sons to carry on his name, and he'd finally realized his dream to open his own restaurant.

Not bad, he mused.

No, he hadn't done too badly for a guy who'd left home because of a domineering father. He didn't ride a motorcycle anymore, because he was now a family man. He'd taken a vow before God and man to protect his loved ones. And that was one vow he intended to keep.

* * * * *

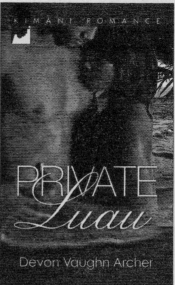

REQUEST YOUR FREE BOOKS!

2 FREE NOVELS
PLUS 2 *FREE GIFTS!*

KIMANI™
ROMANCE

Love's ultimate destination!